POPULAR PUBLICATIONS — FACSIMILE EDITIONS

Dime Detective Magazine #6 (April 1932)

Dime Detective magazine was the flagship detective pulp in the Popular Publications stable, running for almost 300 issues over twenty years. The April 1932 issue contains stories by Frederick Nebel, Carroll John Daly, John Lawrence, and J. Allan Dunn, and includes appearances by series characters such as Cardigan and Vee "Crime Machine" Brown.

Authors:

J. Allan Dunn, Carroll John Daly, John Lawrence, Frederick Nebel, Norman H. White, Jr.

Illustrators:

William Reusswig, John Fleming Gould

EVERY STORY COMPLETE

EVERY STORY NEW

Vol. 2   CONTENTS for APRIL, 1932   No. 2

COMPLETE MYSTERY-ACTION NOVELETTES

Watch for the May Issue   On the Newsstands April 20th

Published every month by Popular Publications, Inc., 2256 Grove Street, Chicago, Illinois. Editorial and executive offices 205 East Forty-second Street, New York City. Harry Steeger, President and Secretary, Harold S. Goldsmith, Vice President and Treasurer. Entered as second class matter Aug. 6th, 1930, at the Post Office at Chicago, Ill., under the Act of March 3, 1879. Title registration pending at U. S. Patent Office. Copyrighted 1932 by Popular Publications, Inc. Single copy price 10c. Yearly subscriptions in U. S. A, $1.00. For advertising rates address H. D. Cushing, 67 West 44th Street, New York, N. Y. When submitting manuscripts, kindly enclose sufficient postage for their return if found unavailable. The publishers cannot accept responsibility for return of unsolicited manuscripts, although all care will be exercised in handling them.
PRINTED IN U.S.A.

"THAT COUPON BECAME A
MARRIAGE
LICENSE!"

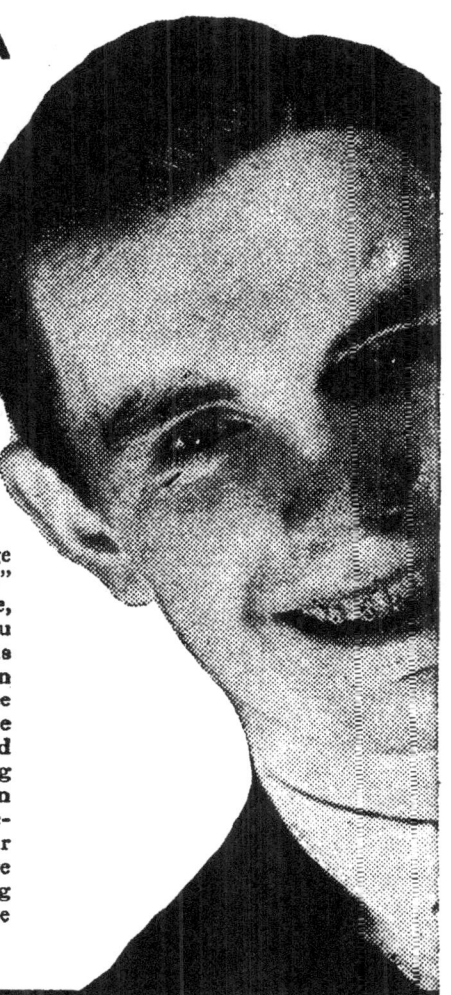

"THERE was only one reason we had not already married—money, money! I was desperate, there was no prospect of a raise on my job. The sad truth was, I knew *that* job was paying the limit.

"One night Sarah handed me a coupon she had clipped from a magazine and said, 'Mark this, then mail it to the International Correspondence Schools at Scranton. The solution to *our* problem is more training for you!'

"I did. Today I have a better job because of that coupon.

It really became a marriage license, for we are married."

Whatever the incentive, I. C. S. training will help you realize your ambition, just as it has helped thousands of men all over the world to advance to better jobs . . . earn more money. If you have the old fighting spirit, I. C. S. training is a powerful instrument in the battle for success. Spare-time study is not a pastime for quitters. It even takes courage to admit you are not getting ahead! Mark and mail the coupon today!

The FIRE FIEND

by

J. Allan Dunn

Author of "Out of the Night," etc.

Out of the blaze it came—live coals and smoldering ashes clutched within Its awful paws. What was this monster—this fiend of the flames —who gripped men's throats with searing fingers—left them there, on that hearth of mystery, branded with burning death?

He lay there, stark, grisly terror
still stamped on his features.

CHAPTER ONE

Murder at the Towers

FAIRVILLE was not a metropolis but its population of sixty thousand was big enough to support two papers, one morning and one evening sheet. And Clint Parker was not a star reporter. But he meant to be.

He had ambitions. Better than that, he had ability, though so far he had not had much opportunity on The Fairville Journal to develop it. As a matter of fact he was still rated a cub and his assignments were none too classy. Still, some day he was going to be a crack space man in Chicago or New York. Meanwhile, he not only dreamed of scoops and stories that would stir the nation but did his best to secure them. Something might break, even in Fairville.

Already it was acknowledged that the daily column on The Journal that told of departures and arrivals was better than that on The Star, especially items other than those which were gleaned from the routine inspection of hotel registers.

Clint had a simple but ingenious plan. One railroad and one depot served Fairville. The depot boasted four red-caps, on duty two at a time. Clint cultivated the good will of two of these, one from each shift. He was able to do them favors in the way of publicity for their clubs and lodges, for their own affairs of entertainment and, more than once, he managed to minimize unfavorable comment on certain actions which became automatically public and to which The Star gave full space value. Therefore Clint was a "fine felluh" and The Star was anathema.

It didn't seem very important or vital, even to Clint Parker, until the day when, buying a package of cigarettes at the depot stand, he saw and heard the girl expostulating with the chauffeur. And, strange as her story sounded, Clint did not have any hunch about how he was to be mixed up in its horror, its tragedy and wild adventure.

She was not a bad-looking girl, young, with a nice figure and a fresh complexion that did not come from a drug store. She had evidently been crying and she was indignant. Probably she was ordinarily well mannered enough, but now, in her belief that she had been unjustly treated, she forgot her surroundings. The chauffeur was listening sympathetically, but he seemed a little skeptical, Clint fancied. Chauffeurs get that way. And the story was enough to stretch anyone's power of credibility.

" 'E 'ad no call to fire me," said the girl in British accent. "No more did 'e 'ave any call to say I was crazy. It ain't right. I've done no 'arm. I was pursuin' my dooty when it 'appened. And it did 'appen for all you and the rest may think. 'E said I 'ad no business in the Camel Room and Missis Gibbons, to syve 'er own job, lies an' ses she 'adn't give me no orders to dust in there. But she did. It ain't fair."

The chauffeur seemed embarrassed. He glanced at the clock and then at the gate.

"Your train's in," he said, setting down the girl's two suitcases. "I've got to be getting back. It was tough luck it happened to be you, Lucy, but you got your fare back and two weeks wages, didn't you?"

"The train don't go for twenty minutes yet," she returned. "Wot's more, you ain't goin' to see me lug those two 'eavy bags all the w'y down that long platform, are you, Joe Spriggs? You used to be more accommodating. And wot's two weeks wyges when you've lost a job and been called crazy inter the bargain? Though it was enough to myke anyone go barmy to see it comin' on out of the very 'eart of the fire and that a blazin' like it was a bit of 'ell. 'Orrible it was, with its gleamin' eyes. It ain't no wonder I screamed and fainted and I'm glad," she added with feminine shift of feeling, "to not 'ave to live in a 'ouse with a 'orror like that in it."

"O. K.," said the chauffeur, who was neatly uniformed, "that's the way to look at it, kid. I'll take the bags in and see you seated right."

"Then come erlong," the girl retorted. "And you mark my words, Joe Spriggs. The Thing ain't 'uman. It's like the monster in the film, only this one was made in 'ell, it was. And there'll be 'orrible things 'appenin' at the 'ouse. You better watch out you don't git burned alive, or worse."

Rufus Washington Lee, who did not seem to feel that he had lost a possible tip from the girl, grinned amiably at Clint, to whom he had already given a list of the passengers he had noticed. He was across the waiting room and did not seem to have overheard the conversation. The girl in charge of the newsstand had been telephoning with a boy-friend and it struck Clint that he was probably the only one who had registered on it.

It sounded like a weird and nightmarish affair, save that the girl was evidently in earnest. To her, at least, the thing had happened. Clint strolled over to Rufus.

"That's the shofer to Mr. Benting up at The Towers," said Rufus. "He totes the help in the station wagon, when they come and when they go. I guess that one done went. They say it ain't easy to keep help up theah."

"Why?" asked Clint. He still lacked a hunch, but his news nose scented a story somewhere.

"I dunno. I know most of them don' stay long and I've heard say The Towers is ha'nted. It's a powerful old place."

CLINT knew that. The Towers was one of the showplaces in and about Fairville. The Bentings were an ancient family. They had once owned most of the land on which the city stood by virtue of royal grant and retained their present property because they had sided valiantly with the revolutionists. There were legends about the place, including the universal Washington one. The Towers was built of good brick that had withstood the years, faced here and there with stone, mantled with ivy and, more like an English house than an American residence, its diminished grounds were all contained within a high brick wall, buttressed, with a stone coping set with vicious spikes which had been curved in a manner most discouraging to would-be climbers. There were iron gates and a small two-roomed lodge occupied by a grouchy bachelor Scot who was gate-tender and gardener's assistant.

There was another entrance for tradespeople, a postern with a grille, available only for passers on foot. The grounds were well laid out, though without ostentation. The trees were mostly old and of big growth; the lawns, too, had the velvet of time in their verdure; the flower beds were old-fashioned, both in arrangement and contents. The house could not be seen from the gates, except when winter thinned the boughs of foliage.

Clint had never been within the gates or the postern and he could not remember any Benting coming or going while he had been with The Journal, almost five months. He did not know any of the family by sight. He doubted if they entertained much. A wealthy and dignified menage, reserved, untouched by scandal, unless the small talk that had drifted to Rufus, and the dismissed maid's excited tale could be called gossip. It wasn't news.

Just the same, Clint Parker told his friend and mentor about it. He was The Journal's big shot as a news gatherer.

He covered the important stories, knew the insides of state and local politics.

"The girl was nuts, in all likelihood," said Davis. "She probably butted into that Camel Room against orders and pitched a weird' yarn she had read in some penny dreadful in her native Londown Town.

"You couldn't get through to interview Benting and, if you did, it might cost you your job. Hes got connections and money and he's a crank on privacy. He almost had me thrown out the only time I went up there and, if I hadn't happened to know something of medieval carving, I'd never have seen the Camel Room. It's a sanctum, sacred to Benting's treasures. I doubt if he lets anyone dust in there but himself."

"Has he got camels in there?" Clint was disappointed that Davis did not sniff something worth while in his report.

"Got a lot of things worth going a mile for," answered Davis. "The wall paper is old—early Colonial pattern. Scenes on the Nile or thereabouts, palms, crocodiles, pyramids, ruined temples and a caravan of camels. And the room is like a museum. Armor, weapons, ecclesiastical paintings and manuscripts, mummies, carvings, religious vestments, antique jewelry, some gorgeous pieces of furniture, chests and choir stalls, and so on. Old missels, books, ivories, chalices and altar pieces."

"Good loot?" grinned Clint. "Wonder some rusticating gangster hasn't cracked the crib."

"Try and get in. He's got mantraps and spring-guns and half a dozen men, not to mention dogs. Besides, valuable as all that stuff is, you'd have to use a moving van to take most of it and you couldn't fence the jewels or the carvings or manscripts. They wouldn't touch 'em. And old man Benting looks as if he'd come out of one of his mummy cases.

Like a reincarnated Pharaoh. Won't wear modern dress. Stays home. Great traveler in his youth, and so on. Quite a blade. He wrote a book—you'll find it in the public library. *Travels in Araby and Abysinnia,* I think."

A call came from the city desk and Davis left Clint to the writing of the Going and Coming Today column. He thought he would like to look at that Camel Room at The Towers, but he forgot it in the rush of work.

EVERYBODY had gone from the editorial and reporters' rooms on The Journal except Clint Parker. He was holding down the ghost watch. The out-of-town edition had been run off; the composing room was standing by with one linotype operator; make-up men and foreman were ready to make over the front page for the regular edition.

Clint's job was to extend the late flimsies from the A. P. There might or might not be something exciting in them. Probably not.

Nothing was expected to break. But Clint was new enough to the game to get a kick out of being at least in nominal charge. He liked the smell of ink and the rumble of the presses as the regular edition was put to bed. He liked to see the turtles go to the stereotyping room, to watch the shuttle of the linotypes, though he was aware that he was considered a nuisance outside his own department. He was still a spurless squire of the Fourth Estate.

The telephone operator had long gone home. There were three supposedly soundproof booths and a battery of phones on the city desk. Clint sat there, in borrowed and very temporary dignity.

A bell jangled. Clint picked up an instrument, traded that for the right one and glued his ear to the receiver. It was always a thrill for him to hear a ring in the ghost watch, with most of the city asleep, unconscious of the march of events. It had never amounted to much with him, so far, but hope springs eternal in the young reporter's breast.

It was the police station. Clint would have called it in a few minutes, perfunctorily. The desk sergeant was speaking. He was a good friend of The Journal, with an eye to his own interests. And this was something that could not be slighted.

Clint's eyes fairly bulged, shining under the green-shaded bulb over the desk.

"What? What? Yes, this is The Journal. Parker speaking. You've sent for the chief? He's not there yet? I will be, in a couple of shakes. Thanks, sarge. You bet. I got to go with you."

He tingled with excitement as he phoned downstairs.

"Hold the front page. I said hold it. Stand by for a big flash. You heard me. No, I'm not bughouse. It's murder, you chump, out at The Towers. I'm on my way. You call up Mr. Martin. I can't wait. Tell Martin I've gone. And hold it until you hear from me."

CHAPTER TWO

The Corpse in the Camel Room

HE CRAMMED the flimsy he had been extending under a weighted spike file and grabbed his hat. It looked hot. They couldn't hold him, send someone else. He wasn't going to give them the chance. They couldn't blame him for starting to cover it and he had a very definite idea, from what Davis had said, that it might be difficult for any newspaperman to get into The Towers unless he crowded in with the police. And it was vital to get in on the ground floor. With the memory of what the maid had said to the chauffeur nothing could hold him back.

He found a taximan gossiping at the lunch counter across the street, idling over his coffee and sinkers, and dragged him away.

"Aw, buy some more later. I'll pay for it. Rush me down to the police station. It's murder, out to The Towers."

"Who? Some dame?"

"The butler! Step on it. I want to catch the chief. You stand by in case I miss him and want you. The Journal pays."

He said it with a lordly manner, but he was not so sure of what City Editor Martin might say about expenses. Or about his taking the bull by the horns, anyway. But there was mystery here, on top of murder, and he knew—or thought he knew something about it. Inside dope.

As they rounded one corner, the chief's car swung round another at the end of the block. It halted outside the station and the chief hurried in. Clint leaped from his taxi and got into the back of Chief Sullivan's car. There was no driver. The chief would be calling the state police. He came out with two men, one in uniform, the other a plainclothesman. He glared at Parker, barked at him to get out of the car.

"Journal, chief," said Parker, and showed his card and badge. "I know something about this case."

"Yeah? The hell you do? You drive, Halloran. Sit with him, Burke. Now then," he added as he got in beside Clint, "what's this line you're handing me? Journal using a kindergarten these days?"

Clint was twenty-four. But the gibe did not rankle.

"I was on watch," he said. "I've called up Martin. But someone's got to be on the spot. Have a heart, chief. Listen, here's what I know."

He would have liked to keep it to himself. But it was his passport to get inside those gates, to get the color of the yarn. And, if it hadn't been for The Journal, Sullivan wouldn't be chief.

Sullivan growled at him.

"That sounds like so much hooey, to me," he said. But he let Clint stay in the car.

The wrought-iron gates were shut, but there was a light in the little lodge and the surly Scot appeared, peering against the headlights that showed him plainly, half dressed, nervous, demanding to know who they were and what they wanted.

"It's the police, you fool!" roared Sullivan. "Open up."

"I canna let none in. What dae ye want wi' us?"

"It's murder! You telephoned the station."

The man blinked at them, sullen.

"I've heard naught o't. An' what's more, there's no telephone i' the house or on the place."

The man might tell the truth about the telephone, Clint thought. It was possible. But he would hardly have gone to bed with half his clothes on. And there had been a light. Still, he might have been sitting up. But that was not likely.

"There's nane can gang in here nor oot o't," he said. "How dae I ken you're the police?"

"You'll 'ken' it by finding yourself in a cell, locked up as an accessory to murder. Look at the sign on the car. We're coming in if we have to smash these gates down."

The detective, Halloran, sounded the shrill police siren and kept it going. Burke got out, with the exasperated chief. Clint stayed where he was.

The sulky Scot unwillingly opened the gates and the car rolled inside. Clint exulted.

"He may be still inside the grounds," said Sullivan. "Burke, you stay here by the gates. Halloran, you'd better scout a bit."

"Ye'd better tak' me wi' ye," said the lodge-keeper, "or ye'll be steppin' into a snare. Mind ye, I'm doin' this under duress," he added.

SULLIVAN got into the front seat. Clint Parker fancied himself temporarily forgotten. The chief drove along the winding drive and suddenly the big house showed. There were lights spotted on its big facade, upstairs and down. He heard Sullivan grumbling to himself and then the chief let the siren bellow. It did not strike Clint as especially a clever thing to do, but Sullivan was a better policeman than he was an investigator.

A wide door opened part way at the top of steps and a man came out. He was more respectful than the lodge-keeper. He, too, was in disarray, a red and white striped pajama top thrust into his pants, slippers on naked feet.

Sullivan charged up the steps.

"Police chief" he snapped. "Where's Mr. Benting?"

"He'll be down directly, sir," said the man. Footman, Clint imagined. Certainly not the chauffeur he had seen at the depot. His speech was smooth but, to Clint's stimulated fancy, it was assumed, like the accent of an actor. He was a hard-looking type, a tough man to tackle, Clint thought as he noted his broad shoulders and narrow hips. He had something of the litheness of a good welterweight and his nose had been broken.

"Where's your phone?" asked Sullivan.

"We haven't any, sir. Mr. Benting don't approve of them."

Sullivan muttered. Clint thought he wanted to call more men now he realized the layout. The killer might—should—be still on the premises, house or grounds, unless he had wings. But trees might grow close enough to the wall for an exit that way. Anyhow, the state cops would be along. And Clint was inside. The man gave him one glance that was almost contemptuous, then ignored him.

"Where did this happen?" demanded Sullivan.

Telephone or no telephone, it was plain that this servant was not surprised at their visit. But he hesitated just a moment as Sullivan closed the outer door. He glanced up at the broad flight of stairs that led from the hall to a dim landing. The hall was set with carven furniture, there were horns of all kinds displayed on the walls, a heavy chandelier of bronze hung from the ceiling.

On the upper landing Clint caught a glimpse of a girl standing at the head of the stairs, peering down. Her face was just a pale oval, but he surmised that she was young. Then a shaded wall lamp flashed on and he saw that she was in a negligée of jade green, that her hair was a shade of red that glinted as she darted away.

But not before Clint Parker noted her expression, that puzzled him, that was going to haunt him. It held terror that melted to appeal, to a hope that died and left terror regnant.

A man, a figure rather, so impersonal it seemed, came down the stairs. No doubt that this was Benting, the master. He was clad in long robes of stiff material that showed glints of golden threads in a faint pattern embroidery. One wide sleeve, as the right hand rested on the bannister rail, revealed a lining of silk, the hue of split pomegranates. It was a strange hand, corded and veined, brown and shrunk, a hand that belonged with the face, a hand that might almost have been that of a mummy, save for the strength in it as it glided down the wide rail, not clinging to it. Clint watched the shoes, pomegranate crimson, turned up at the toes, without heels; shoes that took

skilful practice to maintain in place. Those robes were neither Chinese nor Arabic, Clint fancied. Persian, perhaps. But these thoughts were fleeting impressions that barely registered at the time.

The man's face gripped him. A reincarnated Pharaoah, surely. Regal, majestic, essentially powerful, like the hand, though whether for good or evil, was beyond Clint Parker's ken. It showed no emotions. The lips were full though wrinkled, but you could not class them generous. The chin seemed bursting through the drawn, brown skin; it was like a jutting crag. The nose bridged high, with haughty nostrils; arrogance was on the brow. Only the eyes were remote. They held no glints, they looked like bruised black grapes in their deep hollows.

But, behind them, for all their lack of luster, there was power. Dynamic power that emanated from that masklike face with its spare flesh, high cheekbones and temples, as if light poured through a parchment shade. Power in his tread, deliberate and stately; in all his mien.

EVEN Sullivan felt it, charged with self-importance as he was, with the dignity of his office—as he saw it. He almost cringed as Benting stopped at the foot of the stairs and looked at him, speaking sonorously, talking almost as if his voice was something apart; as if, while he spoke to them, his soul was elsewhere, serenely detached from annoying, worldly matters.

"You are the police?" he asked. "I sent a messenger to you. Rather, one was sent. I myself knew nothing of what had happened. I have been busy for many days—and nights. And I was asleep, lulled by mandragora."

Mandragora? The whole thing was becoming fantastic to Clint, as yet unnoted, and glad to be, by the owner of The

Towers. Lines came to him. Iago, as the poison worked in the mind of Othello.

Not poppy, nor mandragora
Nor all the drowsy syrups of this world. . .

Mandragora, most ancient of anaesthetics and narcotics, essence of the weird mandrake root. Benting had been taking drugs and did not hesitate to acknowledge it. He might be an addict, but he would not be a slave of the habit. It fitted with his appearance, his attire.

Clint wondered who had telephoned. Benting had sent a messenger, he said, and Benting would not lie. He would not have to. But somebody had phoned, from outside. He supposed Sullivan got that.

"They tell me it is my butler," said Benting. There was neither horror, nor remorse, nor any human emotion in his voice. It was as if a god spoke of the affairs of underlings.

He led the way to a room of which the door lay open.

Clint knew it was the Camel Room. He saw the things that Davis had mentioned. He saw a fire glowing in a great fireplace, shining back from armor, and then he saw only the figure of a burly man in blue pajamas, his nude toes, bunioned, inexpressibly tragic, turned stiffly upward, lying across the threshold.

If this was the butler, as it must be, Clint would have thought him a plugugly in life. Stark, grisly terror was still stamped on his features. His eyes protruded, his teeth showed between purple lips. The knuckles on one hand were bruised; his pajamas were torn. It looked as if he had put up a tremendous struggle as, by all appearances, he could. One leg was drawn up. On his throat there were ugly marks, of throttling, of more than that, marks that were seared as if by metal, or fingers of steel that burned.

It looked as if the dead man had put up a fight. Alive, he would have been eminently capable of it. Unless he had been taken entirely by surprise it must have been almost a superman who had bested him, killed him, strangled him with those strange marks on his throat.

Inside the room furniture was palpably out of place, a rug was rumpled, a chair overturned. And there was something else—an automatic pistol. Sullivan picked it up with a handkerchief about the handle, sniffed at the muzzle.

"It ain't been fired," he announced.

When the state detectives came they would rate above Sullivan in the investigation. The chief of police meant to make the most of his opportunity. He might solve the matter, at least get important evidence that he would be credited with in the papers and in court. Perhaps this was one reason why he did not interfere with the young newspaperman. Clint was being automatically taken as some member of the police and he was grateful. He would give Sullivan the best of it.

The chief started his inquisition. In plain life he would have been awed by Benting's grim and forceful personality, but now he was the law, *in propria persona,* and he acted accordingly.

"This man your butler?"

"He was," Benting corrected laconically.

"What was his name?"

"Hoskins—John Hoskins. He was a good man who had been with me for five years."

"Do you know what he was doing down here at this time of night, dressed like he is?"

Benting's eyes were sarcastic.

"I told you I was asleep, under the influence of a sedative. I can guess that he might have fancied he heard some disturbance and came to investigate. That would be his duty."

"Got any reason to expect anything like that?"

BENTING shrugged his wide shoulders under his robe that hung from their spareness like a garment on a rack. His gaze was no longer sarcastic. It was annoyed.

"I consider such a possibility less than remote. The grounds are walled and otherwise guarded. My doors and windows are bolted and proof against entry. There is—"

From outside there came the sudden blast of a gun. It sounded like a small muzzle-loading cannon. Sullivan swung about, a hand on his own weapon. There was the deep barking of dogs.

"That will be a spring-gun," said Benting quietly. "One of your men must have blundered into it. I trust he was not injured. Someone of my household must have been along or those dogs would have barked before. Great Danes! They are trained to eat only what is given them by one man who prepares it. They cannot be poisoned, they bite before they bark. They are two strong reasons why the house is safe."

"If my man's been hurt it's your responsibility," said Sullivan fiercely. "Spring-guns are against the law."

"You should know your law better," replied Benting. "Under the original grant of land to my family we were given right of eminent demesne which still exists inside my walls. For certain special services rendered the Colonial Government forces at a critical moment in the history of this Republic, we were given certain unusual rights and privileges. They still exist. Your men must have been warned. If they were clumsy it is not my fault."

His dull eyes shone now, like balls of obsidian reflecting the flames of burning alcohol. He spoke cuttingly, contemptuously. Clint Parker did not doubt that he knew his position. That got through to Sullivan. He became less truculent,

though he stood his ground stoutly enough in pursuit of his duty.

"Who found him, gave the alarm?" he demanded.

"My secretary, Miss Edith Fenwick, discovered him. It was she who sent a messenger to give the alarm as you call it. I imagine she also, like poor Hoskins, heard some disturbance. She is a well-balanced young woman—"

"We'll let her tell it," said Sullivan gruffly. Clint Parker thought of the look he had seen in the girl's eyes at the head of the stairs. He felt sure she was the secretary. And that look did not click with Benting's praise. "I'd like to see everybody who lives here," the chief went on. "If the place is so well guarded this must have been an inside job—unless," he added swiftly and, to Clint, cleverly, "someone came down the chimney."

The eyes that had been dull, then shining, flashed. Benting was no longer a mummy. His gaze held the lightning of a wrath that seemed about to be emitted in electric javelins to destroy this probing intruder. Clearly Benting belonged to the old order. He resented this interference with his privacy and failed to appreciate the majesty of the law. Murder had been done, but, to Benting, Clint Parker felt, the killing of an underling did not count; life and death were not important factors outside of himself and his equals. He belonged to another era, to an age when a police officer would not dare to oppose a landed gentleman.

CHAPTER THREE

The Chinese Phoenix

CLINT felt himself strangely translated to such a period. Benting dominated the scene; the rest, save perhaps for Sullivan, appeared unreal, like wraiths. In his strange robes Benting seemed the all-powerful noble. Fantastic it was yet, for a fleeting instant, Clint Parker eminently modern and up-to-date young American and newspaperman, would not have thought it strange for Benting to have flashed a rapier from its sheath and spitted the presumptuous policeman.

But he restrained himself, though with evident exertion of will, while the thinly padded skin worked over his protruding bones. Veins swelled and writhed on his temples and his lips twitched as the nostrils of his arrogant nose, high-bridged as Caesar's, or as Tutankhamen's, dilated.

"The chimney," he said coldly, "is at least sixty feet in height above this floor. It has a stone coping in which is set a steel grille. Moreover, you will notice that there is a fire of logs that still burns fiercely. I do not use steam heat in that room because of the damage it would do to the collection. But that fire never goes out throughout the winter, from fall to spring. The back logs preserve it and it is constantly replenished. It is the duty of one of my men to give it fuel during the night."

"Hoskins?" asked Sullivan, whose naturally high color deepened at the acid contempt in Benting's tones, at the evidence that Benting despised him. But he was dogged in his determination to go through with his duty.

"Not Hoskins," rejoined Benting. "But I submit that even your somewhat automatic mentality might realize that, unless the man who killed Hoskins was either Shadrach, Meshach or Abednego, one of the trio who walked through the fiery furnace, according to the Old Testament, he could not descend the chimney nor pass those logs.

"There's been talk," said Sullivan, "of a maid you discharged yesterday, who says she saw someone—or something—coming at her out of the fireplace, right through the flames."

"Do you believe that?" asked Benting, haughtily disdainful.

"A girl named Lucy," persisted the chief of police. "She was talking to your chauffeur in the depot."

"Ah, a girl named Lucy, who was talking to my chauffeur?" Benting's voice was almost toneless, but it was curiously menacing, Clint fancied. "So? Well, I do not engage or dismiss my maids, officer. That is the office of the housekeeper. No maid is allowed in the Camel Room. Those are orders which, if disobeyed, mean *ipso facto,* that they leave my service. My housekeeper, no doubt, saw to that."

Sullivan stared into the Camel Room over the dead body of the butler. Clint, taller than he, looked over his shoulder. The fire growled and leaped fiercely on the wide hearth; its hot vapors swirled up into the breast of the chimney, concentrating as they rushed to the top where a steel grille guarded ingress or egress.

Benting was strange enough, weird in his garments, his port and curious suggestion of another era. But the idea that some fiendish creature could have come out of that blaze was even more fantastic than it had sounded to Clint in the railroad depot. Sullivan gave a non-committal grunt.

"There was the Phoenix, the fabulous ancestor of the Phoenicians and the father of Europa; an embodiment of the Egyptian sungod Ra, fabled to live for five hundred years, according to the Arabians; then to be consumed by fire and arise from its own ashes, renewed in strength and beauty," Benting said mockingly. "The Chinese call it Feng-hwang. So there may be something in it. You might get a clue out of that, officer. Then there were salamanders, formerly believed to be able to live in fire. In the theory of Paracelsus, Salamander was a being inhabiting that element."

His mood had changed; it seemed amused, and then it shifted again.

"These matters tire me," he said abruptly. "Get ahead with your duty, man. I suppose you will remove the body."

"Presently," returned Sullivan stubbornly. "There'll be more here, including the coroner. What's more, there's small sense in making fun of murder with a string of talk about heathen doings. I'll trouble you to get together everyone that works for you. I want them checked off."

BENTING moved to where a twisted cord of crimson hung on the wall and pulled it. A deep gong resounded. At the same moment the front door admitted Halloran with the lodge-keeper and, behind them, a lieutenant of the state police with a subordinate officer. Last of all came Davis.

Clint had been expecting him, not with pleasure. Martin would have aroused the star writer, of course. From now on Clint was squelched. He might not even be able to write what he had seen and heard. Davis would get all that from Sullivan and Clint had given him the angle on the fire—not that that theory stood up.

Sullivan's position as chief of police was largely confined to the protection and patroling of the city and its immediate suburbs, the regulation of traffic. He was a sort of sublimated watchman. Under state regulations, the lieutenant of the state police represented the active detective service. He was now in charge and Sullivan was a supernumerary. But, before he abdicated, he turned to Halloran, who was hatless and whose face was scratched.

"What happened to you?" Sullivan demanded. "What was that shot we heard outside?"

"It was some damned spring-gun contraption," said Halloran. "Scotty here warned me and told me where not to go. But I heard a rustle in the bushes and I started for it. Scotty threw me down just as I tripped over the setwire. It was only one of those damned dogs that prowl round without barking after Scotty calls to 'em. I'll admit he saved my life. I damn near scratched my eyes out in some prickly bush and my hat was shot to flinders. But I'll wager there ain't nobody hangin' round in the grounds, what with my lookin', those trick guns and traps, and those two dogs. Big as calves. They come up and sniffed at me when Scotty said it was O. K. for me to be around. They made for the lieutenant and his cycle bull without a whimper until Scotty called to 'em. They're as good as a machine-gun battery."

Halloran was aggrieved and garrulous. Sullivan checked him. He gave a brief but full report to the state-police lieutenant, whose name was Wilson.

Now the hall was half filled with Benting's household. Clint saw a stout woman whose manner and dark wrapper, with a Paisley shawl above it, proclaimed her the housekeeper. The chauffeur was there, fully dressed, another man beside the one who had admitted them—and he too was more like a gangster's bodyguard than a domestic servant, in Clint's opinion; and then he concentrated on the girl. Her face was pale and her lips were red. Her short but close-cropped hair was auburn; her eyes, he thought, were violet. They no longer held fear or appeal, or any definite emotion. She seemed what Benting had described, "a well-balanced young woman." And a beautiful one, slightly exotic in her negligée of heavy jade-green silk which was embroidered with a device that Clint recognized as having seen reproduced on plates and dishes at his own boarding house.

His pulse went up a beat or so as he suddenly knew what the device was. The Feng-hwang pattern, they called the blue-and-white dishes. Feng-hwang! The Chinese Phoenix! It might be only a co-incidence that she should wear the symbol Benting had deliberately brought into his speech, it might be Clint's stimulated nerves, but it startled him. Then Davis was talking to him as the lieutenant spoke in low tones with Sullivan.

"So you got in, kid? Good for you. Now you can beat it back."

"You want me to write the lead?" Clint asked eagerly. "I told 'em to hold the press."

"They're holding it," said Davis with a grin. "But I'm writing the lead—and the rest of it. Tough luck, kid, but it's too big a story. You beat it back to bed."

"Like fun I will," said Clint. He was disappointed but not too surprised. He knew that Davis could write rings around him in furnishing what the owners and readers of The Journal wanted. He had a strong notion that he might make a better story of it in one way, to appear in a magazine as a mystery-murder yarn.

"I'm on my own time," said Clint. "I'm in and I'm sticking round. I might get on to something. By the way, Sullivan got me in, for The Journal. He didn't know I wasn't going to get to write the story though I might have, at that, if Martin hadn't been able to find you. But give the chief a break."

Davis grinned. "O. K., stick around because we can't hold that press all night and you can cover the follow-up. Coroner's on the way. There'll be an autopsy. Also you can develop those detective instincts of your's, kid."

Lieutenant Wilson proceeded crisply with the examination Sullivan had been about to start. He was sternly official, polite but not deferential to Benting, handling him better than Sullivan had, with more tact and comprehension.

Wilson turned first to the chauffeur.

"You're the only one dressed. Why?"

"Miss Fenwick sent me to tell the police. I hand over the car keys of a night. Mr. Benting had them. He couldn't be disturbed. So I walked."

"Couldn't be disturbed, not even by murder? You're Miss Fenwick? You found the body? How about what this driver says?"

To Clint, the girl's voice matched her appearance. It was low, full, clear. It reminded him somehow of crimson velvet.

"He is correct. I heard a noise. I sleep lightly. I saw Hoskins fall backward as I came down the stairs. Then—I got the chauffeur, who sleeps in the servants' extension at the back, told him to dress and get the police. I knew that Mr. Benting had taken a sedative and would be difficult, at least, to awaken. It seemed to me haste was necessary."

"Sedative, eh? You take them regularly, sir?"

Benting almost smiled. His mood was contemplative now, as if he had ceased to take further interest in the proceedings, or as if the drug had reasserted itself.

"At intervals, officer, as the need prescribes. Mandragora, a most beneficent potion! Mandragora and myrhh was offered to those who died of crucifixion to allay their agonies. It was in the wine offered to Christ upon the Cross. It was used in the second century by surgeons for amputations. Stilled from the magic mandrake root, you know, that—as some say—shrieks when it is dragged from the earth. Yes, I was asleep at the time. And, if you do not wish to question me further than our amiable and persistent chief of police has already done, I shall ask you to excuse me. I am not a young man and all this fatigues me."

"It bores him, ráther," Clint thought. The lieutenant assented. Benting stalked up the stairs. He moved as if his bones should have creaked. The action again revealed that he was skeletonic in his emaciation. Clint wondered how old he was but checked the thought to listen to what the girl was saying.

"I do not think I was afraid—then— except for Hoskins. I had a pistol and I knew he had one but there had been no shot fired. I saw only Hoskins, falling backward. He tried to call out but he was choking. When I reached him he was on his back. I saw his gun on the floor."

"That all you saw, Miss Fenwick?"

The hall was so still, waiting her answer, that a falling pin would have startled all of them. They all seemed to share the idea, the certainty, that her words would be pregnant with importance. She moistened her lips, hesitated.

"I don't know," she answered finally. "It was dark in the room, except for the firelight. It is full of shadows, as you see. There are the mummy cases, the suits of armor. And I was upset. I knew Hoskins was dead. But, I am not sure. It might have been an hallucination—it must have been."

"What did it look like?" insisted Lieutenant Wilson.

"I thought," she said slowly, and once more Clint Parker saw the look of dread in her eyes, "I fancied that I saw a shape by the fireplace. It vanished. It seemed to blend with the smoke and flames."

"A shape. You mean a man?"

"It was more like a great ape," the girl answered. "It was light in color—it was furry—short fur that seemed to glisten. I did not see its face. It was gone in a moment and I knelt by Hoskins, after I had turned on the light in the hall lanterns. I was right. He was dead. Those marks were on his throat. And there was an odor of burnt flesh."

CHAPTER FOUR

Clint Makes Contact

CLINT, somewhat enviously, was reading The Journal as he ate an early breakfast of ham and eggs. He had been up all night and had got a copy hot off the press.

FANTASTIC FIRE FIEND LINKED WITH TOWERS MURDER

That was the flash headline to the signed story by Davis and he, Clint Parker, was not even mentioned. More than that, he had a strong hunch he would get bawled out by Martin for not having called up the city editor himself and for leaving the flimsy without extension and rushing off to The Towers. But, in view of The Star being left little better than a rehash, Martin would probably be liberal minded.

Clint was not at all sleepy. Hungry, yes, but exhilarated and alert. Hot on the scent. Hotter than the scent was.

Clint had met the girl after the body had been taken away in a basket and Halloran, emulating metropolitan methods, had powdered for fingerprints. Davis was having flashlight photographs made when the girl had suddenly fainted. Clint's eyes had seldom been far from her and he caught her, set her on a lounge in the hall, and waved off the housekeeper, though he accepted and used her restoratives. Then, when the girl came to, he corrected her idea that he was a detective or a police officer. He had admitted, a bit ruefully, that he was an obscure newspaperman who had had the luck to get on the spot but not to be considered worthy to write the story. But, he assured her, he was going to solve the secret of the haunted hearth, of the fireplace fiend.

"You can't do it," she told him. "If you meddle with it the same thing may happen to you that did to Hoskins."

"And it might happen to you," Clint retorted. "Why don't you get away from here? It's dangerous."

"I have a certain sense of duty," she said. "And, besides, I need the money I get from Mr. Benting. I don't know why I'm telling you this."

Clint grinned at her. It was a grin at once disarming and informative. It had helped him more than he dreamed of in his newspaper work. It was a certificate of honesty of purpose and it lit up the rest of his face so that one instinctively knew it belonged to a chap who would give you a square deal, not betray confidences or go back on promises.

"I know about that money racket, these times," he said. "And I can savvy your idea of duty. But you told me because we're sympathetic, see; because we understand each other. But, just the same, you don't belong in this atmosphere. I'd like to keep an eye on you, in case you see anything more that's mysterious and threatening. Do you suppose I could see you once in a while, just to report progress?"

She smiled back at him, faintly.

"I don't think you can see me here," she said. "Certainly not as a reporter. Mr. Benting doesn't like that sort of publicity."

"He's going to get it, whether he likes it or not," said Clint. "This is a whizz-bang yarn and they'll be coming here hot-foot from the big-town tabloids. Good picture stuff. They'll have the newsreel wagons here before the day's out. But why can't I see you outside?"

"Why can't you not be in such a hurry?" she replied, not ill pleased with his persistence, sure he was not trying to use her for copy. She needed a friend and she liked Clint. "I go out very seldom."

"O. K.," said Clint. "I'll be seeing you. Leave that to me."

LIEUTENANT WILSON had not found much more with which to solve the mystery. The grounds were searched again though the lodge-keeper protested that so long as the two great dogs were alive and unleashed there was no question of an intruder.

"They'd doon a stranger first," he said. "Wi' a rush, an' then they'd bay the moon wi' their muzzles bluidy wi' the interloper's gore."

Clint decided that the dour-looking Scot had a rare dry sense of humor, despite his aspect. He decided he would cultivate him, trying irrigation, by the Scotch-whiskey method. He did not think the man could be bribed but he might be softened toward an accredited visitor. There was no doubt but that he was well disposed toward Edith Fenwick.

Clint had left with the last of them, just after dawn. The coroner had pronounced the cause of death strangulation and was going to make careful autopsy of the seared prints like fingermarks on the dead man's throat. That would not work out until close to noon. The check-up of the servants revealed nothing much, save that Clint concluded that their generally tough appearance might result from Benting having picked them as bodyguards to prevent robbery of his treasures.

He had made no complaint of being robbed which was, Clint thought, something the police had overlooked—as well as Benting.

There were several curious things about the case. He meant to investigate them thoroughly, one by one.

He considered them over his second cup of coffee and three cigarettes.

Someone had telephoned the police. There was no telephone at The Towers. Benting was a recluse. Orders for necessities were made out by the housekeeper, filled by the chauffeur. Was that message one of bravado from the killer? It looked like it. Murderers, of certain types, did such things.

Benting was a bit of a mystic, a little mad, perhaps. He took mandragora and talked pedantically. But the narcotic had not mastered him sufficiently to prevent his being on the scene when Sullivan arrived. That might be easily explainable. He might be an addict, the effects lessening with use. Clint meant to look up his history, his age, the record of the Bentings, to dip into the book Davis had mentioned that Benting had written.

It would be a good idea to go round outside the grounds by daylight. It did not look as if any one could scale those walls, get past those dogs and mantraps, but it was worth investigating.

And, despite its lack of all logic, there was the fire-fiend theory that Davis had played up, that was going to make a sizzling story out of the case, stir the nation's thrill-seekers. First Lucy's, then Edith Fenwick's reluctant admission, the fear in the latter's eyes. Even Benting's talk of the Phoenix and the pattern of the Feng-hwang on Edith's dress.

What was the motive? Which, among the treasures in the Camel Room, aroused the cupidity of a robber sufficiently for him to commit murder?

What about those scorched prints on Hoskins' throat?

And how close was Sullivan to the truth when he insisted it was an "inside job." He was not so quoted. The state police lieutenant did not endorse his opinion. Nor did he pay attention to the quoted tale of the departed Lucy or the statement of Edith Fenwick about the thing that looked like a great ape, with short, glistening fur, a shape that blent with the vapors of the fire! Davis, good newspaperman that he was, had made the most of it. Wilson styled it an hallucination.

"It's unreasonable," he declared, after they had surveyed the fireplace with the big logs still burning, flinging out great heat; the hearth backed and sided with iron panels on which, as Colonial custom dictated, designs had been wrought of Adams' wreaths, torches and ribbons, with the embossed motto "Lux In Tenebrae." They had gone to the roof and seen the steel grid strong across the chimney coping.

"It's a spooky sort of household," summed up Wilson to the rest of them on the primary investigation. "Benting must be a hundred years old, at least. That Camel Room would give anyone the jitters if you stayed there long enough. That secretary of his is writing his life —to be published after his death, and that would give any normal girl the creeps. He might have slipped her some of that mandragora stuff of his. That's one thing we can't mention without a whole lot of cause. You've got to go easy with any of the Benting outfit. They're still a sort of tradition. But those addicts do have a trick of getting others to use their dope. I think she just had an hallucination."

"How about the maid?" Sullivan had asked.

"Might have snitched a drink of wine with the stuff in it."

CLINT was not due on duty until one. It was now seven. The library would not be open until nine. The librarian was a spinster lady of uncertain years whom Clint had managed to charm by asking her opinion—which he did not always adopt—upon certain research. Without any deliberate idea of deception he invariably thanked her for the help she had given him, and knew that she regarded him much as a maiden aunt might look upon a favorite nephew.

Now, fortified by breakfast, Clint rousted out his flivver and coaxed it into perverse activity. Arrived at his destination, he made an outside survey of The Towers. The grounds were extensive although the once great estate had now narrowed to some few acres.

At the rear, The Towers property backed upon a wilderness of second growth that led to a ravine in which ran the Maridan River, marked on ancient maps as Shadde Creeke. The high wall, everywhere topped by bristling, curving spikes, showed to Clint no sign of having been surmounted, no opportunities for passage by means of convenient trees. He gained nothing by his survey and found his high hopes a trifle dashed. But he made the full circuit and arrived again outside the heavy gates.

The Scotch lodge-keeper and assistant gardener were raking leaves. Clint hailed the former and the man turned and slowly came toward him.

"Ye can't get through," he said, not altogether sourly. "I'm letting no one through the day wi'out a warrant from the Governor an' I'm no so sure I'll recognize that. The laird is ill."

"Mr. Benting?"

"Aye. He's no a stripling to stay up a' nicht an' be rangin' an' reevin' aroond the next mornin'."

"Like you," said Clint with a grin. "I don't want to come in. But you'll have plenty that will before the morning's over. I was just wondering how you were feeling."

"Aye, you would be speirin' after my health. I'm fairly braw, thank ye, considerin' a'. An' the lassie's fine, fra' a' I hear."

Clint grinned at him again. The man was human if he was hard-shelled like a crab.

"It's getting chilly these fall days," said Clint. "I noticed you had a slight cough yesterday. I was wondering if you cared for a tonic?"

He produced a bottle of Scotch he had brought in his car. It had set him back almost a quarter of his weekly salary and he saw the other's eyes brighten cautiously as he reached through the still-locked gates, took the bottle, inspected the label dubiously, eased out the cork with a tool in a knife that fairly bristled with useful gadgets and, finally, smelled, then tasted the contents.

"Laddie," he said, "I'll no deny that I've a wee hoast that troubles me. It was bricht o' ye to notice it an' kindly to think o' the tonic, tho' I'm nae dootin' that ye have ulteerior motives. But I was young mysel' once on a time. I'd no advise ye to imbibe this yoursel' min' ye," he added as he took a second swig." "I'm loyal, mind ye, to the laird, wi' a' his vagaries an' whimsies, but Donald Menzies isna the auld fossil some think him. What I can do for ye, in a' verity, I will."

He took a third swallow, hid the bottle underneath a pile of leaves and winked at Clint before he solemnly puckered his lips and turned away with his rake, whistling Annie Laurie.

Clint was outside the library when it opened. The elderly spinster greeted him, her gooseberry eyes eager. The two girls who assisted her hovered near. Clint felt himself a person of importance in their eyes. The curator wanted to know if there was anything new about the terrible affair at The Towers. Clint was cagey. He knew how to appeal to her.

"Nothing yet," he said. "There may be around noon. The coroner's report, you know. Now I've got to find out what I can about the history of the Benting family. That's the end they gave me to look up. If anything breaks by noon I'll drop in again and let you know."

It thrilled her, as he had expected. She could go to lunch with her cronies and give them the latest inside news. She set herself to find what Clint wanted and piled a dozen volumes on his desk, including one of bound pamphlets yellowed and brittle with age.

"Those are copies of 'The Moderator'," she said. "It hasn't been published for a hundred years. But there's some reference there to the Bentings you might find useful. Have you got plenty of paper and pencils?"

"I'm a reporter," said Clint. "I carry my own. Thanks, ever so much. If I get anything I won't forget where it came from."

She beamed, already seeing a paragraph referring to her as "the librarian whose research had unearthed valuable material."

CHAPTER FIVE

The Tunnel in the Ravine

CLINT was doubtful as to what he might find but was soon interested. Among the books was one entitled "State and County Families" and there he found records of various branches of the Bentings, prominent in the early settling and development of the state.

Search among other books revealed a curious elision of the dates of the coming into the world of Lawrence Bentings, which was somewhat confusing. There was a Lawrence Benting born in 1830, with no record of his marriage. Clint dug deeper. A Benting had helped to endow Harvard. There had been Bentings there for almost three hundred years, almost since the founding of the college at Cambridge, then called New Towne. At that time the name had been spelled Bentynge. But the last Lawrence mentioned as enrolled there was in 1853.

It looked like a loose end. Nowhere could he find the present Lawrence Benting of The Towers registered in club or other manuals or directories. He gave that up. The present Benting had traveled early, as was shown in the literary biography of his book, but no data on his age

or education were given. He might have been privately tutored. It did not seem important.

But, in the old Moderators, Clint Parker found an account of the "valuable assistance" rendered to the Revolutionary Forces.

It appeared that the Lawrence Bentynge of that period had been gravely wounded in action and had retired to his residence upon Shadde Creeke, so called from the run of shad in that then navigable water.

A British convoy had encamped upon the stream and its officers quartered themselves upon the Bentynge Mansion, whereupon Lawrence Bentynge, though indisposed, had "roused himself to play hoste and with praiseworthy patriotism, did ply the said officers with wines and negus until they did babble incontinently" and revealed that they were in charge of a pay train, carrying gold for British troops and Hessian mercenaries. Therefore, in the night, Lawrence Bentynge, "with certain faithful ones of the neighborhood, did set upon the convoy and take the monies," conveying them through a tunnel which had been established for the trade in contraband during the Tax Oppression, to a secret place within the mansion. And, despite the suspicions and threats of the British officers, "did stande them offe until the assistance he had sent for timely did arrive. These monies were diverted to the treasury of the Colonial Forces to their great assistance, bringing great honors to the family of Bentynge."

A tunnel from the Maridan, flowing in the ravine back of The Towers!

It might have been used as entry for the assailant of Hoskins, who had learned of its existence. There might be a sliding panel in the Camel Room beside the fireplace, into which the killer might have seemed to vanish to Edith Fenwick; from which he might have seemed to emerge to the curious maid. It was a vague theory but to Clint, in his enthusiasm, it promised a solution.

There was no time for him to seek for the tunnel. It was close to noon when he was through reading. He saw the coroner and learned that the marks on Hoskins' neck were actual burns, that under them the windpipe had been powerfully compressed with vital arteries. The assailant must have possessed the strength of a gorilla.

When Clint reported for duty at The Journal Davis had not showed up. Martin greeted him briefly, gave him some local assignments.

Inevitably Clint let down. His enthusiasm did not wane so much as it clouded under adverse conditions. The trivial yet exacting details of his work dulled excitement. But it flared up when The Star came on the street with boys blatantly announcing its startling news.

"Second murder at The Towers! Horrible tragedy!"

CLINT PARKER, coming from a dry meeting of the chamber of commerce, snatched a paper from an urchin and tossed him a dime. He almost feared to read the headlines, dreading to see the name of Edith Fenwick. Ghastly as the news was, he was relieved.

It was the chaffeur who had been found on the rhododendron-bordered flag stones which marked the path beneath the windows of the mysterious Camel Room, with his neck broken, the cervical vertebrae snapped in twain. Unquestionably this too was the fire fiend's work for the same searing marks appeared. He must have been attacked from the rear by someone, or something, of almost supernatural strength, slain instantly, left there to be discovered by one of the Great Danes. The dogs had raised no disturbance. Chief Sullivan was quoted now as saying that it was an "inside job," that the killer was inside the walls of The Towers.

Wild theories were suggested by The Star, based upon the fury of the attack, the statement of Miss Fenwick that she had seen something like a great ape in the Camel Room. A brute like that might even scale the walls, hide in the trees, leap on a victim. It was pointed out, however, that there was no rumor of any such creature escaping from private or public menageries, or from some ship that might be conveying a jungle monster. The Towers were being thoroughly searched once more—both house and grounds. Mr. Benting was still ill in bed, his condition reported not far from coma. There was not, nor had there been, any mention of mandragora or drugs. Such references might be costly. They did not seem to bear on the case. The physician who had attended him was reticent.

It was nation-wide news now. Newsmen and cameramen came by rail and motor and airplane, besieging the gates of The Towers, and were grimly refused admittance by Donald Menzies, reinforced by a state trooper. There were half a dozen star reporters on the job, fuming at the blockade; sob-sister writers, invading the offices of The Journal and The Star.

Clint broke through them to Martin. His information could no longer be reserved. He was a paid reporter first and foremost. Edith might be—was—in imminent danger. One thing had been discovered. It was the chauffeur who had telephoned in to the police station from an all-night drugstore and, later, returned to The Towers without going to the police in person. Later yet, he had visited a garage where there was sometimes a crap game and, finding none going, had returned to his quarters. Sullivan had dug that up. Beyond showing a certain callousness on the part of the chauffeur, now himself a victim, it threw little light on the increasing mystery.

City Editor Martin leaped at Clint's news of the old tunnel.

"Have you told anyone about this?" he asked.

"Only you," said Clint.

"Great! We'll keep this to ourselves. If we find the passage it's The Journal's discovery. Then we'll let the cops in on it. It's worth a special."

It was his discovery, Clint thought, before he remembered that he was only a vassal of that modern Mercury, the news.

"I suppose I can go along?" he asked. Martin stared at him as if he had been a robot, some mechanical device that had served timely notice.

"You? Sure, Parker. It was good work. Now then—"

He called off three names, Davis among them, called them into conference. Clint was left out of the huddle. He supposed he'd be left out of the scoop, too.

But they let him go along. The four of them made a detour, left their car on a side road and broke through the brush along the Maridan, looking for the entrance to the old tunnel. The stream had silted in but the left bank, on which The Towers stood, was rocky and should not have altered much, though the creek, from various causes, was now comparatively insignificant. Once, smuggled cargoes of tea and brandy, of lace and silks, had been brought up it in luggers or pinnaces. Now a canoe could barely get through its reaches.

It was Clint, looking logically for the best place for a landing close to the old mansion, who discovered old timbers that might once have formed part of a pier. They scattered then and a shout soon announced an overgrown archway, at first a natural rift in the rock, bricked as they forged in the mouldy passage with their electric torches splaying rays of white light. The place was fungus grown, the floor a mould on which there showed no

footprints. And, a hundred feet in, the tunnel had collapsed!

THEY turned back, silent and disgusted, making for the car. Clint lacked the heart to get in. Only Davis spoke to him.

"Never mind, kid. It looked like a good lead. Good thing we kept it quiet."

Davis was right, Clint told himself as he left them drive off without him.

It was a flop. He was a flop. He walked automatically down the road in front of the entrance gates to The Towers and, as automatically, glanced in. There was the trooper, Sam Brown belted and holstered, trim in his uniform. Donald Menzies was pecking at weeds in the gravel as if nothing had happened. But he beckoned to Clint.

"Friend o' mine," he told the trooper, with a slight hiccough. "Here wi' the lieutenant last night. On The Journal."

He spoke through the gates with a reek or more or less synthetic Scotch on his breath. Clint recognized it.

"She'll be at the drug store at the corner o' Fourth an' Main," whispered Menzies. "Wi' a prescription, mind ye, to be filled. She'll be drivin' the sma' car but she's no started yet. A word to the wise is worth a volume to the foolish, ye ken. An'—the bottle's empty."

"I'll fill it," said Clint.

Clint went and waited inside the drug store, buying cigarettes he needed, hanging around until Edith Fenwick appeared. She looked wan and anxious but she brightened at the sight of him.

"How did you know I was coming?" she asked and Clint managed a grin.

"Luck, Menzies and a bum bottle of hooch," he said. "I want to talk to you."

She handed in the prescription, said she would wait for it. Then they sat in a service nook for soda customers. Clint ordered.

"I know what's happened, of course,"

he said. "You've got to get out of there."

"This is no time to quit."

"Oh no? What chance would you have?"

"I've still got my gun."

"Hoskins had one, but he didn't get a chance to use it. Listen, I'm coming up there tonight. I'm going to be with you. We'll sit up and watch. Menzies 'll let me in."

SHE looked at him with wide eyes— he knew now they were violet—and with parted lips.

"I'll own up I'm afraid," she said, "but I'm sticking. I'm helping the housekeeper to look after Mr. Benting. He wouldn't have a trained nurse."

"You're a wonder," he said. "I'd have been scared to death if I saw what you did."

"That isn't all, Clint." She glanced about but the one clerk was busy behind the prescription desk. "It's Mr. Benting. You saw him. How old do you think he is?"

"How old?" The question staggered Clint but a reaction came swiftly, as he remembered the curious lack of dates in the data he had searched. "I don't know. He might be a hundred. Though he's active enough."

"I think he's more than that. He's changed lately. Not physically, but mentally. You know I'm taking notes for his autobiography, though it's not to be published until after his death. And sometimes he hints that that will be a long way off. There are times when he is a very old man, who can hardly move, and then, the next day, he is vigorous—and sardonic. He tells me that he supposes I expected to wake up and find he was dead, and he boasts of a strange secret.

" 'I found it too late, my dear'," he said. " 'Now only the mind is left, the mind and memories. But I could bequeath you a colossal mystery. How would you like to live for ever? While you are young to stay young, while you can live and love?' Clint, it sounds incredible but I almost believe he has found something that prolongs life in the body, and that he found it, as he says, too late. He has traveled in many strange lands and there are times when he shuts himself into the Camel Room and the next day it smells of curious odors that seem to penetrate and stimulate and invigorate you."

Clint nodded soberly.

"You may be right at that," he said. "I ran through that book of his today. He made some explorations, tombs and things. Says his discoveries may revolutionize everything. He may be the same Benting who went to Harvard in eighteen fifty-two. My God, Edith, it seems uncanny to be talking this way, in a Wregal Drug Store, about such things—but they may be so. All the more reason for you to leave there. But all this doesn't seem, in any way, to explain the murders—except that someone thinks he has the secret of prolonging life, is looking for the formula, the elixir!"

The girl nodded.

"I've thought of that. Someone from the ancient lands he visited, a priest."

"Did he give you that negligée with the emblem of the Chinese Phoenix on it, the Feng-hwan?"

"Yes. It is on the tiles of his fireplace in his room. Once, he said to me, 'I am the Phoenix.' I knew by then that he was taking drugs and I took no notice of it. Now—"

"I've got that prescription," said the clerk.

They parted, Clint promising to return to The Towers as soon as possible. His brain seemed to seethe as he drove downtown. He did not return to The Journal. So far as the paper was concerned he was through.

He went home and got his gun. If the fire fiend appeared again that night he meant to try what speedy lead would do. He was not an expert marksman with a pistol but he would not be caught napping. The butler and the chauffeur had been caught off guard. He made up his mind that he would not be.

CHAPTER SIX

Fiend of the Flames

THE fire flamed high in the Camel Room. The uncertain shadows flickered on the armor, the cabinets, the mummy cases. The caravans on the wall paper wavered and seemed imbued with life.

Clint Parker sat there with Edith Fenwick, keeping a weird vigil. Benting lay upstairs in the narcotic trance that might, the girl said, be broken at any instant, unless this time the worn-out frame might refuse to respond to the drugs he was using to prolong its existence.

The logs shifted; in the hall an old clock ticked. Both were conscious of some force that enveloped them, penetrated them, made them one, but they did not speak of it. Their talk had been confined to whispers and now they were silent, listening to the clicking of the pendulum, the broken murmurs of the fire—waiting.

The house was quiet. A state trooper kept vigil by the gates. The two great dogs, satisfied of his intentions by Menzies, roamed the grounds.

Midnight had chimed—one—two. At three, a man, roused by an alarm clock, would replenish the fire. Discipline still maintained at The Towers though the master lay ill.

The clock ticked on. He had to get her away, Clint told himself. He thought she cared for him. He knew he loved her. He supposed his job was gone but he had some money banked for an emergency, the better part of a legacy left him by his father. It was not much but perhaps he could get her to take it, even if she had to take him along with it. They would go to New York . . .

The backlog shifted and sparks went rocketing up the chimney. The girl clutched the arms of her chair and bent forward. Clint saw her face but he could not see, for a moment, what caused her look of utter terror. She seemed hypnotized by horror, and then Clint saw.

THERE was a fearful figure in the midst of the flames, its color a dirty gray, furry, glistening; a shapeless, stooping creature with enormous eyes.

Those were fixed on the girl. Then the head turned with a curious wrinkling of loose skin and the great orbs glared at Clint. The creature stooped and picked up glowing embers, held them in the palms of its hands and so it came slowly forward, menacing, hideous, unreal but terribly manifest.

He heard Edith gasp, as if a scream was muffled in her throat. The monster advanced and Clint thought of those hideous marks on Hoskins' throat. He fired once and was sure he scored a hit though the gun jerked upward with the recoil in his unaccustomed hand, as he pulled trigger.

Then the creature whirled away from the girl and leaped at Clint, flinging at him the scorching ashes from his palms. They struck Clint in the face, almost blinding him as he grappled with the brute, astounded at its strength as he realized that the gray pelt was loose over a framework of bones that were sparsely covered with flesh, though the energy in its muscles and nerves was terrific.

They clinched and, young and lusty as he was, Clint knew he was no match for the horror. Already its hands were at his throat and he could not tear them away. He slugged at the body of the brute but his strength was failing rapidly. The thick fingers, burning hot, compressed his gullet. He began to lose consciousness and put his last force into one despairing effort. He felt that he drummed feebly with his fists but, to his astonishment, the beast's clutch relaxed. It stood weaving uncertainly, then toppled to the floor.

There was blood on the beast's shoulder but it was high up. Clint had hit him but not in a vital spot. Yet the gray shape had collapsed, lay inert in front the fire. There was a pounding on the front door, steps were coming down the stairs. The two great dogs were giving tongue, not in barks but dismal howls.

The shot had been heard. The alert trooper was shouting for admission. Benting's two remaining servants reached the hall. One of them opened the door.

They crowded in to see the tableau, the girl in Clint's arms, the hideous huddle on the floor. Clint's face was blotched but he was beginning to see fairly well once more. Lights were switched on. The trooper, with drawn gun, knelt by the furry thing.

"Dead as a doornail," he said. "I see you shot him. By God, that's funny! Look at those nails."

He had taken the creature's hand, or paw, and now they saw that what the trooper called nails were tips of metal, like copper thimbles, capable of gaining sudden and intense heat. Clint knelt beside the officer in excitement.

"It's a man," he said. "That isn't fur. It's an asbestos suit. The eyes are mica."

"It came through the side of the fireplace," said the girl. "The whole thing swung on a pivot."

"We'll see what he looks like," said the trooper. "Maybe he ain't dead, just fainted or something."

IT WAS an excuse to avoid waiting for the coroner, Clint knew well enough, but his own curiosity was supreme. The asbestos stuff overlapped and laced with pliant wire in the back. The suit was all in one piece including the hood. It was not hard to unfasten. It had been contrived so that it could be put on and off without assistance. At last the face was revealed.

Then Edith Fenwick shrieked in earnest and the rest shrank back with shock.

For the face was that of Lawrence Benting. It looked more like a skull than ever, sweated with a moisture that might be perspiration or the dew of death. His lips were curled back in what looked like a sneer, his eyes stared like balls of smoked glass.

The bullet had not killed Benting. He began to speak in a thin, painful mumble.

"The gods have failed me," he gasped out. "For all my study and my fastings, my rituals and my prayers, my searchings after the ancient truths, they have failed me at the end.

"Atharvan and Atago—Cacus the Fire Spitter, son of Hepheastus the god of fire—Dso, who lives in the flames—Agni rising, like the Phoenix, from his funeral pyre; they have ceased to listen.

"Moloch the Mighty—Yei—the fire godlings, Ndauthina and Nusku—even Ra's own embodiment, the Phoenix, have forsaken me, though I have worshiped them. Perhaps," he added, his eyes dim but, like opals, showing sudden lights of insanity; perhaps they were jealous, perhaps I worshiped too many."

As he muttered the names of the gods of many races, of classical and heathen beliefs, all masters of the so-called devouring element, his madness was made very clear. He seemed for the time unconscious of listeners; this was a lament rather than a confession.

"Fire destroys yet purifies," he went on. "Agni, chief of Vedic gods, Agni the twice-born, of the cloud and in the wood, descending as the lightning. Thus, as flame comes from the friction of two sticks and instantly devours those who brought him forth, so is Agni born.

"So, when I made sacrifice and passed through the fire was I to be reborn, granted new lease of life. I might have lived forever but the gods no longer care for mortals or their power has lessened. The first I killed, that his spirit blend and strengthen mine as I passed through the purifying flame, was too old. I gained nothing.

"Nor with the next one—the chauffeur. Both of these I killed in the Camel Room, in the presence of the altar, of the leaping element, as is set down in the precepts of Zoroaster. He, the chauffeur, was younger. He was strong but I bested him. I dragged him through the secret way and flung him into the shrubbery so that I might not be suspected; for in these days they do not honor those who make human sacrifices to the gods.

"But I would have won, I would have gained a new lease on life, new strength, aye even youth; if I could have got the girl."

He raised himself on one elbow, his voice sank to a crafty whisper.

"Those others were too gross of flesh and spirit. But a virgin, pure of mind and body—ah, there would have been a sacrifice that no god would despise! And there was so little time. My earthly envelope was growing thin. I could not put it off too long. And now—" his voice faltered away to the lightest of murmurs—now—it is—too late!"

After a convulsive shudder Benting's body twitched once, then stiffened and lay still.

"He was undoubtedly mad," said the coroner when he finally arrived and had made his examination. "His brain shows that it was actually rotting in some of the cortices. It was a blood clot that killed him, not the bullet."

The physician picked up the parchment found in Benting's room together with an empty phial that still smelled pungently. He read off a list of medicaments written in Latin under the title of "Elixir Vitae." "Listen to this," he said. "Buprestis, ixias, sea-hare, opium, pharicum, bull's blood, taxus, opoponax, aniseed, meum, ammi. Pish! The man was mad in the beginning to believe in such nostrums.

"He may have succeeded in prolonging his life but it was only from a supreme belief in his own ego and also in the efficacy of the stuff he was taking. It destroyed his metabolism, his cerebral renewals failed. He became a maniacal homicide. And no wonder. It was a strange case."

The Call to Kill

A Vee Brown Story

by

Carroll John Daly

Author of "The Curtain of Frost," etc.

I saw the knife quiver there in the wood close to Erma's head.

Black night and triple terror hovering to strike. Suddenly through the silence and the gloom a whimper sounds—and then a scream of fear! What do they mean? Can Vee Brown heed the summons—hear the Call to Kill?

CHAPTER ONE

The Death Messenger

JACK FERRIS, of The Evening Globe, got me on the telephone again.

'You're a hell of a reporter, Dean," he said, though in fact I did just an occasional article for the paper. "While you've been keeping Vee Brown's hideout such a secret The Herald-Examiner has hunted him up, and— Don't you read the papers? But—there. It's out now. Run up to Maine and see Brown. There's more than a rumor around that his testimony in Lieutenant Eswal Grim's trial will open up Benny Nevis for first-degree murder.

Get me a story. Something—anything. What he does. What he says. If he's afraid that Benny Nevis might—"

"Vee Brown!" I couldn't help cutting in. "He's afraid of nothing."

"Well—anything. What he does with his time. It's a big trial, and Brown's the star witness for the State. They say that even Mortimer Doran, the district attorney, doesn't know exactly how important or sensational Brown's testimony will be, and won't know until he goes on the stand —next month. But Brown has promised to disclose a few things that will lift the lid clean off racketeering. It's well known that Lieutenant Grim is soft, and will squeal to high heaven to save himself from the chair. It's Benny Nevis, isn't it

—Dean—who will get the hot seat if Grim does talk? It's Benny Nevis who has paid for the Grim defense battery of high-priced lawyers. Picturesque character—Benny! Old-time gangster, who rose to the top through cool, brutal, vicious, physical strength alone. No back-seat driver—Benny. They say that even today he does his own gunning-out in important cases; that his life depends on Grim being acquitted, which means his life depends on Brown not testifying. But yet—"

"I'm sorry to dampen your enthusiasm, Jack," I guess I told him for the tenth time in as many days. "You know Vee won't talk about that."

"Yeah—I know. But this is different. Now that his hideout is known Benny will try to put the finger on him. I hear, down at headquarters, that they're thinking of sending Brown a heavy police guard despite his objections. But listen, Dean. Go up and see him. Tell him The Herald-Examiner made a monkey out of you. Get any kind of a story. Anything! Human interest. I can make a couple of columns out of a paragraph. What does he do up there? Read? Fish? Or—"

I smiled to myself as I hung up. I guess I was the only one in the city who knew what Vee Brown did with his time. For Detective Vee Brown, assigned to special duty on the district attorney's staff, was also the unknown but famous Vivian—writer of sentimental songs the income from which was equal to that of a bank president. Now Brown was at an old farm house up in Maine, recovering from an almost fatal thirty-eight caliber bullet wound just below the heart. That was in his last case, when he had captured the fugitive Lieutenant Grim, of the police department. Captured him alive, at the risk of his own life.

SO I prepared to travel to Maine. Now that Brown's retreat was known there was no reason why I should not visit

him. While I doubted that any worthwhile story would come out of the trip, it was a chance to see him again. His recovery from that bit of lead was a slow, tedious, but—lately—encouraging ordeal. But I wanted to look him straight in the eyes and see for myself if he was in a good physical condition as his letters laid claim to.

Perhaps I flatter myself that my association with Vee Brown gave me something of the man-hunter's keenness of sensing danger; perhaps it was just imagination. But ever since I left the ticket booth in the Central Station I had the feeling that I was followed. Nothing tangible, you understand—and certainly no way to tell if that milling herd of people who passed quickly by or loitered there, seemingly watching me, were other than travelers hurrying to or waiting for trains. Surely I might have picked any one of fifty people, whom I suspected of following me.

It was after I had passed through the train gate, descended the ramp and was on the long, dim stone walk between a couple of trains that I knew the truth. Nothing of perception now; no sixth sense that I was being watched. This time a hand descended upon my arm, gripping it tightly below the elbow, and a voice spoke close to my ear.

"Easy does it, buddy." The hand dragged me to a stop. "You're going up to Maine—and I have a message for you to deliver to a certain party."

I swung and faced the man. Cruel thick lips; steady, colorless eyes, peering through narrow long slits; yellowish white skin. I knew him of course. It was Benny Nevis, who on three different occasions in the last two years had beaten the rap for murder. And back of this sinister gangster and racketeer were the flashing figures of many men and women. Nothing to be frightened about in such a pub-

place—nothing to be alarmed over. But I was alarmed. I looked up and down the platform for the familiar uniform of the station police, opened my mouth once to call out and closed it again.

"You won't do me any harm, nor that boy-detective friend of yours any good by making a squawk." Benny Nevis' hand had left my arm now and the thick fingers fastened upon my jacket. "And I ain't aimin' to have you miss your train. I'm as much interested in your makin' this trip as you are."

"What do you want?" was the best that I finally gasped out as I watched the hurrying figures over his shoulder, half picking in my mind the pugnacious-faced or huge, broad-shouldered men who might serve me in an emergency. But I did not call out. I stood still and listened to Benny Nevis.

"You tell this squirt, Vee Brown, that the finger is on him. That if he shows up in the city for the Grim trial nothing can save him. You tell him that even the fastest man in the world with a gun ain't much good if a lad shoves a rod against his back and burns him out. You tell him that I know, just as well as he knows, that Grim is yellow—and that if Brown testifies to what he knows, Grim will talk before he frys. And you tell this squirt—" Benny was certainly talking— "that I know me and some others will get the juice if Grim squeals. You tell him that if he talks up, I know I die; and you tell him—" and now the fingers tightened upon my jacket and his evil, leering face came close to mine, "that—that I don't want to die."

And Benny Nevis was gone, walking slowly down the platform against the crowd, pushing his way up the ramp to the gate, his hands sunk deep in his coat pockets, his broad shoulders forcing the hurrying travelers roughly aside.

There was nothing for me to do. If

I followed him and turned him over to the police I had nothing but my word of his threats. At the best, he'd be out on bail in a couple of hours. At the worst— Well—Benny Nevis had shot others down and still walked the streets, a free man. It was said that he had more influence on his payroll than any gang leader in the city. And it was also hinted that Benny Nevis kept out of jail—at least, avoided a long stretch—because, despite his rising fame and leadership, he still attended to all big jobs himself. Especially those that involved vicious and brutal murder. He was one underworld character who did not possess a single redeeming feature. So I turned, walked along between the trains, found my car and let the Pullman porter take my one small bag to my berth.

VEE BROWN had certainly picked himself a far-distant stretch of country. A good ten-mile drive from the nearest railroad but an ideal spot, there at the foot of the mountain bordering on the clear blue-black waters of Lake Little Big Elk.

The old lady at the farm house regarded me with that fixed pseudo-dumb stare of old New England shrewdness, and when I stated my errand she blankly shook her head.

"Brown—now." She looked toward the distant mountain. "I mind hearin' the name, I think—or a name close like it. There's some summer folks that have—"

"But he's here with you. You've known him since he was a child, when he used to come up here in the summer. I'm his friend, Dean Condon, from the city, who—"

"If you're his friend, you wouldn't be here." She snapped the words out suddenly, and then just before she slammed the door, "However, I've only lived here sixty-three years, and my mother before me—so I ain't expected to know people hereabouts. Sit down, if you like. Mind the flower pot by the rocker! Pop or the boys will tell you more."

The door closed and I was on the broad veranda.

Of course Vee Brown was there. I had written to him and received answers. Short, terse notes that his wound was coming along slowly, but fast enough to find him in the witness box the opening day of the trial in the city. But I shrugged my shoulders and wandered off toward the lake. It was a beautiful spring day and the crispness of the Maine air was warmed by a brilliant sun.

Ignoring the great stretch of newly plowed fields to the west of the farm house I walked toward the lake, breathed deeply of the sweet-smelling pines and sought the cliff above the water. If Brown was sufficiently recovered, his quick nervous temperament would seek some recreation. Even fishing! I smiled at that thought, drew close to the edge of the cliff, braced myself by a pine, and shading my eyes against the late afternoon sun looked out over the lake. Nothing but the stillness of that blue-black water, the distant shore with its pretty boarded bungalows, not yet open for the summer residents, and—I guess I heard him before I saw him. From below me came the notes of a harmonica.

And there was Vee Brown, first-grade detective assigned to the district attorney's office, sitting on a rock playing a wild, odd, fantastic, yet catchy tune, while a child, balanced upon a huge boulder close to the water's edge, danced to the music.

The little girl capered too near the edge, slipped upon the moss-covered surface, clutched frantically at the air, and sprawled upon the loose rocks of the uneven, rough shore.

I saw Brown jump to his feet, heard his laugh as he rushed to the child's assistance. Then I turned sharply, lost my own balance, grabbed at the tree again—and faced the man who had silently come up behind me.

"You ain't a'goin' down thar," the man said abruptly, while the rifle he held under his arm seemed to jump up of its own accord and point its long barrel right at me. "You ain't a'goin' nowhar, stranger, 'cept back like you come." And when I just stared at his gaunt, huge frame and the touches of gray in his tawny hair, he spat once and said, "This here is private property."

I knew him of course. Brown's description could fit no one else. He was one of the three Bender brothers, the inhabitants of the farm house I had just left.

"You're one of the Bender boys." I just got the words out as I looked at the gun, grinned too, as I thought that the "boys" ranged in age from sixty to sixty-five.

"That ain't a hard guess." He scratched his head, looked toward the sky, back at me again, and said: "Ain't important neither. Everybody here'bouts knows that. I know that. What I don't know is—who you be, and mebbe I don't care much neither."

"I'm Dean Condon." I started toward him with outstretched hand, but stopped as the gun swung from under his arm—and a finger just naturally seemed to curve over the trigger. "Vee Brown's friend. He's spoken about me, surely." And as the old man knitted his eyebrows and scratched his head in a puzzled way: "If you'll come to the edge of the cliff and just give Brown a call, we can settle the whole—"

HE shook his head very slowly. "No. We can't do that. He wouldn't fancy bein' watched over. No more he'd need it, neither. But we've kept the newspapers from him—him thinkin' we don't see them. But now that it's out whar he be—and that's here—and seein' as how we decided not to tell him it's out—wal—we just sorta got to watch him or tell him—and it's better he just get well with nothin' on his mind."

"How do you suppose the paper found out he was here?"

"The maid at the big house across the lake. She seen him with the child there, and she seen his picture—and like as not she talked."

"The child is not—not of your family then."

"Lor', no—stranger. She's city reared Not so over healthy, and up 'fore time, with the help, gettin' the house ready for the Van Warrens, next month. Bright child—Erma. Smart. 'Too smart' the Missus calls her." And doubtfully as he chewed on a bit of grass, "Too smart for country folks like us, mebbe, but she's done Mr. Brown a world of good—and I ain't sayin' he ain't helped her more'n a bit. Peculiar—both of 'em. But that ain't—"

"Suppose we hail Vee and say you brought me up from the house. Then he won't know you were watching him, and I won't tell him anything."

"Say—" the old man snapped his leg, "that's smart. That's real smart." And with a sudden squinting of his eyes: "I ain't sayin' I wouldn't 'a' thought on it in time. I ain't given to hasty conclusions." And in a burst of honesty: "Like as not it never would 'a' come to me. But here I am 'a' talkin'—and you mebbe one of them city racketts."

But I was at the edge of the cliff now, and had shouted down to Vee Brown who sat there holding the child upon his knees,

patting her little blond head, singing softly to her.

He was surprised of course—slightly disturbed too, I thought. Maybe he even wished I hadn't come. But he was glad to see me. Even from that distance I could see the crooked little smile as his lips curved at one corner—the right corner. Then at his invitation and the farmer's direction I found a path and climbed down to Brown.

"No apologies now, Dean." He took my hand. "I'm glad you came of course. And if I were a detective of fiction I'd ask you why you hesitate between telling me that my hideout is discovered—and wonder if it would ease my mind by breaking a confidence—and informing me that Mr. Bender is watching over me."

"How do you know that?" I demanded.

"Elementary, my dear Watson." And this time his eyes grinned too. "But we're forgetting our manners. Miss Erma Van Warren, known to you from now on, by mutual agreement, as Erma."

"I'm going to like you." The little girl jumped from Brown's knees and stood looking at me. "Vee told me how you saved his life, and I promised to like you—because you're not going to take him away from me. And when you both come back in the summer, Vee's to—" And perhaps seeing the surprise on my face, or maybe just a comical expression as she called him "Vee." "Oh, it's all right. Vee and I are going to be married when I grow up. I'm twelve now—almost twelve anyway—I'm past eleven. Are you going to like me?" She looked up out of the corners of sparkling, sharp blue eyes.

"Why—I hope so. I'm sure I am."

"And you won't mind my marrying Vee?" A pause, and then, "In books best friends do mind."

"Oh, no." I tried to be very serious. "I hope you'll both be very happy."

"Then you can come and live with us. I'm going to be a detective too."

"And a very good one." Brown nodded. "It was Erma who found out the protection Mr. Bender is giving me, and about my hideout being discovered. The Van Warren maid, Laura, is an addict of the tabloids."

ERMA ran on, without embarrassment. "I knew Vee the minute I saw him. So did Laura, I guess." And her little eyes knitting, "Anyway, she bought a new dress—and once when she took me into town I saw her talking to a reporter. A long-nosed, snoopy-looking—" She raised her head suddenly, listening. Distinctly came the *putt-putt* of a motor boat, and then the flashy little craft itself appeared around the bend. Erma Van Warren looked toward the setting sun.

"There's no use to put up a holler. I gotta go, I guess. That's Laura's boy friend in the stern. She can't tell much I do lest I tell about him, and the time she comes in nights." And taking me suddenly by the arm and dragging me toward the water's edge and not far from the few piles and narrow strips of lumber that served as a dock: "You're on a paper, aren't you? Not a picture paper though. I like a picture paper better. If, some day, you want my picture, Vee's got one." And then in a very low voice and very quickly spoken: "Help him up the path when he leaves. Pretend like he's helping you. I always do. He's awful wobbly yet." And, again, in a louder voice, to Vee: "Oh, Vee—that reporter's been snooping around, and Laura's been looking for one of my pictures. I hid them all though." And her eyes getting big: "I did so want my picture in the paper. I want everyone to know, Vee, that you aren't all alone and unhappy, like they write about you—

but I was afraid it might give you away."

Erma Van Warren turned suddenly, ran quickly to Vee, where he was hidden from the dock by the foliage, and threw her arms about him.

"Three." She returned to me and took my hand. "Good-by, Dean. I'm going to call you Dean, now—and I'm going to like you, anyway." And she was gone, running across the loose rocks to the dock, where the little boat now waited.

"Queer child," I said. "What did she mean, she's going to like me 'anyway'?"

"She objected to you at first, Dean." Vee Brown grinned. "Jealous, I guess. Said you wouldn't understand—would think her a silly child—and would laugh at her, like other grown-ups."

"Cute, isn't she?" I watched her climb into the boat.

"More than that." Vee Brown came to his feet. "I never had anyone get under my skin like Erma has. It makes a guy think back over the years and wonder if marriage— There was a girl once, Dean." He counted off on his fingers. "Funny that. I might have had a daughter about—well—maybe not quite Erma's age. There's no one to care, Dean. I haven't got the right to let them care. Erma, now— If—if they got me it would break her heart. I shouldn't have— But listen. I did a song for her. About Maine and New York. You see, sentiment is subject to contrast as well as atmosphere. I call it, *Home Is Where That Girl Is.* It goes like this."

And as he sought the path to the cliff Vee Brown hummed. Even without the words I got the feeling of the song. The music of the woods and the lakes strangely intermingled with the roar of the city. But halfway up the path he stopped, and though he pretended it was to admire the lake and to point out the distant, snow-capped mountain I knew he stopped to rest. But he made no objection when he was guiding me up the treacherous, loose rocks. He was so thin and white, and so pitiably delicate and small.

"I have lost a bit of weight." He still had that wistful, childish smile. "But it will have its advantage in my game. A harder target for a gunmans' bullet."

It was then that I told him about my meeting with Benny Nevis.

"He's only one in a hundred, Dean, with the same thought." He laughed at my fears. "The very fact that he expressed such a thought—made such a threat on my life—shows that he is driven to conversational violence rather than physical. Mark that for future reference in your study of the criminal. Love of the dramatic, or hate, often causes the gunman to talk himself to death. Benny Nevis never could draw a gun with me—and he never will be able to."

"But—a bullet from behind a tree; a machine gun hidden in a closely curtained car; the darkness of the city streets and a chunk of lead in your back, Vee. You've often said, yourself, that a bit of lead in the back is—"

"To be sure." He cut in on me. "My pet fancy, Dean. If a detective shoots a murderer straight through those two narrow eyes of his, after safely weathering a fusillade of bullets, he receives an ovation from the press—a hundred dollars in gold is given to him in the ward of the hospital—or, if he is not so fortunate, then his widow gets it. But society is served as well if a policeman's bullet is found in the back of a dead gunman's head as if it is found in the front of his head. But—no more of Benny Nevis! He is not what brought you here, for you were on your way when you met him. It was a story for the paper of course."

"Right again." I smiled. "Your re-treat is 'out' now. So—why not a story for the paper?"

CHAPTER TWO

The Enemy Strikes

BUT it was late that night around the fire in the big old-fashioned living room that I managed to obtain Vee Brown's permission to give the paper a "sure-fire article."

"It's human interest, Vee," I finished with my best eloquence. "The others will find out about the child, Erma. They'll make it sound silly. Besides, there's Erma. She'll get a big kick out of her picture in the paper—and it's a real story. The human side of you, Vee. The Crime Machine that the papers have denied any human feeling to. And Erma saying she's going to marry you when she grows up. Human interest—"

"That part we'll leave out of it." Vee almost snapped the words.

"Why? It's real cute. Maybe a little silly—silly to you or me, but very serious to her, and—"

"And very beautiful," Brown said slowly. "Very beautiful to me too. I have never had anyone care for me like that before—and it won't be exploited for half-dressed, frowsy matrons to giggle at over their morning coffee." And suddenly turning to me: "And what's silly about it? Erma is a remarkably bright girl—bright child, if you'll have it that way. And she loves me, Dean. Loves me as no one has ever cared for me before. She sees something that no one else has ever seen in me—something that I never knew was there. But it must be something decent and good, or she wouldn't see it. You don't get flattery from a child—you don't buy love from a child. She has given me a love, an affection, because of that intangible—

"Don't you see, Dean? It takes that

goodness and sweetness and purity of a child to look into your soul. Don't laugh. I've lived as close to death as any man, but there's something that holds me back, keeps me on a par with a child—like Erma. It's— Why, even now at night I often dream and plan and imagine what I'll do when I grow up. You see, I can't realize that I've ever grown up. It's just life—just seems like a game. A child's game. And, Erma— But close the door. It's all in the chorus." He walked to the baby-grand piano which looked out of place among all the antiques, and which Brown had had sent up to the farm from the city. "You'll get the idea better when the child appears again, just as the warm brightness of her face shines up from the cold dullness of the black water."

For perhaps ten minutes Vee played very softly.

"It'll be a hit, Dean. His eyes brightened when he finished. "But you should hear Erma play. She's a genius. It's been my greatest regret that I never could get my soul into the piano. Oh— in the words and music, yes—but not in the piano. But there— I've got doctor's orders, and I've broken my promise to Erma as to my hours."

And as he turned at his bedroom door, the candle in his hand accentuating rather than dulling the whiteness of his bloodless face: "I won't see you in the morning then. Human interest if you like, Dean. Her youthful presence and careful nursing—but nothing about marriage. And, Dean!" as I was going down the hall. "Her picture, now. Front-page stuff. She was a little brick to hide her photographs. But it will be a big thrill for her. Don't make it silly and stupid. Make it real. I'd have gone mad in this crushing solitude without her."

And my story of Vee Brown and little Erma Van Warren made the first page of The Evening Globe. Not much

credit to me, either—for of a certainty I wouldn't have recognized the story as my own. Jack Ferris had turned it over to an experienced and high-priced feature writer. It was good stuff, and even got under my skin when I read it. According to the write-up, Vee Brown's life was saved that he might be a witness for the State; a witness that would send to prison a police lieutenant who had betrayed his trust, and cause a shake-up that would involve numerous trusted public servants and a well-known racketeer.

A child's devotion to the notorious detective had literally jerked his life from the grave. The "Hard-boiled Killer of Men" had found peace and quiet and health in the love and devotion of a little child.

Yes, I gulped as I read it. Close to three columns of it, with the heading "City Owes Much To Child." And then "Erma Van Warren Saves Life of State's Star Winess. Detective Vee Brown Able to Testify Next Month in Big Racket Case. Guarded in Maine Retreat by Four of City's Best Police Lieutenants."

Oh, I knew that. Knew that since his hideout was discovered the district attorney had sent up picked men to guard Brown, despite his objections. Though I knew that Brown's claim to distinction was the fact that he was just that much quicker with a gun than any other living man, I slept the better for this protection, remembering the paleness of his face, the thinness of his body—and the sinister, leering eyes of Benny Nevi when he made his threat to kill.

I HEARD from Vee Brown, and with his letter was an enclosure from little Erma Van Warren. It began with the promise of having me live with them when they were married and ended with the appreciation of the thrill she received at seeing her picture on the front page of The Evening Globe. But there was a P.S. which disturbed me slightly. It was simple enough and to the point. Erma had written: "P.S. I am wondering how the folks will take it."

And a couple of weeks later there came another letter from Brown.

I suppose it would have happened anyway. The Van Warrens wouldn't have approved. But now—Erma doesn't visit me any more. "Vee Brown, hardboiled detective and killer of men" evidently does not appeal to the Van Warrens.

Four police lieutenants here to guard me seems ridiculous. The same thing that always stood between me and violent death still stands. The thing that has made me the physical, or perhaps the material superior to any gunman or racketeer who ever hid in an alley to kill a policeman. You and I both know, Dean, that that thing is the simple pressure of an index finger upon the trigger of a gun.

But if this guarding me has its humorous side it also has its disadvantages. I can not write music. I dare not chance that my secret may become public. Though fortunately I have finished and sent to my music publishers the song inspired—or if the word "inspired" smacks of conceit—then, the song at least born through Erma. I have had several titles for it, but finally decided upon *When I Grow Up*. It will be dedicated to Erma, and the public will believe that Vivian took the idea from your article in The Evening Globe.

So Vee Brown saw nothing more of Erma in his guarded retreat up in the Maine woods.

Then one day Jack Ferris popped in to the Park Avenue apartment, the lease of which, to prevent talk of how Brown could afford it, was taken in my name.

"Have you seen Vee Brown's little friend, Erma Van Warren?" he asked me abruptly.

And when I told him, no—and my suspicions that the Van Warrens had not taken kindly to the article, for Erma no longer visited Brown, he shook his head at me.

"No. The father was interviewed shortly after the story. He didn't fancy the notoriety maybe, but nothing more than that. Now—the Van Warren's city house is closed, and the family have not gone to Maine. We can't locate either Mr. or Mrs. Van Warren, and certainly not Erma. But although we've missed him so far, Van Warren has spent considerable time at the district attorneys' office, and there is plenty of undercover activity at police headquarters. I tell you, Dean—Erma Van Warren has been kidnaped."

"But why?" I gasped.

"Because a threat of death to the child may keep Vee Brown from testifying at the trial."

"But such a coincidence is—"

"Coincidence!" Jack Ferris laughed. "Why, they read The Globe, and since they couldn't silence Vee Brown in death, they figure they can silence him through the threatened death of Erma Van Warren."

"Brown doesn't know?"

"Of course he doesn't. The police will keep it from him. Letters will be intercepted and an attempt made to trace the writer down. But Brown won't know. The reason is—that he's too valuable to the State. The explanation to to him, if later necessary—that his health forbade such knowledge. Now, Dean—have you heard anything?"

"Me? No. I can hardly believe it. But why should I be informed, if the police—"

"Not by the police, but by the kidnapers. Somehow, before the trial, Brown must be told. Who would they be more likely to get in touch with than Brown's best friend and participator in his cases?"

"But what could I do? If Brown knew, he couldn't help. Not in the condition he's in, and—"

"He could decide if he should sell out

the State to save the child, or— But, even then, kidnapers seldom keep such a promise. It's too dangerous. It's easier and safer to kill and prevent future retribution through identification."

"I have heard nothing," I told him, and there was hope in my words; hope that it was all just a newspaperman's imagination, born through the love for a big story.

"But you will," said Jack Ferris. "And it will be up to you to decide if Brown should know. I can't print it yet. No proof. But, inside me, I know that Erma Van Warren has been kidnaped."

JACK FERRIS was right. Two evenings later I had a caller. "Jacob B. Rietzer—Attorney at Law" the card said, and although I had never met the man, his reputation as a shady but prosperous underworld lawyer was known to me.

He let his lips slip back, showing fine white pointed teeth; let a hand run across thick colorless lips; watched me a moment out of sharp beady eyes; then, after walking to the library door and closing it tightly, took the chair I offered him and placed his soft gray hat upside down at his feet. Then putting the tips of his fingers together and looking once to see that the thumbs of both hands touched, he spoke.

"I am a man of few words, Mr.—Mr. Condon. It has been my duty in life to protect the innocent from the blindness of hysterical justice in our disturbed city. It is my mission again tonight to protect the innocent— A little child. I believe you wrote a most touching article about the gap she filled in a man's life—shall we say, ebbing life. In fact, she saved that life so it might be used to take the lives of others. Now—" he raised his hand when I would have blurted in on him, "Vee Brown has a chance to pay his obligation to the child. It is within his power to save her life."

"What do you mean?" I gasped.

"Oh—I know what you're thinking. I disliked the position in which I was placed. It might set me in a bad light." He placed his hands far apart now and brought them back slowly together before he continued. "The burden was mine. I must carry the message or forever feel the twinge of conscience—that because of what the Bar Association may consider unethical, a little child, a helpless little child had met a death—perhaps a horrible death. For the fear and terror of men who face death in the electric chair is nothing to their rage and bestial cruelty when the cause of that death is in their hands. Plainly, Mr. Condon, I have tried to get in touch with Vee Brown and have failed. Others have tried, and traps have been laid for them. Now—" he leaned forward suddenly and his lips twisted, and his little eyes were pinlike and cruel, "I must talk with Vee Brown by tomorrow night—or the twisted, mangled body of a child will be found in a city street. The emotions of highly strung men can not be long controlled. If the live child can not be a deterrent, the dead one will be a warning."

"You—you mean that Erma Van Warren— That you are going to kill her. A vengeance against Brown."

"Me?" The lawyer straightened slightly. "I am not here as an angel of vengeance—rather, an angel of mercy. I am going to beg your friend, Brown, to save the child's life. Nothing else would have made me chance this interview. So you see, the soul of man is not as bad as it is painted." He came to his feet. "My office, then—tomorrow night at nine o'clock. You will bring this detective, Vee Brown."

"But—" I am afraid I half stammered, "if I don't tell Brown. Then he can't be responsible, and surely you— these others wouldn't—"

"Of course," he shrugged his shoulders, "if Brown does not know he can not be responsible. The responsibility must be shifted, then, from Brown's shoulders to yours."

"You mean—if I don't get him—bring him to your office tomorrow night, you—"

"I wish, Mr. Condon," he said very seriously, "that you would not inject the personal 'you' into the conversation. But a child must be hidden and watched over. Not too easy when the police are combing the entire city. If there is no incentive to keep the child alive—why, it is much more effective to—to get rid of her. That, of course, is the reasoning of warped minds and not my reasoning. But, after all—Mr. Condin, you are not dealing with me—but with warped minds. I am only trying to prevent a—" he shivered, but his lips parted and his teeth showed in a grin, "a dastardly crime."

He was at the door now, his hat upon his head. Very serious, very sedate, very much the established shrewd, honest lawyer.

"But the time. Give me longer—another day anyway. I—I couldn't reach him in time."

"Let us say two nights hence, then. Forty-eight hours. You will tell him?"

"I don't know."

I stood there at the door a moment. But the lawyer had not yet reached the elevator when I was packing my bag.

CHAPTER THREE

Brown Takes the Blow

I REMEMBER the sharp look Lieutenant John Mercer gave me when I reached the Bender farm house in the old Ford from the station. I gulped, but dared not keep the Ford waiting. Mercer was sizing me up to see what I knew— why I had come—if he'd let me see Brown, and I tried to smile beneath his steady, cold, appraising eyes.

"Some book in the bag." I hope my laugh sounded better to the police lieutenant than it did to me. "Just the sort Vee likes. His letters seemed sort of down in the dumps—and besides, I need a bit of Maine air myself. How's Vee—is he in the house?"

"Not so good—and he ain't in." Still those steady eyes were on me.

"Oh—down by the lake, with Erma." And though it tore at my heart I got it out. "How's the romance coming? Great newspaper story."

And his face cleared and clouded almost at once. I read it like a book. The clearing, as it struck him that I didn't know about the kidnaping of the child. The clouding. Well—I knew that John Mercer had two young daughters of his own.

"He's at the lake." And this time Mercer didn't stand directly in front of me. "He's alone, and I wouldn't kid him none about the child. Her folks—" and the lie died in a gulp as he finished. "She don't come around no more. Kidlike, I guess."

But I was past him and off for the pines, the overhanging cliff and the little shelter by the lake.

And I saw him. For once Vee Brown was doing nothing. Just gazing out onto the lake. I was down the cliff and almost on him before he saw me. Then he spoke.

"I wanted to be alone until the very moment I saw you, Dean, then—" and that twisted, wistful, crooked smile—rather more sad now. "I've got to talk to someone about her, Dean. I suppose her parents were right. The notoriety and all that!" He came slowly to his feet as he held my hand. "But complain or not, ninety-nine people in a hundred like to be in the papers. Erma, now. Oh—I know she's only twelve, and all that—but she would have found a way to write to me. She's more than a child, you know. Funny. I never felt that way about people, and now—it's like a part of me was taken out." He grinned just a bit boyishly. "Would the family be more likely to approve of Vivian, the song writer?" He turned toward the lake. "I miss her like blazes, Dean. With fear, I think, more than a longing. Sometimes at night I—" He turned and faced me—then both his hands shot to my shoulders. His eyes flashed, steadied, and peered deeply into mine. Then in a sudden outburst: "Out with it, Dean. Something has happened to Erma."

I told him. It was not his hands upon my shoulders; not the eagerness—the agony, perhaps—of his words. It was his face. The white, bloodless face; the searching, animal-like eyes; the twist of his lips. But while I was telling him a dead, blank sort of expression that I had never seen on his face before was there. He was so white—so drawn—that I thought he'd faint, and I held out a hand to support him.

He didn't faint. He just stood there, when I finished. Looked at me a moment, and then said very slowly. "What were you saying about Erma?"

I grabbed and shook him. Sudden fear gripped me. He hadn't heard me. No—that wasn't it. He hadn't understood. He hadn't been able to understand me. Something had snapped in his brain. His frail little body had— And then his whole frame seemed to tremble. He shook his head once or twice and rubbed a hand over his forehead.

"All right, Dean," he said finally. "It's there now—stamped upon my mind, every word of it. But it didn't fully register at first. I guess the mental, as well as the physical, can digest just so much

shock—then blooey. I think I had a close call. It never happened to me before. The thread that holds the balance in our brains must be very delicate."

"I shouldn't have told you. Not like that."

"But you should have. It's over and done now." And suddenly, looking directly at me: "What do you think I'll do?"

"Why—" I laid a hand upon his shoulder again, "there is nothing for you to do—even if you were in condition to do anything. I just couldn't accept the responsibility, that's all. I know what you think of your job—how you call yourself a Crime Machine maintained by the State. I know what it means to you. How you stand on loyalty; honesty; duty to the people, and—"

HIS laugh was like a sleigh on a dry pavement. "You don't believe that," he said harshly. "I would betray the State that hires me; the people who pay my salary; the men of the system I work with, and refuse to testify against the lowest scum that ever threatened our city government—and I'd do it without a moment's hesitation or doubt—if it would save Erma." He looked out over the lake again, and then half speaking to himself, "But would it save her? The child is extremely bright. A slit in the wood of a heavily boarded window—the chance that she might recognize the face of the man who brought her food or watched over her. No. Once the case has blown up; once I have gone on the stand and perjured myself against the State that pays me; once the Crime Machine has turned into a human being; once Vee Brown, the stolid, cold-blooded, hard-boiled detective —Killer of Men—has betrayed his city— then Benny Nevis' fear of retribution, together with his hatred of me, will bear fruit in a terrible vengeance. For it is Benny Nevis, Dean. We can be sure of that. Erma—" he clutched once at his side, staggered slightly, and straightened almost before I caught his arm.

"Come—" he said, and his voice was husky; his words stuck in his throat. "We must get to Boston and catch the afternoon train back to the city."

"You have a plan?" I asked.

"A plan?" His brows knitted. "No— I guess not. Unless the desire to hurt and maim and kill is called a plan. I tell you, Dean—I could go on for years. No evidence; just the slightest suspicion; just a hint from a stool pigeon in the under-world would be enough to make me—" His tongue came out and licked at dry lips. "Let's not mince words or excuse ourselves, Dean. We'll call it what others would call it—murder."

One of the police guard was fishing off shore, another stretched out on the small smooth plot of grass behind the generous farm house, a third read a book in the library. It was the fourth—John Mercer, who had held me at the door of the cottage before, who stopped us now as we went to climb aboard the old Ford, driven by the eldest of the Bender boys.

"If you're just taking a ride, Brown—" John Mercer eyed the bag I held, "why, I'll wake Jake up from his snooze in the yard and go along with you. Though neither the doctor nor I would advise a ride for your health, even if—" he grinned, "we may have different ideas about what constitutes your health."

Vee Brown looked at Mercer steadily. Looked too at the big hand that was casually laid upon his arm.

"I'm not going to lie to you, Mercer," Brown said very slowly and very calmly. "I'm not going to criticize you for doing what you believe to be your duty and keeping silent about Erma. Though,

after all, we're both cops—and I think you owed it to me. But one thing is certain. I'm heavily armed, so your well-known strength wouldn't help you any in stopping me."

Big John Mercer shrugged his shoulders as he looked at Brown's two empty hands.

"There's been no order forbidding me to carry firearms, Vee," he said. "I was picked for my quickness with a gun." And with a smile that only partly hid the threat in his words: "I've got orders to watch over you. In plain words, I can place you under arrest, as a material witness in the Grim case. Or," and now his lips set tightly, "I can draw, aim and fire in just one second."

BROWN shook his head. "Mercer, you and I both know that you'd be just one-half second too late." And then—in sudden appeal: "My God! Mercer, aren't you half a man? You have two daughters. Would you stay here, knowing what I know now—if it were one of your children? Can't you see that I love that kid as much as you could love one of your own? Can't—Come what may, I'm going."

"The police have been doing—"

"The police have done nothing. They can't do anything. It's my job. I got her into it. I'll get her out."

"If you feel that way, you— Damn it! Vee, you're not even fit for the train ride, and—and—" Mercer must have read the thing in Brown's eyes. The thing I had seen there but couldn't pin a name to. A mixture of hate and horror—and perhaps agony.

"He's right, Vee." I tried to make my voice low. "You're not fit to—"

But Brown turned on me with such a look—one of— But it would be only describable or recognizable to one who had hunted in Africa and seen the eyes of a wounded lioness.

"Oh, hell!" said John Mercer, "I haven't any mandatory orders to keep you here. Go on." And he helped him into the car: "Damn it! Vee, if you've got anything in mind take me along with you. I'll—" But Brown had waved Bender on, and the old car was leaping over the ruts of the country road which led to the smooth concrete.

I shall never forget that train ride to the city. Never forget the look on Browns face—but most of all, the words he spoke in our little compartment in that last stretch before we reached One Hundred and Twenty-fifth Street. It sent the chills up my back.

"Brown," I placed a hand upon his arm when his words were especially terrifying as to what might become of Erma if he could not save her, "you've got a big job to tackle, though for the life of me I do not see what you can do, since the police have failed. But certainly you can not help Erma or yourself—in that frame of mind."

"You think not?" He shook his head. "Well—that's the frame of mind I want to be in. I want to think how that highly strung, delicate child must be suffering. I want to think of— Oh, not too far maybe. Maybe not far enough to burst and let loose the blood that's pounding through my head now." He clutched at his head. "And perhaps, after all," he stretched his left hand out and opening it slowly stared at the palm and the fingers, before he closed them slowly, "I can overdo the thoughts. God! Dean, don't you see? I want to be in the frame of mind to commit a murder."

At One Hundred and Twenty-fifth Street we left the train, despite the fact that our meeting place with Jacob Rietzer was well downtown and we did not have

any too much time to keep the appointment.

"I can't chance the Central Station." Brown shook his head as we found a taxi. "John Mercer is a good man—but he's a cop, and an honest cop. The system is strongly implanted within him. He didn't try to stop me then, when his emotions were aroused—but later, when he thinks of it coldly— No, I wouldn't be surprised if Inspector Carrington, himself, is waiting at the gate down in the main station now."

And later disclosure proved that Brown was quite correct in that thought.

CHAPTER FOUR

The Count of Ten

JACOB B. RIETZER let us into his shabby, ill-smelling office and took his seat behind the highly polished, flat desk. Brown sat—or rather, seemed to collapse in the chair directly across the desk from the lawyer. I sat in the corner—recalling Brown's instructions that I was not to open my mouth, come what may.

Jacob B. Rietzer looked at the watch upon his wrist and came right to the point.

"My dear Mr. Brown, you do not look fit for travel—but I would have come to you if your friends had not made such action impossible. We are alone here and can talk freely. It would be better, perhaps, if I made things clear right in the beginning. That you are fond of the child I—or they, unfortunately know. The article in the paper was opportune or inopportune, according to the point of view one takes. I do not wish to be over-alarming, yet I do not wish to smooth over possibilities. I am speaking with the words of another.

"It is well known to others as well as to the authorities that Lieutenant Grim will talk if convicted—will talk to save himself from the chair. He had a confidence in friends—one friend in particular. That friend has kept him silent on the assurance that you will not testify against him. The thing is simple. If you testify, the child dies—horribly." He moved slightly back as Brown leaned over the desk. "Pray—let us have no dramatics. I am acting simply as an agent—and, I hope, an agent of mercy."

"Let us assure you that I have already helped, for it was the intention of a certain party to send you a token—a little—er—keepsake, to let you know that these warped minds held no conscience—no mercy. Look. Here is the child's ring." He snapped open a box and displayed a silver band with a bright stone in the center of it. "But for me," he said very slowly, very sinisterly too—and I thought there was a smack to his lips, "a finger would have come with that ring. You understand? Your word, now, that you will not testify—and it will be unnecessary to send you other little reminders of the child's danger. But, a week—a day even—that you hesitate, and there will be another message from the child—a message that will not be so easy to contemplate—the finger that wore that ring. You understand and appreciate why you must act at once."

"And if I do not testify?"

"The day the prison doors swing open for Lieutenant Grim, that day the child will be returned. You might hurry things, of course. Your influence—your assurance to the authorities that the evidence against Lieutenant Grim is not sufficient. The child is delicate—impressionable—and, I believe, she cries out for you even in her sleep."

"I see," Brown said very slowly. "Of course it is Benny Nevis who has the child. He realizes that if Grim talks, he gets the chair."

"That is not under consideration, my dear Brown—and problematical."

"I see." Brown sat very stiff, looking at Rietzer. His lips were one thin, red line now. No crooked, wistful smile. And his cheeks were drained of blood. "I have never betrayed my trust. I have never double-crossed the department. I have never put myself ahead of my duty —or anyone else ahead of that duty. Now I will betray that trust. I'll even go on the stand and make Lieutenant Grim's acquittal assured. I'll betray every confidence that has been placed in me. I'll perjure my very soul. I'll go to any length you suggest or request— as soon as the child is set free and delivered up to me."

RIETZER toyed with a pencil. "Ah! A catch. But—do all these things, and then the child will be delivered to you—alive and—fairly well."

"No." Brown shook his head. "My way. Give me the child and I'll resign from the department—swear to anything that will free Grim. My word of honor on it." He half stretched out his hand as Rietzer grinned.

"We progress." The lawyer looked at the hand but did not take it. "But we progress in the wrong direction. If I were acting for myself, or even advising my—er—client, we would say no more about it—and the child would be here at once. But it can only be as I stated."

"And what assurance would I have that the child would be given up—alive? They hate me, you know." And there was agony in Brown's voice.

"That same word of honor. This time, mine." And Rietzer stretched his hand across the table. "Is it a bargain?"

"If you were acting for yourself." And the twist to Vee Brown's lips, now, might have been a smile—but if it was it was a hard, cruel one. "But I can't trust them—can't trust Benny Nevis."

"Have you any choice?"

"Maybe not. I could—might—trust you But you are only an agent."

"But a rather well-informed agent."

"Yes—you speak for Nevis. But you know only what they tell you. You do not know that the child is alive, even— know for yourself, I mean."

"But I do know it," Rietzer said evenly. "She was alive and well. A little weak, perhaps—fading slowly, perhaps— crying rather pitifully, perhaps—and counting on you, Vee Brown, less than an hour ago."

"How do you know?" Brown's eyes flashed now. The old determination seemed to be there.

"I know." The lawyer half looked toward me.

"Ah!" Brown straightened. "I think, perhaps, that the statement of Lieutenant Grim—if he talked—would involve you greatly. Maybe up to murder."

"What of it?" Rietzer sneered. "I am giving you the information you seek. I am trying to help the child—not you. I guess I have as much reason to hate you as anyone. I— Well—you have nothing on me. At least—now." He leaned across the desk, his lips slipping back like an animal's, the polished gentleman gone. "You'd better speak quickly, Vee Brown. A wrong word from you now, and— But let me assure you. You will agree to the terms—agree to them gladly—beg for them—within a week. I am a student of human psychology. I can read your affection for that child far more in your face than I read it in the columns of The Globe. I— Don't you see, man? You've got to act quickly. She has seen one of— She—" And seeing the fire creep into Brown's eyes: "They dare not keep her much longer. Better agree to the best terms you can get."

"Yes," said Brown very slowly, "the best terms I can get. She has seen one of the men—a man who knows she can stand up in a court room, and with a single childish cry of fear, take forty years off his life. I can only guess that the man is Benny Nevis—and I can't convict him on a guess. I can only guess that you are involved—but I can't convict you on a guess."

JACOB RIETZER leaned back in his chair. "No, you can't convict me on a guess."

"No." Brown's whole body, from the waist up, shot forward across the flat desk. His right hand moved quickly in, and out again. At least there was a flash of a white hand in a blue coat sleeve— and now, that right hand which was empty before, held a gun. A heavy, black, snub-nosed automatic.

"No—" said Brown again, "I can't convict you on a guess. But I can kill you on a guess. Rietzer—where is the child?" And the gun shot across the desk, and the nose pounded against the lawyer's chest.

"I don't know." And the smile that Rietzer started, vanished like the children's game of rubbing an expression off their faces. "Good God! Watch that gun. You're a sick man. Your hand trembles like—"

"Like the hand of death," Brown cut in. "Maybe you don't know, Rietzer. Maybe I don't care much. I see little chance of saving Erma now—now that you've given away the fact that she saw a face. So—" and his words lacked energy, "tell me where she is if you know— tell me before I kill you. For I'm going to kill you, Rietzer. Yes—" he nodded and his words were almost dreamy "I'm going to kill you Rietzer—on a guess."

"What good will that do the child?"

"None." Vee Brown straightened now and his hand steadied and even a touch of color came into his cheeks. "But it'll do me good. Purely a selfish idea, Rietzer. Besides—it will be a notice to the others. Everyone, Rietzer, who has a hand in—in Erma's death. They'll know—and think.

"You are right. I love the child—as as much as if she were my own. More, even, than you think—than you could understand. I would have betrayed my trust; something dearer to me than life— my life—and certainly dearer than your life, to rescue that child. Now I'm going to count ten, and if you don't tell me where the child is, so I believe you—then you're out. And if you understand human nature—human psychology—you might explain to me before you die—why I, because of that affection for a child, will get a certain satisfaction; a certain pleasure, besides serving notice on Benny Nevis that men are going to die."

"It's murder, Brown—just murder. And you've always said you've never killed but in self-defence. Never—"

"Rietzer, you've lived long enough and played the game long enough in the underworld to know the racket. In the jargon of your kind, you're on the spot. On the spot, Rietzer—you understand. I'm going to count ten. *One*—"

"You couldn't do it. Not you."

"*Two*—" said Brown. "Maybe you're right and I won't be able to press the trigger when the time comes. *Three*— I doubt if I'd believe you, anyway. *Four*— Keep your hands so. No need to wipe the sweat from your face. *Five*— So you feel fear then."

"You couldn't do it. You can't do it. Cold-blooded murder!"

"*Six*— No, perhaps you're right. Don't tell me before I reach ten. Then we'll both find out. *Seven*— You're on the spot, Rietzer—just as you've put others there. It's a tough spot. *Eight*— If you have the guts to keep your mouth shut to ten, you'll find out if I haven't the guts to close a finger on the trigger. But I'll

be the only one to know if I have. *Nine*— Rietzer!" and Vee Brown's voice raised to a falsetto, stifled sort of shriek. "And I hope to God you've got the guts to keep quiet, because—"

"I'll tell, you devil. You'd have done it—you wanted to do it. I read death in your eyes." Jacob Rietzer involuntarily put a hand to his throat—and so did I. My own face was wet and cold.

THERE was a light banter in Brown's voice now, though a thickness to his words. "You disappoint me, Rietzer. There was a test there, and for my own satisfaction I— But come! We won't go through with it again."

"I was a fool to bring you here. I—"

"Come—come," said Brown. "We won't cry over spilt gin. Open up. If it's the truth—if I take the child safe, there'll be time for you to skip. If you lie, if you— Well—I'll come back—and then there'll be no childish game of counting numbers. Think one moment before you speak, Rietzer. If I don't believe you at once, you'll—" He shrugged his shoulders. "If you do lie, and fool me for the moment, I have a way of knowing you'll wait here for me."

"And if I give you the truth, you'll— let me go—at once?"

"Just as soon as I know where the child is."

"So—so. She's—" Rietzer looked at Brown a moment, and then: "She's in a warehouse off Tenth Avenue." He gave us the street number. "Benny Nevis is there with her. So help me God, I'm telling you the truth!" He fairly shrieked the words as Brown's gun shot up.

There was sudden terror in Rietzer's eyes. An upward jerk of an arm above his head, as if to ward off hot lead. Then, as the dull thud came, Jacob B. Rietzer sank in his chair, his flabby chin folding up on his chest, a dull red beginning to trickle down his forehead.

"Brown! Vee!" I was out of the chair now. "You—you don't know what you are doing. That blow—was—was it necessary?"

"Necessary?" Vee Brown came to his feet and half swayed, but raised a hand when I would have supported him. "Perhaps not, Dean—but I think that it was. Very necessary, indeed, to save his life. There—you do not understand me." He clutched me by the arm and pinched it. "You must put up with the foibles of a sick man. He will be quiet for a bit. Long enough, maybe, for us to find Erma. For he told me the truth, Dean. I know it. I read it in his eyes. It is much as we were taught. Dying men speak the truth! And Rietzer was— But, come." He led me to the door without even a backward look at the lawyer slumped there in the chair.

"We are not so fortunate as the detective of fiction, Dean." He ranted on as we descended the stairs. "I carried no handcuffs, nor was there a length of rope in the corner—left there inadvertently by a janitor who, just being discharged, had intended to hang himself. My belt, to be sure—Dean, might have served the purpose. But then, I have lost considerable weight and I am afraid my trousers would not have—" He bumped against me, steadied himself, shook his head and rubbed a hand across his eyes.

"Vee—" I placed a hand beneath his arm, half pulled his frail, fleshless body toward me, "the police. Telephone them. They can do better, and—"

"No—no—no!" He repeated each word louder than the others. "Don't you see, Dean. Benny Nevis is desperate. Benny Nevis will know of my appointment and will await word of the outcome of it. And when he doesn't hear from Rietzer, what will he do? He'll know, Dean. He'll know things went wrong. And he'll move the child, or he'll—he'll kill her. It may be minutes only, but once Benny gets thinking—thinking that I have refused,

and perhaps locked Rietzer up, he'll— When a man who knows Rietzer thinks of him, he'll think of him as yellow—think of him as lacking guts—think of him as squealing."

CHAPTER FIVE

Footsteps in the Dark

I HAD to help Brown down the street and lift him from his knees when he stumbled, getting into the taxi. But he gave the driver directions, offering double pay for quick time. Then he talked to me.

"Do you know what day it is, Dean? Of course you don't. I had forgotten myself. Tonight the song is released. It will go on the air at eleven-thirty. A coincidence that, Dean—or an omen? An omen! Do you know, Dean—I am going to kill Benny Nevis." A moment of hesitation. "It doesn't matter so much, does it? But I hope it won't be murder."

Brown suddenly came to life. He tapped on the window, ordered the taxi to the curb and paid the man as we got out.

"A block or two away—and a lonely neighborhood even at this time of night. Come. Undoubtedly Rietzer was to telephone someone. Not directly to the warehouse, even if there is a phone. They wouldn't chance a wire being tapped by the police. That should give us time. Rietzer's message would have to be relayed to the warehouse." He dragged me into a dark hallway and held my arm.

"We'll have to separate. No, Dean—there's no other way in fairness to—to Erma. There's a back alley to the warehouse—a fence, surely—and maybe a gate behind. At least, that's how they'd take her out if they decide to move quickly. I'll take the back, of course; you the front. The door there—you must simply guard it, Dean. Don't try to enter. You have a gun?" And when I confessed that

I hadn't: "No matter. Take this one." He thrust a heavy-caliber automatic into my hand. "I have another of course," he added, as if it was as natural for him always to carry two guns as it was for a near-sighted man always to have his spectacles, and I guess that it was.

"Remember, Dean, you are not a moving-picture hero. You are dealing with crime—the lowest kind of a criminal. You will be shooting at rats. If they should come out that door with Erma, no heroics on your part—no stand or I'll fire business. You're a fairly good shot and will be shooting from darkness into light—and into a rat, each shot. Remember that, Dean. For an honest man it is much harder to shoot another in the back. It only takes a keen eye and a steady finger to shoot a man smack between the eyes, but it takes guts to shoot him through the back of the head."

"Brown—" I caught the brightness of his eyes, the sudden red in his cheeks, "you can't go alone. You're not fit to go."

"I am not fit to go." For a moment that crooked curve to the side of his mouth—and he was gone, his small body flashing across the dim stretch of street light and being lost in the alley of the warehouse. Then just the blank darkness across the street—and silence.

Five—ten minutes passed, and no one came out of that warehouse. There was no light visible within. Dull, musty windows; a silent, dreary, deserted street. And I heard the whir of a motor, saw for a moment the curb lights of a car—then they went out. But just the same I could make out the dull outline of a low, black car, parked halfway down the block.

Then the shadow moving rapidly and silently down the street—past the door of the warehouse, to the driveway beyond. A sudden, quick turn—the whiteness of a face, and a man had disappeared into the driveway on the opposite side of the building from where Brown had gone.

WAS this the forerunner of danger? Was this the messenger that Brown thought would come from Rietzer? Was this the man who— But the child? It was easily possible that someone might have been waiting on the floor above—someone who visited Rietzer immediately after we had left—someone who had seen him slumped there in the chair, unconscious. Someone who might have found him already recovered from the blow on the head Brown had given him. And Reitzer! He might have talked. Might have told that Brown was going to the warehouse. But would he? Would Rietzer disclose the fact that he had sold out Benny Nevis to save his own life? Would he need to? Wouldn't he say that Brown had— But, Brown—inside—waiting. Or was he inside? Wasn't it just possible that Brown was lying some place back in the alley—unconscious—sick?

And I did it. I crossed the street quickly, slipped behind the high wooden fence that divided the warehouse from the dilapidated tenement next door, ran a bit down the alley, listened, ran a bit more, stopped dead—and heard it. Someone was opening a window. A window on the other side of that fence.

A quick, ineffective look in the darkness—and I realized, if there was a box to stand on, I couldn't find it. Then stretching up both my hands I jumped, grabbed the top of the fence and pulled myself up in time to see a man climbing over the sill of a window. Then he disappeared in the dense blackness.

I didn't wait. I climbed to the top of the fence, dropped to the other side, ran the few feet to the window, and keeping my body slightly to the side lifted my gun and chin over the sill simultaneously—and peered into the darkness. Then I threw up a leg and climbed into the black dampness of the warehouse.

I heard the man before I saw him. That is, the creak of the boards came to me before I stepped forward, rubbed my nose against a wooden upright, caromed slightly to the right and spotted the beam of a flash along the floor through a doorway now directly before me.

I reached that doorway before the pencil of light could disappear from my view. I have stalked game in Africa, but never with the same feeling that I now followed that man. The old, worn boards on the floor of that musty-smelling building gave up their dead. Desperately I tried to keep in step with the figure ahead—in step with that moving circle of light along the floor. I succeeded fairly well, or if I did not succeed—the beat of my feet was taken by the man as the tread of his own. Certainly I strained my ears to follow his footfalls.

He stopped suddenly. I think it was more the steady gleam of the light on the single spot, rather than the deadening of his footsteps that warned me. For, once or twice after that I thought that his feet moved. At least I heard the creak of the old boards—maybe from my own feet as I stood poised on the uneven floor beneath me, seemingly none too flat or steady.

But the noise died away like a distant moan. A great silence. Then plainly—eerie, perhaps—at least terrifying enough to send a cold shudder from my head to my feet, the long drawn sigh of— An animal? A man? A woman? All those thoughts at once—and all wrong. For, as that sobbing moan came again I knew it as the heart-tearing cry of a child. A long drawn, pitiful little moan of agony. Mental, perhaps, more than physical—but just the same, of horrifying agony.

I raised my gun—and the light of the flash raised too, wavered a moment on the wall, picked out the knob of a door—the

door itself, and into the circle of light I saw the hand of a man. Then three low taps.

The heavy tread of feet behind that door; the low, assured whistle of a man who has nothing to fear—and the door opened. Clearly framed in the light from the room beyond were broad shoulders, the salmon-yellow whiteness of a face, the thick lips and the hard cruel slits of eyes. It was Benny Nevis.

THE slim shoulders of the tall man I had followed passed into the light, a mean narrow face turned sideways, an arm stretched up to close the door—paused as the hand of Benny Nevis stretched out and pulled the arm down, leaving the door open.

"We'll be movin' the boat," said Benny Nevis. And I noticed particularly, at the time, that where his words were meant to be free and easy there was a certain nervousness to them—a hesitancy, perhaps, and a wavering uncertainty in the thin slits that partly hid the eyes beyond.

"There's only you and me, 'Slim'," Benny Nevis said as the two figures passed into the room and were lost to view. "Yeah, I know—" he interrupted the man called Slim when he started to talk. "I've been amusin' myself with the kid." And almost viciously: "Every squawk she makes is just like it comes out of the squirt, Brown. I hate his guts. But I'm through. The threat to Brown is as good if she's alive or dead—and we're a lot safer if she's dead. Who's to tell? Only you and me here."

"And Joe. He's—" Slim started, but Benny Nevis cut in on him again.

"Shut up, you fool. I let Joe go for just such a reason. Dead men tell no tales, Slim—and I guess that goes for women and children too—and even the kid here. Look—she's comin' to again. Somehow, I want her to know, when—"

So— That was all I wanted to know.

Benny Nevis had told me that he and Slim were alone there. I slid quickly forward, reached the door Benny had so obligingly left open, stepped into the light and took in the picture.

The two men were close together now, their backs to me. Benny had an arm on the shoulder of the man, Slim. A buzz as of softly whispered words came to me. But it was the child, Erma, I saw. Tied in a corner, crouched back against the wall—her golden bobbed hair matted about her head, the whiteness of her face showing even through the streaks of dirt made by the tears. Her little hands clasped before her—just her feet bound together with a thick rope. And her eyes! Wide and frightened, and perhaps not quite understanding. And then I knew that they were understanding, for they raised suddenly, stared a moment—and she knew me. But before the words could come from her mouth I spoke.

"Both of you put your hands in the air—and stand so." I leveled my gun and resisted the temptation to shoot them down. No—I had not forgotten Brown's instructions to shoot. I remembered them clearly, and also remembered his other words. "It takes more guts to shoot a man in the back of the head than in the front." Somehow, I just couldn't bring myself to shoot. Besides—there seemed little necessity for it now. I was master of the situation.

Two pairs of hands went into the air as one. Two heads turned, but only one head all the way. That was the head of the racketeer, Benny Nevis.

"Ah!" he said, "the little playmate of the boy-detective, Brown."

I should have been warned then, maybe. But I wasn't. For there was little of surprise in his voice, nor was there in his eyes that fear that Brown described in cornered rats.

Almost at the very moment that Erma gasped out her horrified warning to me the thing happened. I saw it on the floor. The shadow—the long shadow of an arm. I saw it swing through the air above my head as I involuntarily turned. There was a leer upon the face of Benny Nevis. I had been trapped. He knew I was there, had coaxed me on with the words that he and Slim were alone, while a man in the darkness beside that door waited for me to step into the light. The footsteps I had heard when Slim's feet had not moved.

I knew it all in a single mental flash, before the blow struck. And just as the blow came I squeezed my finger on the trigger of my gun.

I saw the man called Slim whirl and stagger against the wall—then the dull thud—a million flashing lights, but no pain. And finally the rising floor, as it seemed to come up and dash against my face. After that, blackness. Just a sinking—ever sinking blackness.

CHAPTER SIX

The Quivering Knife

A MAN was talking. It was Benny Nevis. I caught snatches of his speech.

"You're hardly even scratched, Slim. The kid's gotta die now—and him too. No, there's been enough noise. You say Rietzer was yellow. And, Brown— You saw Vee Brown bein' helped into a taxi. That means that lad came here alone. Of course I saw him from the window— knew that he followed you in. I had Joe stand so—in the doorway; waitin' in the dark. Just a lucky shot that damn reporter made. He ain't got the stomach for such work."

"Yeah. Lucky for you—not me." Slim was speaking rather weakly as I opened my eyes. "I'm done for, Benny. I can taste the damn blood in my throat."

"Nonsense!" said Benny. "There's Doc

Beck. He'll fix you up and hide you out. Tell him I'm good for a grand."

"Let me give it to him. Let me empty my rod in his stomach—in his stomach, Benny. The lousy, yellow rat. I—"

"No—" said Benny. "There's been enough dynamite. Don't you think, if I'd wanted noise, I'd of let Joe typewrite his name and address on him? No—you know the out. Not that way, you fool. Through the closet, there—behind them packing cases. The car's outside Sweeney's cellar. Beat it—I've got to finish the job alone."

In a dull, hazy way I saw Slim slip across the room, float, rather—for although the boards creaked, his feet never seemed to touch the floor. That was funny. Like a slow motion picture he glided past me through the air. I tried to raise a hand to brush the mist from my eyes, wondered if I was paralyzed—then realized suddenly that my hands were bound tightly behind me; that my feet likewise were lashed together. And now that my vision cleared somewhat I saw that the door I had entered was closed, and that across the middle of it—resting in iron supports—was a heavy bar of wood. Erma and I were alone in that room with Benny Nevis. Alone and helpless.

"Hello!" Benny Nevis put a cigarette in his mouth and stuck a lighted match to the end of it. "You've come around, eh?" He looked up at the single light which hung from the ceiling. "Well—you put the finger on Slim. I'm afraid he won't go far." He shrugged his shoulders. "If the worst comes to the worst, they'll lay this job here on him."

He walked close to me now and glared down at me.

"Yeah—this job." He finally snarled the words. "I'm goin' to put you out, feller. Vee Brown's buddy, and the kid he did the goofy act over. Maybe he's too mean to die. Maybe he's too quick

to get. Maybe he's the Crime Machine that they talk about. But it'll take more stomach than he's got to look at you and the kid. He got Grim, and Grim's yellow—and Grim will talk as soon as the judge names the date for the roast. And that talk will hand me the chair—if they get me. But I'm through with the city. Yeah, I'm through with it, just like it's through with me." He grinned. "Your laws ain't much good. They ain't made to cover my kind. For what are they goin' to do about this here job—you and the kid snuffed out? They can't touch me for that—there ain't no law that can hold me for that. You see, don't ya? They can't burn a guy more than once."

"You let Erma go," I said through thick lips. "You let her go, and I'll promise you that Brown won't testify. My word of honor. It isn't too late. You haven't— Let her go, and you're safe." I fairly screeched the words now, as for the first time I saw the knife in his hand. "I tell you, if you don't, Brown will follow you—get you—kill you."

HE balanced the knife on the palm of his hand. "Yeah? I ain't so sure that when Brown looks you and the kid over he'll feel like killin' anyone. I ain't sure it won't break that master eye—that quick-drawing hand—that deadly aim. I ain't sure Vee Brown's the man he was, since the kid was took. He didn't have the guts to make it with you tonight."

"But," I said, "it's your chance for freedom. This idea of vengeance against Brown— Is it worth your life? My word you'll go free!"

"Your word, eh? Brown's word! Not much good—either of them. Him a dick. But what about the kid? Smart kid, ain't she? Damn smart! She spent her time tellin' me how she'll know each one of us again. Little tricks to identify us by. Sits there bright-like, running things over in her mind and entertainin' me with 'em

Yep—talkin' herself smack into the grave. Threats too. Brown this—and Brown that.' And pausing a moment as his face twitched in passion. "What was that?" He swung suddenly now, a gun in his hand, looking toward the door. But I had heard nothing—unless— It seemed as if one of the great beams that served as a ceiling had creaked, but nothing to see there but shadows and blackness beyond the circle of light.

"No matter," Benny went on. "I'd have time for the job if half the police in the city were poundin' at the door." He walked across the room now, to Erma. I heard her cry out.

"Close your eyes, Erma," I shouted, setting my teeth tightly—but I could not close my eyes. They just would not stay shut. Rigidly those lids stayed open—rigidly, too, my gaze—my stare of horror was focused upon the child.

Benny kicked her roughly and spoke.

"Look up, kid. Open them glims—them pretty eyes that will soon be closed for good. Do you know why? Because you took care of and saved the life of a rat that didn't have the guts to save you, because they'd take away his pretty gold shield and give him thirty days for perjury—and maybe write mean things about him in the paper. Leastwise, that's what he thought—though I'd of slit your pretty, squawkin' parrot throat anyway. Once—for nursin' the boy-detective back to life; once—for— But open them glims. Well—maybe a little touch of sharp steel will make you think different. I want to see you die, kid."

And as the knife went up I screamed. I couldn't help it. And as the knife poised in the air and Benny half turned his head to leer at me, I cried out.

"Don't you see? She's only a child. Don't—"

And I heard Erma's whisper. "Vee—Vee—" and then something I couldn't

catch. Certainly she didn't cry or sob or moan.

"I like that." Benny Nevis looked at me a moment. "I like the way you're takin' it. Child, eh? Ten or eighty, tongues make words. Words that—" And the knife again. A shriek from me, that never really came but died with horror in my throat. My burning eyes that tried to close but couldn't—and the flashing steel.

And above my cry of horror, that came this time—was a terrific roar which seemed to shake the small room; a puff of orange-blue flame some place above the child's head. My glance went to the ceiling, caught the whiteness of a hand, the blackness of something in it, the curling smoke. Another roar and spouting flame —and I looked at Benny Nevis.

He was kneeling, but now his head was down upon the boards of the floor, his hands stretched out before him. I saw his right hand move—the fingers move. Though he must have been dead I saw those fingers uncurl from the knife—saw the knife quiver there in the wood close to Erma's head. Then I looked up. For again came that same sound—as if a beam moved. And this time it did move. There was a pair of legs, a small frail body—and Vee Brown dropped into the room.

Almost as soon as he hit the floor he had thrown off his coat and tossed it over the thing that had been Benny Nevis.

"Praying to Mecca." Brown seized the knife quickly and cut the ropes that held Erma. "There. My Goodness! You stand up just fine." He steadied her. And then holding her at arm's length he looked straight at her a moment, into those wide staring eyes. "Erma—Erma!" he cried, and swept her into his arms.

IT WAS some time that I lay there forgotten, while he talked to her—desperately — quickly — frantically. And I thought that I knew the truth. Something had stopped working in the child's mind.

Finally Brown set her down on her feet and shook her, then he raised his right hand and brought it sharply across her cheek. It jarred her, and I saw her eyes blink. She looked at him, threw her arms about him and cried out.

"I knew it, Vee. I just knew you'd come, Vee." And the next moment she was sobbing in his arms.

"I'm surprised at you, kid." Vee was laughing now as he held her, her back to the weird shape upon the floor. "Why—we've often talked about it and gone through it together. Now, let's pretend that it's just a dream. Look! There's Dean, all trussed up like a big Thanksgiving turkey." And so he went on—talking to her—laughing—and finally the sobs stopped, and she just clung to him and rubbed her matted head against his shoulder.

"There're the papers too," Vee said, after he had cut my ropes. "They'll want your picture again, Erma. It isn't every girl who has helped catch a desperate criminal. And they'll want you to talk to them. And— Goodness me! What will they say if Vee Brown—the great detective, Vee Brown—is going to marry a girl who can't—"

"But I can," she said as we cautiously left the old warehouse. "I'm not afraid any more." And then she lied magnificently, and I think that the lie did her good. "I wasn't ever afraid—not exactly afraid. I knew you'd come. But I thought—"

"Sooner, eh? And I would have too. But I wasn't so strong, you know—and I had to wait a bit because I had to climb up to a window. And how silly it would all be if I fell—and how the papers would laugh and—"

"You're not well, yet," Erma said, and then—which might have been funny if it wasn't so human; so pitifully serious: "You shouldn't have come, Vee. You're not strong enough."

Erma slept while we were in the taxi, breathing easily but for an occasional spasmodic jerk, when she clutched Vee tightly as he held her close to him.

"And that's age for you, Dean." Brown ran a hand through her hair, smoothing out the snarls. "I thought for a moment it was going to be too much for her. Ten years—five years from now, perhaps it would have changed her whole life. But in another hour—this time tomorrow—it will be just a glorious adventure. Remember two things I told you. You'll want them for your article. That gunmen love the dramatic; they want to talk too much. And this time Benny Nevis talked himself to death. Oh—I heard your shot but couldn't find my direction. It was the steady drone of Benny's voice that finally led me to the loft above that room. And a loose plank. We might do no better than quote the Bible there. Benny looked for the mote in my eye, you see—but not for the beam above his own. Cheap, that attempt? Well—maybe. But you see what I mean. He was so attentive to the small things that he didn't see the large ones. Not even a two by four above his head."

"And the other thing you told me? You mean—"

"Exactly. That society is served as well by a bullet, or bullets, in the back of a criminal's head as between the eyes. Though—" he shook his head, "I was wrong about it taking guts to shoot a man in the back of the head. At least, this once. It was really the simplest—the most natural thing in the world to do—perhaps even a bit pleasant. But headquarters must be notified, and Erma's father and mother of course. You can have the scoop for your paper, for I won't let her see reporters tonight." And as he pulled the little head closer to him: "Benny Nevis was a mess, wasn't he—Dean?" And, damn it—he laughed!

There was no understanding Brown. A

few hours before, he was a sick man—ready to drop on his feet. Now, after all the hell he had gone through—well—there was even color in his face.

NOT much later the three of us were alone in our penthouse, atop the exclusive Park Avenue apartment. Erma was propped up on the couch, fresh from the tub and wrapped in one of Vee's bathrobes. So—we awaited her mother and father, whom police headquarters were able to locate very quickly when Brown telephoned them the news of her safety.

Brown was laughing and talking to the child like a boy.

"The best treat yet, Erma. That's the reason I went for you tonight." He was looking at the electric clock above the fireplace as he tuned in the radio. "Special for you, Erma. Special program and everything. Vivian—who— There, you rascal, you mustn't wink at me. It's just you and Dean I trust now. Listen!"

And it came. Clearly from the broadcasting studio the announcement that the audience was to be doubly thrilled, and the studio doubly honored. The charming Letice Lee, from Broadway's greatest musical-comedy success, would sing Vivian's latest composition. First time over the air—or, for that matter, the first presentation anywhere. And then the magic words that brought the color back into Erma's cheeks; the sparkle of youth again into her eyes.

"This song, When I Grow Up, is dedicated by the composer and author to Miss Erma Van Warren, of Maine and New York. Miss Erma Van Warren."

Brown whispered to me. "I stipulated that they must repeat the name twice there, and once again, when the last chorus is sung."

As the song started the door bell rang. But Erma did not hear it. Her face glowed—her chin was held in her little hands, and her bright vivid eyes seemed to travel right through the radio, out over the air—

Brown followed me to the apartment door. There was a little cry, and a sob. A woman shoved by us, rushed toward the library door. Brown reached her, held her back, and pointed.

"Wait—" he said. But the woman could not wait. As she rushed toward the child, Brown sighed. "All the medical attention Erma will ever need is coming over that radio now," he said.

A sob—a cry—soft kisses, and the voice of Erma.

"Oh, mother! It's been written for me —by Vivian, the greatest song writer. And, mother—he's—" A gulp, as loyalty to Vee downed her pride. Vivian got the idea from the story about me and Vee, in the paper. That's why it's for me."

While Mr. and Mrs. Van Warren took turns, or both held the child at once, and the district attorney himself stood framed in the doorway, Brown said to me: "Now —as an authority, Dean, what do you think was the big moment in this—this case?"

"Why—" I hesitated. "Not the shooting, perhaps. That was not the decisive moment. You wouldn't have been there if Rietzer didn't talk. No—I think it all rested on that single moment when you held the gun against Rietzer's chest. When you told him he was on the spot. Perhaps, the final count of nine, when you threatened him with death. You did it well, Vee. I don't think it would have gone over with me—but, after all, it was a glorious bluff."

"Was it?" Vee looked up at me, and his lips parted in that crooked little smile as he turned his eyes toward the child. "I guess that's the way to write it for your paper, Dean. Bluff! But I wonder if it was."

The
SCARLET
COMET

by

John Lawrence

He threw himself forward,
his gun slashing down
viciously.

Along a metal path it thunders—the crack limited of the G. E. Line. Five steel cars hurtling through the night—and in one of them a lurking killer. For death and mystery ride the Scarlet Comet as it threads its danger way from coast to coast.

CHAPTER ONE

The Man in the Lobby

PAUL BRYANT swung along Forty-second Street, the head of his stick buried in the pocket of his Chesterfield overcoat. From under the brim of his hat, his quiet brown eyes regarded the after-luncheon crowds mildly. His inspection was purely impersonal, but from long habit, each passing face received a careful, if momentary examination.

A clock in a drug-store window caught his glance. It was 2:30, yet he did not hasten his pace. The depression having cut monstrously into the free-lance criminal investigator's business, it made little difference these days at what hour he reached his office.

He turned northward at Lexington. Halfway up the block he stepped from the curb, picked his way carefully across the street, mounted the curb at the other side, and headed for the Chandler Building.

Behind him sounded a sudden screeching of brakes, and from the corner of his eye he saw a yellow cab suddenly cut into the curb, jamming to a blunt stop. He turned quickly, in time to see a little man in a derby hat catapult from the taxi, duck low, and dart into the crowd, just as a second cab shrieked to a stop behind the first, and a scowling, heavy-set man leaped out in furious pursuit.

The little man raced toward the lobby of the Chandler Building, crouching. And Paul's hands came out of his pockets abruptly, as he saw the pursuer whip a black revolver from under his coat.

The appearance of the gun changed the situation abruptly for Paul. Before, the little drama had had the appearance of comedy. But there was nothing funny about the revolver. With a sudden bound, he threw himself forward to head the gunman off, jammed his way expertly through the crowd, and angled in on the door, just as his man yanked it open, sprang through.

Paul stooped in a flash; his stick shot out, jammed between the flying ankles of the man. There was a frantic shouted curse, as his legs tied themselves into a knot, and his momentum carried him into a floating dive. The door swung closed in Paul's face, just as the heavy-set man crashed sprawling, face down on the cork floor inside the building, the revolver spinning from his hand, directly across to the feet of the elevator starter.

Paul yanked the door open. The startled crowd inside were still undecided whether to shout or run. They milled stupidly about. Paul pushed his way as quickly as he could to the center of the floor, caught just a glance of the would-be attacker as he scrambled up and ducked into the crowd at the far side of the lobby.

Unfortunately, the building was jammed. By the time Paul reached the side doors, the other had vanished. And, as far as a moment's inspection could determine, the little derby-hatted man had vanished also.

The investigator stood around the lobby for a few minutes in the vague hope that one or the other would reappear.

When they didn't Paul shook his head sadly. If ever a man stood in need of the services of a criminal investigator, the little derby-hatted fugitive was that man. And he had disappeared.

Paul went outside, looked round for the two cabs perfunctorily. They had gone.

There was the gun that the elevator starter had recovered, but Paul could see little to interest him in that. If he asked to examine it, explanations would necessarily ensue, and further waste of time. Paul gave it up.

The incident seemed closed, a total loss. Paul took a handkerchief from his pocket, wiped the perspiration from his pleasantly lined face, and went back into the lobby. He boarded an elevator.

At the tenth floor he got off, walked slowly down the hall, pulling off his gloves. Before the glass-panelled door marked "Paul Bryant—Investigations," he stopped.

For a moment he hesitated, unable to clear his mind of the matter, then dismissing it sternly, he shrugged, opened the door and stepped inside.

Sam, the red-headed guardian of the reception room, looked up anxiously as he closed the door, his eyes shifting to a point over Paul's shoulder.

Paul said quietly: "What's wrong with you, Sam?"

"A—a caller, sir." Sam inclined his head toward the row of chairs against the wall. Paul turned in surprise—and looked into the grimy, anxious face of the little derby-hatted man.

IT WAS the first time Paul had had a chance to recognize him. It was Moe Leavitt, a pawnbroker, and as unpleasant a character as Paul could number among his wide acquaintance. Leavitt shot from his chair, waddled eagerly across the room. "Bryant!" he cried quickly, "I got it for you business—quick!"

Paul looked him over in disgust. "I don't want your business, Leavitt," he said shortly. "If I'd known it was you, I would have let that fellow alone."

Leavitt's eyes went wide. Evidently he was not aware of the identity of his deliverer. "Huh?"

"Let it go," said Paul. "And you can go, too, any time now."

"Nah, nah!" interposed the other. "Bryant—you shouldn't talk like that yet. Wait—don't take off the hat and coat. Real business, I got, already—"

"I can't use it, I tell you."

"Wait!" Leavitt's tones were anguished. "Wait, yet a minute, Bryant—

Look—you should just go and esk that I get back my own proppitty. Robbed, I'm being robbed!"

"What's wrong with the police?"

Leavitt's face registered extreme pain. "The police—they are not for the poor. They would not listen to me. Besides, it's not business for the police—yet."

Paul stuck his hands in his coat pocket resignedly. "All right. Go on, if you must."

Leavitt threw up his hands. "Go on, he says! Today, right now, he may be leaving the country!"

"Who?"

"J...the goniff that gives me the double cross! The low-down, thieving son of a—"

"Wait a minute!" Paul said sharply. "If you insist on telling me this, start at the front."

Leavitt wrung his hands. "You got to help me, Bryant—I have a deal with a fellah—we're partners—now he's got all the goods, and he's running away, even. I go to his office—a big goy gives me a push in the face! I come down here— they follow me with gunmen in taxicabs even!"

"What's the deal?"

"What do you care?" cried the other wildly. "He won't talk back to you. You flash your badge—"

"On who?"

"On—on—I'll take you by his place!"

"What's his name?"

Leavitt shook his outstretched arms. "Questions, questions, and he may be on a boat already!" he whined. "All I want is my own propitty, Bryant—I guarantee! I'll pay you good money!"

"How much money?"

"Two thousand—five thousand dollars!"

Paul grunted. "It must be good and crooked. I don't want any part of it, Moe."

The little Semite grabbed for Paul's

arm as he started to unbutton his coat. "Make it then ten thousand!" he begged frantically. "Ten thousand—but come now—we may be too late already!"

Paul tried to disengage his arm. Leavitt only clung tighter. Paul said quietly: "That's enough of that."

It had no effect. Leavitt raved on, two big tears trickling down his grimy cheeks. "More, then—whatever you want! Ach! I am bankrupt if you don't help me—I have no time to go to nobody else—I ...Oi!...Oi!...Oi!"

Paul grew suddenly tired of the byplay. He swung Leavitt round, grasped him firmly by the collar of his coat and the slack of his trousers, and lifted him from the ground. Sam, a little tardily, sprang up, jerked open the door, and Paul tossed the pleading, struggling pawnbroker gently into the corridor, closing the door quickly on his bleating.

"If he comes in again," Paul told Sam, "give him a dose of the ammonia gun."

Sam grinned.

Paul went over and hung his coat and hat in the cupboard. "Any calls, Sam?"

"No, sir."

"Where is the paper?"

"On your desk."

Paul washed his hands and face, ran a brush over his lightly curling brown hair, whisked a few flecks of dust from his gray suit, and closed the little cupboard door. Then he went in to his private office.

HE wandered over to the window, looked down at the busy entrance to the Grand Eastern Terminal, shook his head sadly, and went over to the flat-topped walnut desk. He sat down, spread the paper open, and began his daily hunt for a little business.

Crime items, according to a recently inaugurated custom in the Bryant Agency, were marked with blue pencil. The rare ones in which a reward was offered for anything, rated a red border. Business having faded to practically nothing, Paul was no longer above trying to drum some up, even to the extent of looking for a spot for himself in the daily news.

On the first page, the usual gang killing.

On page three, what seemed like an ill-advised statement of some Federal official, evidently driven to rashness by the recent notoriety given the successful activities of the jewel smugglers, to the effect that: the criminals having overstepped themselves to the extent of attempting a wholesale shipment of diamonds, to the surprising value of two million dollars, which even now was suspected to be en route, certain capture awaited them on arrival. The back of the traffic, he announced boldly, was about to be broken.

On page seven, the account of the conviction of Marshall Lounsbury, a patricide in whose detection and apprehension Paul had been instrumental. This he read with interest.

Rather, he read halfway through with interest. Then, giving up the struggle, he laid the paper aside, lit a cigar and tilted back in his swivel chair. Moe Leavitt held his interest.

As a business requisite, Paul was reasonably well aware of most of what went on in New York's underworld, particularly among the lesser fry. Owing to a policy of charging extremely stiff fees, Paul drew more clients from Wall Street than he did from Broadway, but in spite of his splendid reputation among the former, there were times, such as now, when he had to look almost entirely to the white-light district for his livelihood. Consequently, the quiet-mannered investigator was more than well acquainted with both the character and activities of such denizens of Broadway as Moe Leavitt.

And the thought of the shady pawnbroker offering ten thousand dollars for a few hours work did not square with either. There was no doubt that the Semite was a dealer in stolen goods, among other things, and only from this angle could Paul see any reasonable explanation of his sudden generosity. Some deal involving a large amount of loot was evidently in progress, and Leavitt was getting the double cross.

If that were so, there might be a possibility of getting in touch with the legitimate end of the case—the person from whom the loot had been lifted originally!

Paul racked his brain. Scores of minor robberies had been committed recently, but none that could be classed among the figures that would make Leavitt's ten thousand dollar offer seem reasonable.

Then the phone rang.

Paul lifted the receiver. "Mr. Bryant speaking."

"Is Moe Leavitt there?" questioned a low, husky voice, obviously disguised.

"Why, I don't know. Who is calling?"

There was a moment's hesitation, then: "This is a friend of his. I was to meet him there."

"Well, he's left. I'm sorry."

Again a hesitation. "Did he engage you, Bryant?"

"That is entirely my own business," Paul said quietly. "Why do you ask?"

"Because something has cropped up, Bryant. If he has engaged you—forget it. Or neither of you will live for twenty-four hours. Is that clear?"

"Perfectly."

Before he could say more, there was a click in his ear and the wire went dead. Paul placed the receiver back on the hook, let his quiet brown eyes rest on the instrument for a minute. Then he pressed the button for Sam.

CHAPTER TWO

Murder by the Clock

PRESIDENT ARNOLD SALM'S eyes under his bushy brows were filled with anxiety, as he shot unseeing glances over the milling crowds. So were those of the fellow director with whom he stood conversing in low tones in one corner of the Grand Eastern Station. Both men fingered open watches nervously.

The Scarlet Comet Limited was leaving in a few minutes on her maiden, and, if all went well, sensational trip across the continent.

She lay now, a shining steel caterpillar, on Track 1. Every device of modern engineering had gone into her special construction to prepare her against the gruelling journey. Extra tenders were on the train, to obviate even the most infrequent of stops. A double crew rode with the crack engine, for relief. Every comfort and service yet designed was available to the small, but exclusive group of passengers.

Under the staggering guarantee of fifty-two hours from coast to coast, President Salm had succeeded in soliciting the patronage of the very cream of intercoast business men.

In deference to the wishes of these men, publicity was avoided, insofar as the actual hour of departure was concerned. To avoid the mobs of curiosity seekers, only employees and actual passengers knew the hour of the impending start. No signs showed in the blackboard beside Track 1. Occasionally a passenger slipped quietly by the two men, exchanged a greeting. At Salm's nod, the iron door was pushed aside by a trainman, the passenger went through, and the gate was closed again.

Yet publicity was, of course, the main reason for the sensational attempt. The

Comet was President Salm's final gamble against the badgering array of circumstances that had arisen in the past two years to eat slowly and discouragingly into the profits of the line. The country-wide depression, following the collapse of the stock market; the intense competition, both from rival roads and from the ever-encroaching air services; the refusal of the I. C. C. to allow higher freight rates. Inevitably these things had translated themselves into howls from dividendless stockholders, which in turn had bred a faction on the board that clamored for Salm's removal from office.

Taking the responsibility on his own shoulders, Salm had grimly appropriated the many thousands of dollars necessary for the construction of the super-train, had boldly issued announcements in the name of the line, and had the project well under construction before his enemies could find any means to check him. And now it was ready.

A successful run would mean advertising, prestige, publicity, worth many times over the amount expended; would establish the New York Eastern in the minds of the public as the greatest road in the country, and indubitably increase the business of the road.

A failure—well, President Salm preferred not to think of a failure. So carefully indeed had he planned it, had the plans checked and rechecked, that it seemed more than probable that Salm's venture would be crowned with success.

As four o'clock drew nearer, the waiting room took on a gradually higher pitch of activity. Literally thousands of people scurried across the floor. The circular information desk in the center was besieged by mobs of bewildered travelers; the voices of the track announcers droned out more quickly, as the arrival and departure of trains stepped up to its customary afternoon peak.

Red-caps were at a premium. Progress across the room became more and more difficult. The great throaty roar of the busy terminal fell in rising waves on the ears of the two executives, as they stood waiting nervously, their eyes on their watches.

It was six minutes to four. Only six more minutes of waiting till. . . .

Suddenly, from under the information-desk clock, with shocking clearness, two crashing staccato reports roared out, in the very heart of the swirling humanity. Salm dropped his watch, whirled toward the sound, panic in his heart.

Above the bedlam of noise, came a hoarse, bleating cry of agony. Like a receding wave, the roar of the shocked crowd was silenced by the sound. The scream fell to a guttural gurgling, ended horribly in a retching cough. There was a single moment when it seemed that utter silence held the room. Then the body of a man flopped heavily to the floor, his head cracking on the marble.

NOISY hysteria took hold of the milling mob.

Salm turned wildly to the nearest employee—the trainman at the gate—and shouted: "Ring for the police—and the hospital!" and followed by the other official, threw himself into the crowd.

The station was in confusion. Hoarse shouts, feminine cries blended together in an undertone of panic. Some trying to draw back, others pressing forward, created a whirlpool in the center of the great waiting room, with the ugly, ominously still thing on the floor as a vortex.

Arnold Salm, fighting, shouldering his way through the panic-stricken mob, forced his way frantically to the center of the press. Dishevelled and hatless, he burst through the inner fringe.

On the marble floor lay the body of a small man, on his stomach, his head turned crazily over one shoulder. Blood was trickling from his mouth, and a bloody froth, already drying, coated his lips. One hand was hidden under him, clutching his abdomen. His eyes were wide, staring. They seemed to glaze even as Salm looked at them. A widening pool of blood oozed from under the man. There was a heavy automatic pistol on the floor beside him—and a derby hat.

Then the organization of the railroad took hold. With astonishing dispatch, the railroad police snapped into activity, summoned by the attendant Salm had sent. On the very echo of the last scream, doctors had been called from distant parts of the building. Now they came running, burly men forcing a way through the crowd for them.

Two doctors arrived from different directions simultaneously, knelt beside the stricken figure together. Their quick diagnosis could not help but agree. They signaled for the stretcher, and the limp, lifeless hulk was quickly hurried toward the small hospital on one of the upper floors of the terminal.

At the same time, the railroad detectives went into action. The revolver was recovered; a dozen keen-eyed men filtered through the crowd, seeking witnesses, questioning those who had been in the vicinity. At least four or five men must have been actually touching the murderer when the shots were fired, yet the press around the booth seemed to have hidden him as effectually as though he were invisible. A dozen contradictory descriptions were received. At least two witnesses claimed the man had shot himself.

Grimly unmoved, the detectives took down everything that was offered. Yet even at this stage it was apparent that there was little of value to be found.

The city police were notified—of murder.

President Salm swung round, looked up at the clock, as the body was being rushed away. It was exactly four o'clock. He made his way back to Track 1. The trainman had not yet returned. He threw open the iron door himself. The red lights on the rear platform of the Scarlet Comet were just swinging out of sight around a bend in the tunnel. Salm wiped his forehead, let the gate go shut again, and made his way toward the line of telephone booths, his eyes worried.

Five minutes later, he had his general superintendent on the wire, advised him of what had happened. "There's something going on, Jim," he said. "I don't know what it is, but I've got the wind up badly. Somehow I don't think that killing stands alone. Why would anyone choose our terminal for a murder?"

There was a silence on the wire for a moment, then hesitantly: "I can't say that I agree with you, Arnold. The police will no doubt clear things up, but if you are worried, why not get that fellow Bryant. Paul Bryant, his name is—you remember—he worked for us on that forgery business a year or so ago."

"Yes, yes," said Salm, "a capable man. Do you happen to know where I can get hold of him right away?"

LESS than five minutes later, Paul arrived.

He stepped from the elevator at the hospital floor, took a card from his vest pocket, and laid it on the desk before the white-gowned nurse. "Mr. Salm just phoned for me," he said quietly.

The girl looked at the card, gave him one quick glance of approval, and handed it back. "Last door on the right, Mr. Bryant."

Bryant hooked his stick under his arm, went down the hall, stuffing his gloves in his pocket. He rapped lightly at the door indicated.

It opened quickly, and Arnold Salm

looked out, anxiously. His face relaxed a little as he saw Bryant. He stood hastily aside, dabbing at his mouth with a handkerchief. "Good of you to make it so quickly, Mr. Bryant," he said.

"What's the trouble, Mr. Salm?"

"Murder."

If Paul was surprised, he did not show it. He removed his hat, as he noticed the sheeted figure in the center of the room. He took in the scene quickly.

Several detectives from the city force were huddled in one corner, examining the contents of the dead man's pockets. Two of the railroad men stood idly by, watching. Bryant stepped forward, laid his hat, stick and gloves on a chair, and went over to the trestle-supported stretcher. He removed the cloth from the face of the dead man.

It was Moe Leavitt.

One of the railroad detectives edged over curiously. Paul dropped the sheet, turned back to the president.

"How did it occur, Mr. Salm?"

Salm told him.

"They've identified the dead man, of course?"

Salm looked at the detective. The man stepped forward interestedly. "No. We haven't yet. Do you—"

"His name is Moe Leavitt. He conducts—or rather conducted, a shady jewelery shop on Forty-eighth, near Broadway. Probably a dealer in stolen goods. In other words—a fence."

The railroad detective's face lighted. He said "Thanks," hastily, and turned and went over to the group in the corner.

Paul followed him; the others grouped about the table stood back for him. One man murmured a greeting, but Bryant was absorbed in the exhibits.

Beside what had come from the clothing there was the death weapon, an automatic pistol of some foreign make with which Paul was unfamiliar. On the extreme end of the barrel was a smudge,

covered with white powder. One of the headquarters men had been trying to bring out a latent fingerprint.

A huge ring of keys, a package of cigarettes, four lead-pencils and two watches, he noted without interest. And there was a scrap of note-paper, evidently recently torn from some larger piece. On it was written in pencil:

Meet me at your shop at 4:30.
J. G.

CHAPTER THREE

In the Wake of the Comet

BRYANT looked at his watch, then up at the headquarters men. "Which of you is in charge?"

The same man he had already spoken to answered.

Paul went on: "It's just a little before 4:30 now. Why don't you send to his shop, and try and pick this J. G. up for questioning?"

"I was thinking of that," said the detective, and turned toward the door.

"Wait a minute," Paul said; "Send one of your men across to the Chandler Building and ask the elevator starter for a revolver he picked up during a scuffle in the lobby early this afternoon. There may be fingerprints on it, and if there are, apart from the starter's own, I think they'll be those of the man that killed Leavitt."

The detective looked at him blackly, suspicion in his eyes: "Say, what the hell? Are you trying to kid me, wise guy?"

"No. I'm sorry. I'll explain later. You'd better move, though. The killer might get the same thought himself."

The man hesitated. "All right, but if you—"

"Do as Mr. Bryant says!" broke in Salm, and the man hesitated no longer.

"I'll go myself," he said, and strode

to the door, yanked it open—and narrowly escaped collision with a frightened-faced youth who almost fell over the threshold as the knob for which he had been reaching was pulled from his grasp. The boy shot a quick look around the room, located Salm, and took a hasty step toward him. The detective growled, and went on out.

The boy stood looking miserably at the group that surrounded the table. He licked his trembling lips.

Salm caught sight of him, swung angrily round and snapped impatiently: "What are you doing here, Colton?"

"The—the yard super sent me, sir—I—I've got to speak to you alone, sir."

Salm frowned, took the boy by the shoulder and led him over to the door. For fully a half minute, the boy spoke into the president's ear in a strained whisper.

Salm's face went white. He snapped out some orders to the boy, opened the door and pushed him hurriedly through it. Then he turned quickly to Bryant. "Mr. Bryant—this way, quickly!"

Bryant laid down the note, and philosophically crossed the room and went out the door the president held open. As it closed behind him, he looked down at the old man's twitching face in bewilderment. "What now?"

"Wait!" Salm burst out miserably, drawing him toward the elevator, "I—I'll tell you in a minute. I don't want anyone to hear."

Colton was standing there, holding the elevator door open. They hurried in, dropped to the main floor. As they raced across the waiting room they saw that it had returned to normalcy. Paul glanced curiously at Salm. The president's lips were a thin white line, and there was sweat in large beads on his brow.

The boy ran ahead, pushed open the iron gate at Track 1. Then as they passed through, Salm threw a hasty glance behind him, and blurted out: "Another man's been killed, Mr. Bryant—another one!"

"A murder?"

"Yes, yes!"

"Hold on, then!" Paul grasped the old man's sleeve and stopped him. "You'd better tell someone to get those police detectives down at once."

"No! No!" Salm cried wildly, "I—I've got to talk to you about it first!" He clutched Bryant's arm tensely. "Please come and see him first. There—there's something that—I'll tell the police right away, afterwards—"

Paul took one look into Salm's frantic eyes, then without comment, turned and did as the old man wished. They went swiftly down a long passageway at the extreme right of the tracks. A small office was set in the stone wall, near the end. Salm was half running when they reached the office and went in.

A BURLY man in shirt-sleeves started up from a chair, a uniform cap in his hand. There was a doctor in a white coat standing at the end of a couch.

And on the couch lay the huddled monstrosity that had recently been a human being. The first sight of it took even Paul's breath away.

He fought down his horror, stepped closer to examine the victim. The shirt had been ripped away. Three bullet holes gaped blackly in the flesh of the left breast. The face had been brutally, seemingly deliberately, smashed into a ghastly crimson pulp. From hair line to throat, there seemed no skin. Nor was that the end. The fingers had been severed, as though by the stroke of a giant cleaver, from the hand. Only a gory, mutilated stump remained.

Paul looked over at the doctor, asked through frozen lips: "The hand?"

"Run over by the wheels of the train."

"The face?"

"Beaten deliberately with some heavy instrument, I think."

Bryant turned back to Salm. "You'd better get the police at once, Mr. Salm. Who is this man, doctor?"

The doctor shrugged. "Someone's removed every identifying mark from his clothing. You can see that the features reveal nothing."

"Where was he?"

The doctor did not answer. He looked over at Salm. The president cleared his throat. His voice seemed to have dried, flattened. "He was found on the roadbed, about a quarter of a mile out of the station, between the tracks over which the Scarlet Comet Limited had just passed."

Paul's eyes lit up faintly. "That simplifies matters. You'd better stop that train at once. Have her brought back to the station. Has she a wireless set aboard?"

"She—she had everything there is. But —I—God, Bryant—I can't stop that train! You—you don't know, of course, but—it means my absolute ruin if—if anything happens to throw that train off schedule—anything!"

Paul frowned.

"I appreciate that you want your trains to run on time, Mr. Salm," he said quietly, "but don't you think you are losing your perspective? This is murder. You can't play ducks and drakes with murder. Obviously the body was dumped from the Comet, or whatever you call it. Equally obviously, then, the murderer must be aboard."

"Maybe not," pleaded Salm. "Maybe the body was just taken there, and left accidentally on the track."

Bryant turned to the doctor. "How long has he been dead, doctor?"

"It's impossible to judge with absolute accuracy. I would guess he died just a few minutes after four o'clock."

Bryant looked back at Salm. The president looked down at his hands, twisted a handkerchief between shaking fingers. Bryant said kindly: "Don't make it any worse, Mr. Salm. Surely you can see our man must be on the Comet. If he gets away—Lord knows what the law will do to you."

"Our first stop is eight hundred miles away—we'll have them watch the train at that stop—catch him—"

Paul shook his head. "There's another angle, too, Mr. Salm." He nodded toward the couch. "The man that did that is not a normal man. I don't say that he is, but he may be, a homicidal maniac—or it may be that he had some definite purpose in his handiwork. At any rate, I should hate to have the responsibility of letting him roam around among your other passengers."

Salm carried the handkerchief to his lips. "God, Bryant," he said desperately, "you don't understand. With this train, we're trying for a record between here and the Coast—we've advertised it— guaranteed to shoot the regular schedule to bits! We've got big men—important men, riding with us, under that guarantee. If we stop—for any reason at all—it means my finish—and a terrible, terrible blow to the road. Isn't there—can't you figure out some way—"

Paul hesitated. Finally he shrugged, walked over to the door. "Come outside a moment, Mr. Salm."

THE president followed him outside, his eyes suddenly lighting with hope. Paul closed the door behind him. He said quietly: "I think you're making a terrible mistake, Mr. Salm, but if you insist, I'll do as you say. First of all—how many people know of this?"

"Only those in that room. The yard superintendent discovered the body and brought it in himself. He was unseen, and he waited to communicate with me before going any further."

"Can you depend on them all to keep quiet about anything we may decide?"

"Absolutely. They are all utterly loyal to me."

"I suppose you realize that the minute you notify the police they will stop the train themselves?"

Salm avoided his eye. "They won't," he said, flushing, "if I just tell them the body was found in the yard, and don't bring it to their attention that it was thrown off the Comet."

Bryant shook his head. "That's a damned serious offense if you're found out, Mr. Salm."

The president's face was the color of putty. "I can't help it!" he burst out. "If I stop that train—no matter what justification I have—my enemies will find a way to put me at fault! They'll capitalize on it—throw me out of office. The stock market's got most of my money, Bryant—I can't, frankly, face the loss of this job. There are other angles, too, but —I'll—I'll go to jail, rather than stop that train, or have it stopped!"

Bryant slid his hands into his coat pockets. "You are absolutely determined?"

"Absolutely!"

Bryant shrugged in resignation. "All right. What time did this precious train leave?"

"Four o'clock."

"We have nearly an hour to make up then. What's her speed?"

"She can make up to eighty-five. A steady seventy, anyway."

Bryant snapped his watch shut. "All right, Mr. Salm, I'll try. You realize, of course, that if I don't lay hands on your killer before we hit Frisco, it means the end of my career as a private investigator? That it may mean a jail sentence for both of us as well?"

Salm swallowed hard. "Why, why— yes, I suppose that's right. I—I hadn't thought of it—"

"It's all right. I just wanted you to realize all that. Also that if the man is the type I suspect, the minute he thinks that I'm on his trail he'll do his best to murder me, too."

"Oh—oh, I hope not—"

"Well, don't worry—I don't propose to let him. But—if I do crack it—remember all this when I send in my bill. Now, wireless the conductor to expect me within three hours. You'll have to arrange a momentary stop for me to get on. Also, tell him to put the wireless out of commission till I arrive. No messages are to be sent or delivered from now on, without my seeing them. Tell him you'll wire exact instructions about the stop, as soon as we find out how soon I can get there."

Salm said: "How are—"

"Have you got your car here?"

"Yes, but—"

"Go in and tell those people to keep mum, to lie, if necessary, about where the body was found. Also, no one is to say a word about my being on the case. Send a boy up to the hospital to get my hat and gloves, then you're going to drive me out to the Long Island airport. And hurry!"

CHAPTER FOUR

Aboard the Death Limited

AS HE stepped from the cockpit of the plane, the free-lance criminal investigator glanced at his watch. It was just 7:10. He pulled a small suitcase out after him, took off the flying gear he had used, and tossed it back into the plane. He shook hands with the pilot that had flown him out, walked a few yards away, to be clear of the slipstream.

The pilot grinned, gave the plane the gun, ruddered her around and bumped forward. Gradually, he picked up speed, roared across the weed-dotted field, slipped gently upward, then pulled for altitude. He rose in a long bank, swept back over Paul's head, then straightened out, back toward New York. He waved a cheery farewell.

Paul sat down on his suitcase by the side of the track and lit a thin cigar. The sun had just set, and a cold breeze stirred across the fields about him. He had estimated a ten-minute wait, but it stretched a little.

It was exactly 7:30 when the distant keening of the whistle reached his ears; then the rumble of the approaching wheels, and the melancholy clanging of the bell.

The pounding wheeze of the engine grew louder and louder. Finally it swung roaring around a bend several hundred yards down the track. Like a live thing, breathing fire, it seemed to be tearing straight for him; then the wheels shrieked as the brakes bore down more heavily; lighted windows started to flash by him, and the monster slid to a long, protesting stop.

Paul's eyes flew along the side till he located the single opened vestibule. Even as he found it, a figure in a uniform cap swung down to the ground, peering anxiously through the gloom. Paul picked up his suitcase, hurried forward.

The moment he was seen the man's arm started moving up and down, in a wide arc. He called out: "Mr. Bryant?"

"Yes."

"Let's go," said the conductor hastily.

Paul threw his grip aboard, just as the engine gave a grunting lurch. He scrambled quickly up the iron steps. There was a snarling puff from the stack, the great wheels started to revolve once more, as the conductor swung himself up onto the stairs. The angry *cha cha* of the engine grew quicker and quicker; the train seemed almost to leap forward; the pounding of the tires on the steel tracks rose in a crescendo—and the ill-fated

Scarlet Comet rushed once more into the night.

The conductor forced the door shut, came up the steps and released the iron plate that fell across them with a bang that was hardly noticeable in the larger racket of the threshing wheels.

Conversation was already impossible. The conductor pointed to the door leading into the car, and Paul stepped through, the other at his heels. As the door swung closed behind him, the noise dropped astonishingly. Paul started to brush some of the soot from his clothing.

"I'll open up a compartment for you," said the conductor considerately, "and you can brush up, if you like."

NOT till he had completed his ablutions, and they sat facing each other in the tiny stateroom, did the lantern-jawed official disclose any curiosity. Then, with characteristic directness: "My name's Brock, Mr. Bryant. I'm absolutely in the dark about all this. Mr. Salm's wire said you would enlighten me."

Paul shook hands. "The long and short of it is that you have a killer aboard—a murderer."

"My Lord! Who?"

"That's what I'm hoping to discover."

The conductor wiped the inside rim of his uniform cap with a handkerchief. His gray eyes were troubled. "Who—who did he murder?"

Paul told him what he knew. The conductor jumped up hastily. "I found some bloodstains between two of the cars just after we'd started! I thought someone had had a nose bleed!"

Paul said: "That's fine. We can start from there. Let's see them."

"I—I had them cleaned up."

"Well, let's see where they were, then. Is it far from here?"

"No. The train is short. There's only five passenger cars. This is a test trip. You know that, eh?"

"Yes," said Paul, "I know that." Then, as they passed out into the corridor: "Where is your first stop? Are any passengers booked to get off?"

"Colorado Springs, around dawn tomorrow. No one is getting off. Everyone goes through to San Francisco. This is a test—"

"I know. Where did you find the bloodstains?"

"Between the first and second cars."

"Can you give me a room near there?"

"Yes, surely."

Paul halted. "I'd better take my bag."

The conductor pointed a thumb forward. "You can send a porter for it."

As they started forward again, a young man lurched in sight from the rear. "Mr. Brock!"

They turned. The young man had a square of yellow paper in his hand. "A wire—" he hesitated, then: "Is this Mr. Bryant?"

"Yes. Our wireless operator, Mr. Simmons."

"Glad to know you," said Paul.

"This wire is for you, then, Mr. Bryant." Paul spread it open. It read:

PAUL BRYANT
ENROUTE SCARLET COMET:
FOUND BLOODSTAINED SPANNER AND LARGE RUBBER SHEET IN GRASS FOUR HUNDRED YARDS FURTHER OUT. NO FINGERPRINTS.
SALM.

Paul stuck it in his pocket, looked seriously at the operator. "I hope you understand the necessity for keeping absolutely mum about this, Mr. Simmons."

"Yes, sir. I do."

"Don't send or deliver anything till I see it, eh?"

"Right-o."

The operator turned again toward the rear. Paul and the conductor worked forward, through two cars, till Brock checked him, pointed a bony forefinger at the faint traces of the gruesome stains he had discovered.

From all indications, the body had been squeezed through the side opening at the intersection of the two cars. It cleared Paul's mind on that point. He had wondered how it had reached the track.

They stepped inside the second car, at Paul's signal.

"How about a room near here?"

The conductor drew out his diagram. "I think H is vacant, right here. I'll make sure."

It proved to be available, and a minute or two later Paul sank gratefully into the cushioned seat in Compartment H. The porter was dispatched for the suitcase in the rear. The conductor sat gingerly on the little seat.

BROCK looked at his watch, coughed. "Dinner will be ready pretty soon," he suggested.

Paul's eyes narrowed. He seemed not to hear. "Let me see your diagram, will you, Mr. Brock?"

The conductor handed it over and Paul studied it carefully.

Dr. Zelig was in compartment A. Mr. and Mrs. Murray and servant occupied B, C, and D. Mr. S. Silver had E. There was a vacancy in F, though it was reserved from Colorado Springs onward. Thomas Fahey held G. And, of course, H appeared as vacant.

Paul copied the information quickly onto the back of an old envelope, and handed the diagram back to the conductor. He got up, tucked the paper in his pocket. "Now maybe we'd better try and get some of that dinner, Mr. Brock."

"Good! Do you mind if I wash up a little?"

"Fall to," said Paul.

Paul took advantage of the interval to memorize the names on the diagram.

The conductor finished, emerged righting his cap. Together the two men made their way forward to the diner.

The conductor halted in the doorway, turned back to Paul, and spoke in an undertone. "At the end table on the left— Mr. and Mrs. Murray, and their man. They're in your car."

He went on. A waiter pulled out two chairs for them, and they sat down. Paul studied his neighbors covertly.

Murray was an elderly man—in the early sixties, Paul guessed. His hair was thin, and pure white; his complexion was pasty. His eyes were pale gray, the type that shows no emotion. How the young and lovely Mrs. Murray could endure the unpleasant old man was baffling to Paul. She was at least thirty years younger than Murray—probably forty. A striking blonde, of Junoesque proportions; flashing brown eyes, and a really enchanting mouth, none of which, Paul realized, was wasted on Murray. The old man kept such a constant gaze at her that the girl seemed a little restive under it.

As for the third member of their party, it took Paul a minute or two to determine what it was that made the man seem odd. He was dark, heavy-set, and the glance he had given Paul as he came in showed a pair of alert blue eyes. It was not until after the investigator had ordered his dinner that he realized that the man was not eating. His mien was that of a man constantly on guard. Guard! That was it, of course. The man was a bodyguard!

Which bred the questions: who was Murray? And why did he need a bodyguard? Brock did not know.

Duties claimed the conductor as they finished eating, and Paul made his way back to his compartment alone.

THEY were making good time and the train lurched and swayed as they thundered onward. Halfway back to his compartment the radio operator overtook Paul, handed him another message.

PAUL BRYANT
ENROUTE SCARLET COMET:
GUN FROM CHANDLER BUILDING SHOWS PRINTS OF JOSEPH MUNRO ALIAS BLACKIE. WHAT ACTION SHALL I TAKE?
                    SALM.

Paul smiled. "Wire Mr. Salm to have Munro arrested, on a charge of attempted assault, and try and hold him till I can get back. Also tell him to sweat Munro to find who hired him to attack Leavitt this morning."

Simmons nodded gravely. "Right."

"Have you got all that, or shall I write it?"

"I've got it."

"If he has trouble with the police, tell him to contact Inspector McMurtry, a friend of mine."

"O. K., Mr. Bryant."

Paul proceeded on his way.

He had negotiated two of the cars that separated him from his own coach, had his hand on the vestibule door of the third, when he caught sight of a hurrying figure coming toward him through the glass. It was Murray's bodyguard.

Paul drew back, let the man open the door. He affected no particular notice of the man, would have passed by, but a detaining hand was laid on his arm.

"Excuse me—Mr. Bryant?"

Paul looked down at him curiously. "What makes you think my name is Bryant?"

The other grinned sourly. "Hell, I've seen your face a thousand times, around N'Yawk, Mr. Bryant. My name's Burton. I'm with the Munsing Detective Agency."

"Oh," Paul said, more pleasantly. "What could I do for you, Mr. Burton?"

"That I don't know," said the other frankly. "I was hoping you could give me a tip-off—" He broke off suddenly. "I say, would you mind coming back to my room a minute. I'm not supposed to leave Mr. Murray—that's the mug that hired me. I'm just up here in number two."

"So am I," said Paul. "Lead on."

They made their way back together, Burton's stocky figure in the lead. At the door of Compartment C, the bodyguard stopped, would have opened the door.

Paul inclined his head toward the front. "Suppose we use my room."

Burton nodded. "O. K."

Paul opened the door and followed the bodyguard inside. It was not till he had closed the door behind him that he noticed the square white envelope, tucked in the corner of the flat seat.

He reached over and picked it out quietly, as Burton seated himself in the cushioned seat, and produced a vicious-looking cigar.

"My situation is this—" Burton began.

Paul said: "Excuse me, just a minute, Burton," and turned toward the door. There was no writing whatever on the envelope. It was unsealed. Paul drew out a folded sheet of bond paper, turned it open, and read.

So the great Bryant is on our trail! What you expect to accomplish at this late date, Bryant, is a mystery to me. We want no more killing, but if your wretched snooping gets in our way, I promise you you'll be the next. This is no piker deal, Bryant, and you won't get one inch leeway. Remain in your room tonight—all night—and you'll be all right. Stick your nose into things that don't concern you, and I'll kill you without a second's hesitation. Surely you realize by now that we mean business.

There was no signature.

Slowly, his lean face without expression, Paul slipped the note back into the envelope. For a moment he looked at it speculatively, then slipped it into his breast pocket.

THE threats gave him little concern, though he was fully aware that the writer of the note was quite capable of trying to carry them out. What did interest him, was this certain proof of the fact that the killer was aboard the train. Until now, strong as the intimation was, he had had no actual certainty.

And from the angry tone of the letter, he was beginning to worry them—or him. There was comfort in that.

No sign of his feeling showed in his expression as he turned back to Burton, sat down opposite the bodyguard. "Sorry," he said quietly. "Now what was it you wanted to tell me?"

Burton cleared his throat. "Well—I'm hired to protect this bird Murray—d'ye see what I mean? I dunno what from— he won't admit there's anythin' to look out for. But I figure like this—why would he lay big jack on the line for a private shomus, if he ain't afraid of nuthin'. D'ye see what I mean?"

"Why, indeed?" said Paul.

"Well," Burton shifted uneasily in his seat, pointed with his cigar, "they go and stop this train to leave you get on. Now I happen to know this here is a test trip. So I figure like this: there's somethin' big in the wind, and Bryant's the man to tip me off. Y'see, here's the lay: Murray's scairt of somethin' You come noseyin' aboard, meanin' they's somethin' to be scairt of, and I'm s'posed to be protectin' Murray, and if they's anything I should watch out for—how's for tippin' me off? Mebbe I could make it right with you—some way? D'ye see what I mean?

"Not exactly, no."

Burton grew red, ran a finger inside his collar, "Well—if there's trouble around—we must be workin' on the same proposition more or less, and mebbe you could use me somehow. For nuthin', of course," he added hastily.

Paul stared out of the window. Burton was no mental genius, but he could, probably, handle a gun. And from the looks of things, an able gunman looked pretty good to Paul.

"It just happens that I could, Mr. Burton," he said slowly, "but you'll have to work more or less in the dark. I can't tell you what it's all about."

Burton scratched his head. He did not answer.

"In return," Paul said, "I'll share the responsibility of keeping Murray out of trouble."

Burton brightened. "Say, that O. K. with me," he said promptly. "O'course—why I hesitated, well I got to look out fer my principal—y'see what I mean? But if you're workin' with me—well, that's O. K."

"Very well. Here's what I'm worrying about at the moment. We're stopping at Colorado Springs at six tomorrow morning. No one is supposed to get off the train. We've got to see that no one does get off."

"Yeah, yeah," said Burton attentively.

"The only vestibule door that will be opened is the one in the rear of this car. I have reason to believe that someone in either this car or the one ahead, will try and make a break. Can you handle a gun pretty well?"

Burton's eyebrows went up. "Why, sure, I can look after myself. Is it as bad as that?"

"It's very bad. There'll be no hesitation on this job. If we have to shoot, we will."

"Well," Burton said, "that suits me."

Paul got up. "Then, I'd advise you to turn in and get a few hours sleep. I'm sure nothing will happen till close to six."

Burton got up too. He shook his head. "I got my sleep this afternoon, Mr.

Bryant. I got to stay up all night—stay awake, I mean."

"Well, I'm turning in, anyway," said Paul. "You might look in at five to be sure the porter has roused me out."

"I—well, for—"

Burton's eyes were on the doorknob of the room. His mouth hung open in mid-sentence. Paul looked around.

The handle was turning, slowly.

CHAPTER FIVE

The Extra Passenger

BURTON'S hand flashed to his armpit. Paul reached for the snub-nosed automatic in his hip pocket.

Then the door whipped silently open, and a young man darted swiftly inside. He had actually closed the door behind him, before he realized that the room was occupied. Then his eyes fell on the two guns covering him. "Oh—oh, my God!" he said bitterly.

"Stick them up high," snapped Burton.

The man shot his hands above his head.

Burton stepped quickly forward, ran an expert hand over him for weapons. He drew a blank.

Paul pocketed his pistol. "What's it all about, young man?"

The intruder swallowed hard, licked his lips. "I—I thought it was vacant."

"Well, what if it was?"

The young man did not answer. His pleasant blue eyes sought the floor.

"I'll call the conductor, Mr. Bryant," said Burton.

"Wait a minute," Paul said, then to the boy: "You can put your hands down. What's your name?"

Silence.

Paul frowned. "You're asking for trouble if you take this attitude, you know. Would you prefer that we call the conductor?"

"No—I—no."

"Sit down, then," Paul said reassuringly, 'and tell us about it."

Their prisoner sank wearily into one of the seats.

"There's nothing much to tell. I haven't any ticket. I was trying to duck the conductor."

"You've lost your ticket?"

"I didn't have a ticket. I sneaked aboard."

"How, for heaven's sake?"

The boy looked up in faint surprise. "There's nothing much to that. I told the fellow at Track 3 I was seeing someone off and sold him the idea of letting me through. Then I ducked across the platform to Track 1. I saw some—acquaintances getting aboard, and there was no one to stop me so I did too."

"And you expected to beat your way to the coast without being caught?"

The boy shrugged. "I had to see a man on this train. I couldn't catch him anywhere else. Before I could locate him the train pulled out."

"Who did you want to see?"

"Abe Lyman."

"The motion-picture man? Is he on this train?"

The boy nodded.

"If you know him, won't he lend you enough to pay your passage?"

"No. He's down on me too. I thought I could talk him into seeing my side of the case, but it was no dice."

"What case?"

"I got fired from Atlas Pictures last week. I've been trying to see Lyman ever since."

"Are you a movie actor?"

"No. A director."

Paul sat down patiently. "If you are on the level, I may help you," he said quietly, "but take my word for it—you are in a bad position right now. Give me the story about this Lyman."

THE director laughed bitterly. "I'll give you the story, all right. Lyman is nothing but a catspaw. Everybody thinks he's the big shot in Atlas. I thought so, too, till now. He's just Green's office boy."

"And who is Green?"

"Green? Why, Jake Green, the capitalist."

"Green then, is behind the Atlas picture company from which you've just been fired, eh?" said Paul wondering why he was listening to the tale.

"You said it. It was Green that had me fired."

"Why?"

"Well—I guess he thought I was making a play for Mary Millicent."

"Were you?"

The boy flushed. "Well—yes. She hates Green—she told me so. She has to be friendly with him, or he'll fire her. He's a damned old bloodsucker."

"And," added Paul, "jealous of your attentions to Miss Millicent. Why? What is his relationship to Miss Millicent?"

The boy colored darkly. "She's just a friend. Nothing more—and I'll kill anybody that says she is."

"Say listen!" Burton broke in disgustedly. "What's the use o' tryin' to give us all this hooey, mug? You think we don't know who you are? You think we don't know what ya done? Why, hell—"

"Relax, Burton," Paul said sharply. "Let the boy finish his story."

"Aw, hell—"

"That'll do, Burton!" Paul's voice was impatient. Burton fished out another cigar, bit the end off viciously. Bryant turned to the boy. "Now what's all this about Miss Millicent? I don't follow pictures myself, but I understood she was quite a well-known star."

"She is! She is! She's the best actress in pictures," he declared vehemently.

"Green picked her up as an extra, and he pushed her along. Naturally, she appreciated it, and tried to be decent to the old mucker. Yet when she told him she wanted to marry me—he threatened to ruin her."

"How? A well-known star like Miss Millicent—"

"That's just the trouble. She's a high-priced artist. If he had her fired, she'd have a hell of a time getting located again, with every studio trying to cut down on everything. If she weren't quite so good, she wouldn't have the same trouble."

"I suppose she told you all this?"

"Sure."

"And she wants to get away from her —friendship with Green."

"Yes."

"To marry you."

The boy nodded.

Paul got up, wandered over and got himself a paper cup full of ice water, digested the young director's story.

If true, there seemed nothing at all to connect him with the case in hand. If not true—well, it was rather a shock to Paul to discover how easy it had been to get aboard unnoticed.

JAKE GREEN'S name was no strange one to Paul. Operator of a bucket shop before they were chased out of existence, he had amassed a huge fortune which he had consistently employed in shady enterprises ever since—at least, so Paul was convinced. Persistent rumors had, at one time or another, linked the banker's name to that of various racketeers in New York, to the effect that Green's money was financing a good many of the liquor shipments from foreign countries. Yet there seemed no handle to all this, as yet. He turned back to the youth.

"You haven't told me your name, yet," he reminded him.

"McNeil. Oxford McNeil."

Paul fished—and got a surprising bite. "Where is Green now?" he asked.

"Why, they're on this train—both he and Miss Millicent."

"Oh, indeed?" Paul said casually. "Whereabouts?"

Burton said: "Say, listen, Mr. Bryant—"

Paul silenced him with a gesture. "Burton," he said wearily, "why don't you take a look at your employer? He may be in trouble."

"Eh?" Burton suddenly got up. "Say, that's right! Wait for me, just a minute, will you? I'll give a look. You'll wait, huh?"

"Of course."

Burton went out. Paul smiled at the young director. "You were just saying that Green and Miss Millicent were on this train."

"Well, they are."

"Are you very fond of Miss Millicent?"

"I am, if it's anything to you." McNeil flushed.

"Would you—kill a man to protect her?" Paul persisted.

The director looked at him steadily for a long minute. "I don't know," he said finally.

Paul reached absently for a cigar, found he had none. His fingers came in contact with the slip of paper on which he had copied the conductor's diagram of the car.

"By the way—what car are Green and Miss Millicent in?" he asked idly.

"Why, this one."

Paul's fingers closed sharply on the diagram, and he drew it out. "Oh," he said. "Oh, indeed. Do you happen to know which compartment?"

"They have different compartments!" snapped McNeil. "Green has B; Miss Millicent has D."

"There it was, at last. Paul's eyes fastened on the diagram. There was no room for doubt. The so-called Murrays were Green and Miss Millicent!

Green! And the initials on the note found in the pocket of the murdered Moe Leavitt were—J. G. Could it be— Paul recalled the unpleasant face of the old man he had seen in the dining car. That he might have planned the thing was readily conceivable, but that he would have the physical stamina to carry it out— it seemed incredible. Yet why the secrecy? Why the bodyguard?

"How did you find out where they were quartered, McNeil?"

"She—she told me."

"She knows you're aboard, then."

"No. I saw her a moment in the station before they left."

PAUL considered. "What time did they get on the train?"

"Well—I guess around 3:30. Maybe a little earlier or later."

"And you followed them on."

"Yes, as soon as I could wangle it."

"How long was that?"

"Just a minute or so."

"Did you leave the train again before it pulled out?"

"No. I was trying to get in to speak to Miss Millicent. I wanted to ask her where Lyman's room was, but Green kept popping in and out. I was afraid he'd see me and have me thrown off, so I decided to hide till we'd left."

"Where did you hide?"

"I gave the chef my last twenty-dollar bill. He let me hang around the kitchen, and he told me this compartment was empty."

"Did Green get off the train at all, after he once got settled aboard?"

"Yes, sure. You see he had somebody come ahead of him and get him settled. The rooms were all ready when he and Mar—Miss Millicent came on. He went

off directly after that, back towards the gate."

"Good," Paul said, then as the doorknob rattled: "Don't repeat this—to anyone, understand?"

The boy nodded as the door opened and Burton reappeared. "O. K.," the bodyguard said. "He's readin' a book to Mrs. Murray."

The investigator yawned. "Burton," he said, "I'm going to turn in for a few hours sleep. As far as this young man is concerned—I'm going to take a chance on him, for the present. You will say nothing about his being here, till we decide what to do with him."

Burton breathed heavily through his nose. "Awright!" he said warningly. "You prob'ly know yer biz'ness, Mr. Bryant, but I wouldn't care to sleep in no room wit' this mug."

"Well, if he murders me, you'll know who did it and you can make the pinch, Burton. In the meantime—good night. I'll see you just before we hit Colorado Springs. Keep your eyes open."

"Sure, sure. Well—good night," said Burton, a little doubtfully. Paul opened the door, and he went out.

When he was gone, Paul turned to the baffled director. "You slip down the hall into Compartment F, McNeil, while I have these bunks made up." Then as McNeil would have broken into voluble speech: "Save that till later. Do as I say, now."

The youth complied readily. Paul pressed the bell.

He sat down, took a sheet of paper from his bag and wrote:

Arnold Salm
Grand Eastern Terminal
New York City
When you catch Munro, tell him Jake Green has confessed saying that Munro is the killer.

Bryant.

There was a tap at the door and the grinning porter entered. Paul tucked the message in an envelope.

"Make them both up, George, upper and lower. And get me a half dozen good cigars, like a good fellow. Also give this to the wireless operator, and tell him to send it personal." He held out the envelope with a ten-dollar bill.

"Yas, suh!" said the porter, then dubiously: "Did y'all say bofe bunks?"

"Yes, both bunks. I might get restless in just one."

Paul went out, leaving the porter scratching his head. He started on a hunt for the conductor. There were certain instructions that he wanted to convey. Also he wanted to make sure the conductor would not come bursting in on him, and discover his roommate.

Half an hour later, he rolled in between the sheets, called a cheery goodnight to McNeil in the upper berth, and switched out the light.

CHAPTER SIX

Murder in B

AT 5:30 Burton knocked on the door, and Paul let him in again. The investigator was fully clothed.

Burton said: "We're due in three quarters of an hour."

Paul nodded. "This is what I want you to do, Burton—stand watch between the first and second cars and see that no one gets off. The conductor is making arrangements to have the rear cars looked after."

"What are you going to do?"

"I'll take care of the rear of car two. That's where the door is going to be opened."

"You think the mug you're after will try and escape here, eh?"

"It's his only chance. This is the only stop before Frisco. If we can prevent

him now—I'm sure I can break this case tomorrow morning. This is no tea party, Burton—they'll shoot to kill, and we've got to be ready to also."

"Are there more than one of them?"

"I don't think so. But there might be. At any rate, no one is to get off this train —alive. Do you follow me?"

"Sure. I get it."

"That's all then. Make yourself comfortable, if you like. I've got some figuring to do."

The two detectives sat in silence as the miles rolled by underfoot.

At a quarter to six, Burton said: "I guess I'll have to take one more look at Murray," and put his hand on the knob.

"Wait a minute!" Paul jumped involuntarily to his feet. For a moment, he hesitated, frowning. He had not realized that the threatening note had made such an impression on him. Yet the warning had been to stay inside the room. There was undoubtedly danger waiting outside, of some sort. Paul did not like to see Burton face it. He said: "I'll go with you. And watch yourself. Something is due to happen, anytime."

Burton blinked.

PAUL led the way outside, his hand on his gun, now in his side coat pocket. Nothing happened.

Burton unlocked the door of the sleeping man's cabin. As the light fell athwart the bed, the sleeper sighed and stirred uneasily. Burton closed the door.

The porter emerged from Compartment F. He started at the sight of the two guns in the hands of the detectives. Paul said quietly: "How long till we're in, George?"

"Fi' minutes, suh. I was just comin' to get y'all."

"Good. I'll go with you, now. All set, Burton?"

"All set, Mr. Bryant."

Paul followed the porter, who was muttering to himself, out into the corridor. The last he saw of Burton, he was heading grimly toward the front of the train, clutching his revolver firmly.

The lights of the town became more numerous, flashed more frequently past the windows. Paul and the porter stood alone on the swaying vestibule, as they thundered over the various switches and cut-backs.

The speed of the train began to slacken.

Just as they roared under the sheds, the conductor emerged from the car behind. His face was a little pale, and his eyes were red-rimmed. It was apparent that he had had no sleep. Paul opened the vestibule door, and they stepped inside, where speech was possible.

"I've got every porter standing in the rear vestibule of his car with his hand on the emergency bell, Mr. Bryant," he said quickly. "All the doors are closed. I don't think anyone can get off back there without our being warned in time. How about these two cars?"

"I've got them taken care of. What about the crew on the tenders up ahead?"

"The engineer is watching them."

"Did you arrange with the station police to guard all the exits from the platform?"

"Yes. They'll be out of sight, but no one can escape from the cordon they will have drawn around the yard."

The train gave a lurch, as the air brakes gave a preliminary screech, throwing them forward. Paul said: "You'd better come out on the platform with me. Have you a gun?"

The conductor had. They stepped outside again. The conductor stood in the well of the rear vestibule—the front of the third car. Paul stood in the other, opposite the door that was to be opened to take on the passenger.

Then the brakes began to take hold more viciously, and the long chain of steel cars shunted against each other violently. The harsh grinding of the brakes rose to a crescendo, and once more the whistle gave a melancholy wail. Paul reached forward, drew the trembling porter toward him. He leaned down, and shouted in his ear: "How long do we stop here?"

The porter held up three dark fingers.

"Don't climb down," Paul warned him, "till you see your passenger coming."

The darkey nodded violently.

Paul slipped the safety catch off his automatic, slipped back into the well, and waited.

With a great clanging, and blowing off of steam, the Scarlet Comet came slowly to a clashing stop, stood panting in the Colorado Springs station.

The porter looked round anxiously. "Will—will I open the do'?"

"Yes."

THE cool night air blew in Paul's face, as the darkey swung the steel covering and stepped on the catch that shot the metal floorpiece back, then stood waiting.

Paul strained his ears, but he could hear no sound above the hissing of steam from the train.

A minute passed.

Then footsteps sounded on the platform outside. Like a flash Paul was down the steps, his eyes raking in all directions. Only one man was in sight. He was limping, carrying an old-fashioned carpet bag. Otherwise the entire platform was vacant. Paul turned back to the porter. "All right, George. Bring the little stool down. Here's your passenger."

The porter complied as the lame passenger came up. He had a broad-brimmed hat on and gave Paul a queer look through heavy spectacles.

Paul hefted his gun in his hand. Rarely had the investigator been as taut as he was at this moment. If there were to be an attempt at escape—it must come now.

He put his head inside, instructed the conductor to slip out the other side of the train and take a look. The door rattled open and the railroadman's boots crunched against the gravel. Slowly, the three minutes were eaten away. Paul saw nothing that could be construed as suspicious.

Finally there was a warning blast from the whistle.

The train gave a great grunt. The cars rattled noisily together and began to move once more, the engine puffing in loud spurts.

Paul waited till the last moment then swung aboard, just as the conductor did the same. They mounted the steps together.

As he stood in the vestibule, watching the porter once more secure the door, Paul took out his handkerchief, and mopped his streaming forehead. He smiled thinly at the conductor. "Nothing doing, I guess."

The conductor pocketed his gun, stood expectantly.

"You might take a look through the last three cars and check up with the porters. I'll take a look up front," Paul said.

Paul pushed through into his own car, walked slowly toward the front, his eyes and ears alert for anything unusual, but without result.

At the other end of the car Burton was still peering grimly through the window of the vestibule, his pistol gripped firmly. As Paul came in sight, he turned quickly, then unashamedly wiped the sweat from his forehead. Paul motioned him forward, and the two entered the front car—to confront the porter who was hurring back toward them.

"Anything up here?" Paul asked.

"Nothing at all, sir. No one even came out of their room."

They returned to their own car. Burton shook his head. "I'm glad that's over—and I don't care who knows it."

Paul smiled, but without enthusiasm. "I guess we outbluffed them. You saw nothing, of course."

"Nobody even moved, as far as I could see, Mr. Bryant."

Paul hesitated, his hand on his doorknob. His eyes were troubled. "Look here, Burton," he said suddenly, "I've got some lines out in New York, and I'm afraid things are not breaking right here. I should have heard by now, if they were. I know Bill Richardson, at your agency. If I don't hear, by tomorrow morning, would you send him a wire, and ask him to do something for me?"

Burton blinked. "Why, sure. What's it all about?"

"I'll tell you in the morning," Paul said, "I may not need him at all, but again—I may. Good night once more, Burton."

"Wh—what?" stammered Burton. "Wait a min—"

"Good night," Paul repeated, closing the door behind him.

McNeil was still in the same position in which he had left him. Paul pushed the bell for the porter.

From the darkey, he ascertained that the name of the passenger who had just come aboard was Brodden. He wrote it in on his diagram.

His gun in his hand, Paul sat down on the edge of his bed, to wait. They had promised him death, should he interfere. He had interfered, apparently. Paul waited.

An hour slipped by, to find the investigator working on his third cigar, still in the same position. It was getting light outside, as the great train rushed once more into the rising sun.

More time slipped by.

Then with startling suddenness, from

outside the door, came a hoarse, panic-stricken scream.

"Help! Help! Murder!"

In one spring, Paul was through the door, a biting curse on his lips.

THE porter George, his hands held over his eyes was staggering backward from Compartment B, while queer strangled cries forced themselves from his throat.

"What is it, George?" snapped Paul. "What's the matter?"

"He's daid," gasped the porter. "He's daid!"

"Who?"

"Mistah Murray!"

Paul ran for the door of B. "Get the doctor in A, George," he said sharply, "and stop that sniffling!"

The porter stumbled to the next door. The corridor was rapidly filling with heads. Paul paused.

"Inside your rooms, everybody!" he commanded, "and don't stir out till the conductor tells you you may. Burton!"

"I'm here!" said Burton miserably.

"Go get the conductor, quick!"

Doctor Zelig shot from his room, attired in gown and slippers. He was a short, portly man with a full beard, and a vaguely Russian appearance.

"In here, doctor," Paul called.

They entered the room together.

On his bunk, lay the man known both as Green and Murray. The bedclothes were in a twisted heap on the floor. After a second's test of the pulse, the doctor pronounced him dead.

But the cause of death was the horrible thing. The man's face and throat and chest, were covered with the most ghastly blisters, enormous, and still angry red, in spite of the whiteness of the rest of the flesh.

"What—what happened, doctor?" Paul asked.

The doctor bent closer, examining the welts. "He's been frightfully burned by something," he declared, "but I don't know what."

"Is that what killed him?"

"Yes. It must have happened very suddenly. This man's heart was evidently not too sound at best. The shock stopped it."

The door opened to admit Burton and the white-faced conductor.

"My God!" said Brock, and faltered on the threshold as he saw the grisly sight on the bed.

"Close that door!" Paul snapped. "Doctor—how long before you can fix the time of death."

"It will take me a few minutes."

"Burton—you stay here with Mr. Brock. Let no one in or out, except the doctor and myself. I'll be back presently. Proceed with your examination, doctor."

Paul closed the door behind him, and went directly to the stateroom marked D. He knocked.

CHAPTER SEVEN

The Chamois Box

THE door opened. The perfectly white face of Mrs. Murray confronted him. Paul shot the words at her like a bombshell: "Mr. Green has been murdered, Miss Millicent."

Her brown eyes filled with terror, and her hand flew to her throat. She tried to speak, but could not.

"Please sit down on your bunk."

She backed away from him, her mouth still trying to frame words, but no words came. Paul closed the door.

"Who killed him, Miss Millicent?"

She managed: "I don't know!"

"Was it Mr. McNeil?"

"No, no!" she cried. "No! It couldn't have been!" She burst suddenly into sobs, threw herself on the bed, utterly hysterical.

Paul regarded her compassionately. "Sorry I had to frighten you like that, Miss Millicent," he said. "Everything will be all right, I think. Just stay in your room."

He went out.

"Everybody please come to your doors," he called.

One by one they responded. Only the death room, and the two vacant compartments.... Paul's eyes narrowed suddenly. There should be but one vacancy now!

There was no one standing at the door of Compartment F!

For a half minute, Paul waited for the man known as Brodden to put in an appearance. Then he spoke quickly.

"All right. Back inside, everybody. Mr. Brock!" As the others drew inside, Brock emerged. Paul stepped to the door of F. "This is Brodden's compartment, isn't it?"

"Yes."

Paul knocked, hard.

There was no answer.

He glanced at Brock. The conductor was staring with growing horror at the door handle.

Paul opened the door, and walked inside.

The room was absolutely vacant. The bed had not been slept in. Not even the queer luggage that Paul had noticed in Brodden's hand was in the room.

"Wha-what—" began the conductor.

"Search this train!" snapped Paul. "Find this man Brodden! It's utterly impossible that he could have gotten off. He must be aboard somewhere. Take Burton with you."

He signaled to Burton. "Brodden has disappeared. Help Mr. Brock to search the train. Check every last name on the passenger list. If there is anyone extra— let me know at once!"

The door at the end of the corridor

suddenly burst open, and Simmons, still in shirt-sleeves, came hurriedly in.

"Mr. Bryant!"

Paul turned, took the extended wire from him.

PAUL BRYANT
ENROUTE SCARLET COMET
MUNRO CLAIMS GREEN HIRED HIM ATTACK LEAVITT BUT HE FAILED. MUNRO HAS CAST-IRON ALIBI FOR HOUR OF ACTUAL KILLING. WHAT SHALL I DO?
SALM.

Paul said: "Tell him to let Munro go, that that is all I wanted to know."

Simmons saluted, and turned away.

Burton plucked at Paul's arm. "Did you say Brodden had disappeared?" he asked incredulously.

"Yes. Don't ask questions. He must be aboard somewhere; it's up to you to find him."

Paul returned to the murder room. The doctor was just rising from a kneeling posture. Paul kicked the door shut behind him.

"Well, what time was he killed, doctor?"

The doctor eyed his watch judicially. "Between 5:30 and 6:30 this morning."

PAUL sat down weakly on the settee. "For God's sake doctor, make it more definite. The whole question hangs on whether he was killed before or after six o'clock!"

The doctor shrugged. "I'm sorry. I cannot. Only with much more delicate instruments than I have with me, can it be determined more closely."

Paul sighed. "All right. Do you mind staying here a few minutes? They are searching the train, and I want to be sure no one hides in here."

"Very well," said the doctor.

Paul returned to his own room.

It was almost with a shock that he

found young McNeil sitting nervously on the bed, now fully dressed and smoking a cigarette.

"What—what's up?" McNeil asked anxiously.

"Green's been killed."

McNeil leaped to his feet. "I didn't do it, Mr.—whatever your name is."

Paul said: "Be quiet. Nobody said you did."

The investigator lapsed into silence.

Paul had no illusions. His back was to the wall. If he failed to break this case —these cases, if they were not connected, he could expect no help from President Salm. He had committed a dozen legal offenses in his conduct of the business. And he had made the fatal mistake of underestimating the intelligence of his adversary. Paul groaned inwardly. Only that threatening note remained, with which to trap his man. He put his hand in his pocket where he thought he had secreted it. He frowned faintly. It was not there. Quickly, he went through pocket after pocket. His annoyance grew to anger. The note had disappeared.

Paul's lips set in a thin straight line, and his hands clenched into fists.

There was a tap at the door.

"Come in," Paul said.

The conductor entered, Burton at his heels.

"The train—" he began, then stopped, his eyes bulging. "What—who—" He pointed at McNeil. "Who's that man?"

"Oh, I forgot to mention Mr. McNeil to you, conductor. For the moment, forget him. Take my word for it that he is all right. Did you find Brodden?"

The conductor stared at McNeil. "Not unless that man is Brodden," he said curtly. "There is no trace of anybody else on this train that is not accounted for."

"This man, I told you," said Paul, "is all right. Don't think about him. We'll take his case up later. Burton, do you mean to say you haven't located Brodden?"

The bodyguard shook his head. "He—he's disappeared! And what I want to know," he went on bitterly, "is what I'm going to tell the home office about—"

"We'll talk about that later," Paul snapped. "Now clear out. Mr. Brock, kindly find McNeil a vacant compartment —fix him up in Brodden's for now, and then come back here. I want to talk to you."

"Now, wait a minute, Bryant—"

"Please remember," said Paul curtly, "I am acting for the president of this road!"

The conductor hesitated, then: "Come along, you."

The room emptied.

After a few minutes Brock returned. "Well," he began, "I di—"

But Paul had an idea. He got up quickly. "Wait here—just a few minutes, like a good fellow," he said scothingly. "I'll be right back," and he closed the door behind him.

HE went once more to Mary Millicent's compartment, knocked, and at the timorous invitation to enter, again stepped inside. The girl's eyes were red with weeping, and as she saw Paul, she seemed to shrink into herself.

"What—what do you want?" she asked in a strained voice.

Paul sat down on the settee. "Miss Millicent, I'll have to have your help in solving this crime. Do you mind my asking you a few questions?"

She looked at him fearfully. "N-no, but I don't—"

"First, did Mr. Green know that McNeil was aboard?"

"What?" the girl sprang to her feet. "He—he isn't on board! He can't be! You said that before!"

Paul eyed her carefully. "Am I to

gather that you didn't know McNeil was on the train?"

"No!" she cried almost hysterically. "No!" Then her face went ashen. "Oh, my God!" she gasped. "He—you don't think he did it?" She clutched at his arm. "You—you don't think he did it!"

"I don't know," said Paul quietly. "So far, he seems to be the only one with reason—except yourself." For the moment Paul had no intention of mentioning the missing Brodden. "I want you to dig in your mind—see if you can't think of some reason why he should be killed. That is—a reason why someone else should kill him—someone who knew also he was on this train."

The girl's eyes sought her twisting fingers in her lap. She was silent a long, anxious minute. Finally she said almost pleadingly: "Mr. Green insisted that I tell no one—no one even knew we were leaving New York. We—were traveling under an assumed name." She colored. "I guess you know that. Mr. Green phoned me yesterday morning, told me to be at the train by four. I had to pack in a hurry, take my baggage to his office. Someone else took it aboard for it was there when I got to the train. Mr. Burton was waiting for us there, too. He had made all the other arrangements, so maybe he did that too. Outside of him, we didn't see a soul—except I saw Mr.—Mr. McNeil in the station."

"Was Mr. Green nervous? Did he seem to fear someone following him?"

She hesitated. "Yes," she said in a low voice, "he was. That was why we had to leave town so suddenly."

"Have you any idea what it was?"

"No. He did not tell me."

Paul was silent. His questioning was leading him over ground with which he was already familiar, and there did not seem to be an opening. . . .

Suddenly the girl sprang up. "Oh!" she said. "What a fool I've been—the chamois box! There's a box—a box covered with chamois. Mr. Green was very anxious about it."

"What was inside?"

"I don't know. Oh, do look and see if it's gone! It was in his small black bag! It looks like a good-sized jewel case."

Paul breathed a sigh of relief. It was the one link in the chain of speculation that he had been forging. He smiled, got up.

"I am reasonably sure we shall find it gone, Miss Millicent," he said. "If it is —then there are others who fall under suspicion—which you may say is a break for you—and Mr. McNeil."

The worried look came suddenly back into her eyes. "May I see him—may I see Mr. McNeil?"

Paul shook his head. "Sorry, Miss Millicent. Not just yet. Soon, perhaps."

He went out.

As he reentered his own compartment, Brock turned on him angrily. "Look here, Bryant," he said, "I've had about enough of this! The president may have sent you, but I'm responsible for this train— and I'm not going to have you monkeying around and keeping me in the dark, any longer! Who's this stowaway? What's behind all this killing? Or don't you know?"

Paul smiled. "You've hit just the right minute to ask, Brock. First, I want you to come with me, while we search the dead man's room for a chamois box. Then we'll come back here, and I'll tell you everything I know, and what I want to do. Just at the moment, it looks as though we may be forced to sit tight till we pass through the next small town, but then I think I can clear up everything for you. Now let's go for that box. I am quite sure we won't find it—or, if we do, it will be empty."

The latter surmise proved to be correct.

CHAPTER EIGHT

The Diamond Set-Up

THE double tragedy, if such it could be called, had been successfully kept from the passengers of the other coaches, due to the infinite tact and mental agility of the conductor. Even the search for the missing Brodden had been conducted by the experienced Brock without revealing the situation. Only the occupants of the second car, and a few of the first, were aware of what had actually taken place.

The day wore on. They chatted, smoked, made use of the valet car, the club car, the other superlative conveniences of the limited, blissfully unconscious that a hideously murdered man rode with them; that the murderer, not only of this man, but of another, possibly two others, or even three, if the missing Brodden were to be counted— was somewhere in the train.

Night came on. The dining car filled, emptied. Numerous trays of food were sent forward. The occupants of the first and second cars were dining in their staterooms.

Paul sat in his room, chatting with the conductor. By eight o'clock, the two had come to an agreement. In spite of all their efforts, the train would have to stop. But the loss of time was to be limited to a scant five minutes. That much Paul had promised.

The conductor went at nine. Paul looked in the mirror. It was not his usual dapper self that stared back at him. He had had no time to shave, and his eyes were red-rimmed from lack of sleep. Yet he smiled, grimly.

He went across to Compartment C, knocked. There was no answer and he went in. The burly bodyguard was sound asleep, his feet on the seat opposite him. Paul shook him gently.

"Tired?" he asked, as Burton opened his eyes.

"Eh? No, no—I'm O. K." He sat suddenly erect. "What—what's doing?"

"Nothing yet. We're stopping at a little town a few miles up the line and taking on some Secret Service agents. Thought I'd tell you."

Burton scowled, rubbing his eyes. "God, Bryant," he said sadly, "that puts you and me on the spot. Me, anyhow."

"How do you mean?"

Burton shrugged. "My job. God knows it's bad enough to have Murray or Green or whatever his name was, bumped. Now we have to shout for help to crack the murder. It makes us look like a couple of ninnys."

Paul put a hand on his shoulder. "I wouldn't do it, if I didn't have to, fellow," he said soberly, "but we've got to have a general search. I've just discovered that a chamois jewel box in Green's possession, was rifled. By a queer legal quirk, only the feds can search people on a train. We'll have to have them. When we find what was taken from the box, it will put us on a short trail to the killer, and probably explain a great deal."

Burton nodded gloomily. "When do we get there?"

"Where?"

"Where we take them aboard?"

"About eleven o'clock."

Burton glanced at his watch. "Two hours yet, huh?"

Paul nodded. "About ten minutes before we pull in, I have something for you to do. I have to see the conductor about it first. I'll be in to see you before we arrive."

"O. K."

Paul went out, turned toward the front of the train, changed his mind and went into Compartment F. McNeil was nearly bursting with impatience. The suspense was wrecking the boy's nerves; his face was haggard.

Paul sat and talked with him for some time. When he left, McNeil was more composed.

One by one, Paul visited every passenger in the first two cars, talked with them, studied everyone closely. His watch showed ten minutes past ten when he finally returned to his own room.

HE took out the flat 38 from his hip pocket, slipped the clip out, confirmed the fact that it was full, and cogged a shell into the chamber.

Slipping the gun into a side pocket, he stooped to retrieve a shell that had fallen from his pocket, when suddenly the train gave a terrific lurch, catapulting him almost head foremost into the little washroom. Paul looked quickly out of the window. They were still in sparsely settled country.

The train lurched again. The wheels screamed shrilly, as brakes were applied. There were hoarse shouts of surprise from the other occupants of the car.

Paul threw open the door. A fearsome hissing sound began, and coming toward him, Paul saw an angry, rolling cloud of steam. Instantly, his mind clicked.

"Everybody—come out of your rooms!" he shouted. "There's been some accident—the train's on fire—hurry outside, quickly!"

Dense clouds of black smoke followed close on the heels of the steam, and through it, Paul saw the angry lick of a tongue of flame.

"Hurry up!" he shouted as loud as he could. "This car might blow up!"

The Millicent girl ran screaming from her room, collided blindly with the opposite wall. Paul leaped, turned her toward the front, gave her a push. The other doors were banging open; other passengers raced toward one end or the other. Men were shouting. The hiss of a fire extinguisher began.

Then suddenly the lights went out with a blue sputtering.

The dense clouds of smoke rolled into Paul's eyes, blinding him. He groped toward the rear of the car automatically. Halfway down the car, he tensed, dropped to one knee. There was a powerful flash lamp in his hand now.

The clanking of metal came to him.

Paul switched on the lamp.

There was a dark figure, struggling with the water cooler. That was all Paul saw.

The next second there was a roaring crash as a gun exploded. The flashlight was shattered to a million pieces. Again the orange spurt of flame but Paul was no longer there. With a sudden sideways step, he threw himself forward, left his feet in a dive—and crashed into the man at the water cooler, his gun slashing down viciously.

But he missed. And the miss nearly cost him his life.

There was a muffled roar from the man's gun, and a searing pain dug into Paul's shoulder. Again he swung his gun grimly, caught the man a glancing blow on the head. A hard fist smashed into his mouth; a knee came up seeking his groin, but Paul ducked it, staggered back. Again the gun roared, and a bullet snicked by Paul's ear.

Paul cried a warning, threw down his own gun, and squeezed lead. Not till the automatic was empty did he relax his grip. A stream of hot slugs raked the corridor, knee high. There was a hoarse curse in the darkness, then a scream, and the fall of a heavy body.

Paul flattened himself against the side wall.

"Lights!" he shouted.

The car was flooded with radiance. There was a huddled figure on the floor, just visible through the clouds of swirling smoke. It did not move.

"All right!" Paul cried. "Blow that smoke out." The doors at the end of the car were thrown open. Then: "Get the train under way again."

The smoke gradually cleared away. Bryant approached the man on the floor cautiously—but he was out. Paul turned him over on his back. There was blood on his face, but the features were plain— Burton, the bodyguard!

In his clutching fingers was a chamois sack.

Paul straightened up. "Dr. Zelig!"

The doctor shouldered his way in hastily.

"See about this man."

The doctor dropped to one knee beside the form of Burton. After a moment he got up. "Just creased across the forehead and a broken leg," he said. "He'll be all right."

"All right—give us a hand will you?"

TOGETHER, they carried the unconscious man into his compartment. Paul came into the hall again. "All right everybody," he called. "You can come back now."

The men at the ends of the car collected the oil-soaked waste they had used in creating the synthetic fire, and returned to their duties.

The train sped steadily onward.

Paul went inside, undid the pucker cord on the chamois sack, and spilled the contents onto the bed.

The doctor gasped.

No less than forty tremendous diamonds of the first water flashed on the counterpane. For a moment, Paul was stunned. The flashing, scintillating fire of the stones was sufficient evidence of their genuineness.

"Good God!" said Zelig. "They—they must be worth millions!"

"Two, I believe, doctor," said Paul. "Two millions."

Half an hour later, Burton opened his eyes, groaned feebly.

Around the car stood Brock, Paul, the doctor and McNeil.

"Do you want to confess, and save us a lot of trouble, Burton?" Paul asked.

Burton eyed him steadily. "You got nothing on me, Bryant," he said surlily, "Brodden's the man you want. What's he lammed for? You'll have to explain that in court before you can hang anything on me."

"You forget the chamois bag I caught you taking from the water cooler."

Burton sneered. "I picked it up off the floor. Somebody else dropped it."

"I see," said Paul wearily, "that you still think you have me fooled. All right, I'll tell you what you've done, Burton. If you think I haven't enough to put you in the chair, you're crazy. Listen.

"Somehow, you learned that Green was taking this train—that he had a fortune in uncut diamonds with him. You also learned that the Munsing agency was sending a bodyguard to the train, with Green's dunnage, so that he, himself could slip aboard unnoticed. You got here first. Apparently it is not much trouble to get aboard one of these trains. Anyway, when the Munsing man arrived, long before train time, you shot him with a silenced gun, after he had opened up the three staterooms.

"Then, according to the ghastly plan which you had apparently thought out thoroughly beforehand, you beat his face into an unrecognizable mass, removed every identifying mark from his clothing, and wrapped him in a rubber sheet.

"You appropriated his identity, with his papers. Green and Miss Millicent had apparently never seen the real bodyguard, or if they had, you made some appropriate excuse and got away with it.

"However, there was something that you were not aware of—though it made little difference to you. There was another man that knew of Green's impending departure, and who I believe, owned or had an interest in, these stones. His name was Moe Leavitt. Evidently he was making things hot for Green, for Green hired a torpedo to shoot him. The torpedo failed. Then, in the station Leavitt caught up with Green, probably threatened him with exposure for something. Anyway, Green shot him—right in the station, and went aboard the train.

"To get back to you—when the train pulled out, the battered body of the real Burton was lying in your compartment. As soon as you found the coast clear, you ducked out with it, slipped it through the vestibule coupling. Later you did the same with the rubber sheet and the spanner with which you had mutilated him.

"Naturally, when you threw them out, you did not expect pursuit, thinking that no one would connect the mutilated body with this particular train. Unfortunately, this was such a particular train, that attention was focussed on it at once. The president sent me to look into things.

"**Y**OU knew my face, of course, like most crooks do, and as soon as you saw me boarding the train, you knew I was after you. But your stolen identity looked like a good thing, right then, for it would let you into my confidence, or so you thought.

"You did fool me for a while, Burton—more than I like to admit. Your scheme for killing Murray—or Green, I should say, was the smoothest and boldest piece of work I have seen.

"You were lucky enough to draw the position, for the stop at Colorado Springs, between the first and second cars. Had I not given it to you, I have no doubt you would have talked me into letting you go there. You figured, and rightly, that I would be most concerned with the spot where the expected passenger would board the train. You also knew that I would be waiting at the open vestibule a few minutes before we pulled in, and a few minutes after we had left the station.

"As soon as I left you, instead of proceeding directly to your post, you ducked into your stateroom, pulled on a very simple disguise, consisting of a large hat—to hide your features—a long coat, a pair of glasses and a carpet bag. Quite adequate in the darkness.

"When the car came to a stop, you simply opened the door, slipped down close to the train, walked back to the opened vestibule, and got on again, right under my nose. I presume you had reserved this compartment long before you left New York, in the character and name of Brodden, though whether you had intended it for this purpose or merely as a means of escape, I don't know.

"When you passed me, you walked boldly into the train, stepped straight into Green's compartment, took the lethal weapon from that carpet bag, and murdered him instantly. Then you dropped your disguise in your own compartment, and returned to your place between cars one and two, once more as Burton, the bodyguard.

"Later, when you had the time, you threw the disguise out on the roadbed, as well as the container that had held your weapon. We have men searching for them now, Burton.

"The note you sent me was, of course, solely for the purpose of making sure that I would *not* stay in my room last night—you judged my character well enough there.

"And to complete the story, Burton, I'll tell you how you killed Green. You had a container, probably one of the lead ones they use in laboratories, full of liquid air. To kill Green was the work of a second. A stream of this stuff against anyone's throat for a half moment is fatal, and—it leaves no trace, save the blisters, which are more inclined to be misleading than helpful.

"Tonight, I was sure you were guilty. To make sure I asked you about a mythical Bill Richardson, supposed to be on the Munsing staff. There is no Bill Richardson, Burton, as far as I know. Now, you fool, do you think you can wiggle out of that?"

Burton was silent for a long minute. Then: "All right, Bryant, you win, damn you," he said, "but here's something you don't know.

"Leavitt, Green and myself were playing in together. We were smuggling in a million dollars a month worth of uncut diamonds. I got a chance to buy in on a wholesale lot in Paris—two million dollars. Through the mugs I had working for me, I made it, got them across, and had them delivered to Green. Green tried to double-cross us, to duck out with the rocks to Frisco, and lay low.

"But we had his wire tapped. Green had never seen me, so I was in a better position than Leavitt, but the Jew insisted on making a try for them himself. I didn't say anything, but I had my own plans—you've seen them."

"You were double-crossing Leavitt, too, eh?" asked Paul.

"Have it your own way," said Burton wearily.

There was silence in the room for a moment. Then Paul turned to Brock.

"He's your prisoner, Mr. Brock. I guess that clears everything up. The rest of you can go."

Slowly they filed from the room. Brock called some of his own staff to take charge of the wounded criminal.

At length, the doctor got around to dressing Paul's shoulder wound, and the investigator stepped slowly from the room of death.

To his surprise, a door down the hall was open. Mary Millicent stood there. She beckoned to him.

He went toward her, and she stood aside for him to enter. Slightly puzzled, Paul went inside.

She closed the door and stood with her back to it.

"Well," said Paul, "what's the trouble now, Miss Millicent?"

"What are you going to tell Mr. McNeil?" she asked.

Paul shrugged. "I have nothing to tell him, Miss Millicent."

She looked into his eyes doubtfully. "You mean you aren't going to tell him about—me—"

"Why should I?"

Two big tears suddenly rolled down her cheeks. "If—if you only won't," she cried sobbing. "He—he thinks—he has such ideals of me—I've been a fool—I'll live up to his ideas of me—"

Paul said: "Why sure, Miss Millicent. That's fine. The best of happiness to you both. I'll send him to you now."

Then with a satisfied smile he turned and left the compartment.

MURDER ON THE LOOSE

A Cardigan Story

by
Frederick Nebel

Author of "Phantom Fingers," etc.

"This isn't going to get you anywhere," Bradshaw said patiently.

It wasn't an agency job and Cardigan had orders to leave it alone. But a dirk-stabbed body on the floor of his own hotel room wasn't the sort of thing he could ignore. Even when mixing in meant his job—and the taste of buckle and tongue in a fancy torture trap.

CHAPTER ONE

Mystery Blade

CARDIGAN sat in the depths of the wing-chair, absent-mindedly tinkling cracked ice in a drink composed of Scotch, seltzer and a slice of fresh lime. The twelfth-story room was moderately cooled by a breeze that puffed in from the East River, four blocks away:

with it came the sound of an elevated train slamming south on Third Avenue and the lesser but nearer racket of a Lexington Avenue street car.

Dr. Korn said, "H-m-m . . . it must have been instantaneous. Yes, I'd say it was instantaneous."

Cardigan took a drink.

Fogel, the house dick, broad as a church door, mashed a handkerchief between sweaty palms and hitched a fat white neck uncomfortably in a hard collar. "Cripes," he said. "Cripes."

"Distressing," said Ownes, the night manager, rolling his eyes and pressing his palms piously together.

The man on the floor said nothing. He was dead. Stabbed through the heart.

Cardigan took another drink, untangled his legs, got up, strode to the little white pantry. Korn and Ownes looked at each other and heard the clear-cut chink of ice against glass, the fizz of a siphon. Cardigan reappeared carrying a fresh drink and saying, "Help yourself, gentlemen. The makings are all in there." He made a semicircular detour around the body on the floor and resumed his seat in the wing-chair.

Ownes said righteously, "This is murder, Mr. Cardigan!"

"Sure. A guy busts into my room and another guy who was already in here or came in afterward gave him the works. What am I supposed to do?"

Ownes made a hopeless gesture, and Fogel, shoving out his cleft chin, said, "This sure is funny, this is."

Cardigan looked at him. "You woudn't be making any cracks, would you?"

Dr. Korn's interest was purely clinical. "An expert thrust, a very expert thrust— just one." He held up a finger. "Once."

Cardigan was still looking at Fogel. Fogel buttoned his coat, slid his gaze slantwise away from Cardigan, went to a window and regarded the cool spire of the Chrysler Building. Cardigan looked at the folds in the back of his thick white neck and consumed a quarter of the drink.

There was a rap on the door. Ownes started, turned. Fogel turned from the window, threw Ownes a look and then thumped his flat feet across the carpet and opened the door.

"H'lo, Fogel," Lieutenant Bone said.

"Hello, Abe. Hello, Frank."

"Hello, Gus," Sergeant Raush said.

Hatchet-faced Abe Bone dropped a dour gaze on the dead man, lifted it to Dr. Korn, moved it to Ownes, moved it on to Cardigan.

"Oh," he muttered. "You."

Cardigan saluted with his glass. "*Skoal.*"

Bone said impersonally, "I thought you were in St. Louis."

"I was. For several years. I'm back."

"Yeah, I see. How come you're in this room?"

"I live here."

Bone showed no surprise. "Who's the stiff?"

"I don't know. I walked in my room twenty minutes ago and fell over him. I called the desk downstairs, and Fogel and Mr. Ownes came up and brought Dr. Korn with them."

Bone looked at Dr. Korn. "Dead when you got here?"

"Oh, yes. Quite. Dead for several hours, I'd say."

BONE'S slab-cheeked face remained expressionless. He knelt beside the dead man, studied the wound, studied the face. His own expression never changed. His hard, bony hands probed pockets and brought forth odds and ends which he laid on the carpet. He rose suddenly and crossed to Cardigan.

"When did you come in here?"

"Eleven-ten."

"'D you touch the body?"

"Felt it—the pulse—that's all."

"Who is the guy?"

"I don't know."

"Was your door open or locked when you came in?"

"Locked. It locks automatically when you go out."

"What's your theory?"

"A guy was in here or came in while this egg was frisking my room and let him have it."

Bone said, "What would this guy or the other guy be after?"

"Haven't the slightest idea."

"Miss anything?"

"No. The room's just as I found it, except that door to the in-a-door bed was open. One or the other of the guys didn't have time to complete a frisk."

"Find a gun?"

"There's one under the stiff."

Bone drew a handkerchief and pulled the gun out by the barrel. It was a 32 Webley automatic, fully loaded. He wrapped it in his handkerchief and thrust it into his pocket. He looked at Cardigan with hard, sour eyes.

Cardigan drained his glass, rose and carried it to the little pantry. He reappeared empty-handed and said to Ownes, "Of course I'll want my room changed."

Bone said dismally, "If this guy broke into your room, he must have been after something."

"Sure. Most crooks that break into rooms are after something."

"Never mind that. There was another guy after something, too."

Fogel put in, "So he says."

"You keep your oar out of this!" Cardigan snapped.

"Never mind him," Bone chopped in. "I'm talking to you."

Cardigan looked at Bone. "I've told you."

"You haven't told me enough."

"Then that's just too bad, and what do you think you can do about it?"

Bone was bleak. "I can pinch you—"

"In a horse's neck you can. Dr. Korn told you the guy's been dead several hours. My key was on the rack downstairs. I got it at eleven ten and came right up."

"Two guys were after something," Bone said. "Each on his lonesome. They crossed, and one of them got rubbed out. One guy might have been on an ordinary break, but not two, Cardigan—not two. What did the one guy get?"

"Nothing."

"What was he after?"

"I don't know."

"What might he have been after?"

"I don't know."

Fogel said, "Hell, Abe, he'd never tell you, he wouldn't. I know him, I do."

Cardigan said, "Just one more burp out of you, you cheap keyhole artist, and I'll take a swing at you."

"I told you never mind him," Bone cut in.

And Cardigan swung on Bone saying, "There's a dead man. I found him in my room when I came in. I don't know him. I don't know what he was after. I notified the desk a couple of minutes after I found him. I got the doctor up. I acted according to law in every respect. So now try using your head instead of your mouth for a change and figure it out for yourself!"

His expression changeless, Bone said, "I'm figuring it out, Cardigan. I know you. Any time you think you can pull the wool over my eyes—"

"I'd hold him, Abe," Fogel suggested. "I'd hold him. I'd make him tell."

Cardigan pivoted, took one step and a swing at Fogel. Fogel sat down on the floor, and Bone and Raush jumped and caught hold of Cardigan's arms.

Bone snapped, "Now cut it out, Cardigan."

"All right, then tell this crackpot to keep his mouth shut. Leggo!"

Bone and Raush stepped back and Cardigan said, darkly, "I'm moving to another room. Try any rough stuff and see where it gets you. Just see."

DAYLIGHT was filtering through drawn green shades when the telephone bell jangled. Bedcovers erupted, and out of them appeared Cardigan's tangled shock of hair. A long arm slewed outward; a big hand picked up the instrument from the bed table and drew it to the bed.

"Hello . . . Well, what the hell's the idea of waking me up so early? . . . Oh, it is? Well, now *I* think that eight o'clock it too early— . . . All right, George, all right. What's on your mind? . . . You did? Big headlines 'n everything, huh? Swell . . . Didn't know the guy from Eve's daddy . . . Yeah, Bone was there, sour-mugged as ever. And Fogel . . . You know the guy you canned three years ago. And is he sore? Uhn-uhn! . . . I'll tell you when I get down the office, George . . . Goom-by."

He hung up, swung out of bed and plowed into the bathroom, clearing his throat raucously. He took a cold shower, cursed it, rubbed down with alcohol, dressed and went down to the coffee shop. He drank half a pint of tomato juice, ate three eggs, four rolls and drank two cups of coffee. It was nine o'clock when he came out on Lexington Avenue and said 'hello' to the *chasseur*.

He walked north to Thirty-ninth Street, stopped and looked backward. He didn't see anyone tailing him. He walked on north to Forty-second Street, turned west. At a stand in front of Grand Central Terminal he bought a newspaper, saw his name mentioned twice, got the gist of the story and walked west to Fifth Avenue. He boarded a taxi and gave an address.

Fifteen minutes later he got off at the corner of Seventy-fifth Street and West End Avenue. He walked north for several blocks, passed the Whitestone Hotel, stopped at the next corner to light a cigarette and look around, then turned back and entered the Whitestone. From one of three house phones in the lobby he called suite 708, then took an elevator and got off at the seventh floor.

A man with carroty hair and freckles on a sun-tanned face opened the door.

"Well," Cardigan said, "so it's started."

The man was in pajamas and dressing gown. His voice shook, but his mouth remained firm. "Yes, I read it. Come in."

Cardigan tramped into the living room, scaled his battered fedora onto a divan, toed an ottoman out of the way and dropped into a mohair armchair.

"Drink?"

"Not till the eggs get down," Cardigan said.

The man had locked the door. He was tall, broad-shouldered, had a muscular jaw and steady blue gaze. He dropped to the divan with a faint outburst of breath, shrugged and slapped his palms to his knees.

"I'm sorry, old bohunk." He leaned back. "What did he look like?"

"Tall, thin, yellow hair—about forty."

"That would be Tracy. He must have tried to lone-wolf it."

"Then who got him?"

"Bradshaw, Sterns—or the woman."

"Leave the woman out. Bradshaw or Sterns."

A brindle bull walked in from the bedroom, flopped down and stared at Cardigan.

Cardigan said, looking at the dog, "Charley Wheeler, I don't know what you're going to do."

The carroty-haired man shrugged. "I came back for Mary. I'm not leaving this man's burg till she's well enough to pull out with me. I don't like the way those guys have turned on you, though."

"You worry about yourself, Charley. Don't think that the cops or these heels or anybody else is worrying me. Not me. I like it. It's not often I get the chance to work for an old pal."

Wheeler said, reflecting, "She ought to be O. K. in a week. Anyhow, we're booked on the *Gigantic* for Southampton next Tuesday. What do the cops think?"

"Nothing worth a damn. Abe Bone is on it—and Abe's hard as nails and twice as nasty. I gave him the run-around last night, but he didn't fall like a tree."

"They can't hang anything on you, can they?"

Cardigan laughed shortly. "I should say not. They might try, but—" he rose and raised palms toward Wheeler— "they'll wish they hadn't."

Wheeler stood up and looked grimly at Cardigan. "I hope to God we can make that boat, Mary and me. If there was any chance in the world of me sliding out by telling the cops, I'd tell 'em."

"They'd never recognize you, Charley. That plastic surgeon did a swell job, and your hair's a knockout."

Wheeler held up his hands. "They have my fingerprints. They'd find out. The papers'd get it and spring it: 'Big-Time Charley Wheeler, Former Beer Baron—'" He shook his head. "I'd never stand a chance, old bohunk."

Cardigan came over and towered close to Wheeler. He laid a big hand on Wheeler's shoulder. "You'll make that boat with Mary, Charley. You had the guts to come back and get her. I always said you had guts. You'll get her."

The brindle bull, scarred and battered, got up and went back into the bedroom.

CHAPTER TWO

On the Loose

WHEN Cardigan tramped into the inner sanctum of the Cosmos Agency George Hammerhorn, the brass hat, lifted a leonine blond head and said, rusty-voiced, "Now what the sweet hell have you gone and got yourself into again?"

Cardigan said, "Morning, George," and went to an ice-water cooler, drew and drank two glasses of water while Hammerhorn regarded him with agate-hard eyes.

"I said, by cripes—"

"I heard what you said," Cardigan cut in. "Now keep your pants on and don't get loud-mouthed, for, after all, I'm only working for you, and for two cents I'd start an agency of my own."

"Who said anything about starting an agency?"

"I did."

"Piffle, piffle, piffle!"

"All right, piffle all you want, but get over the underfed idea that you can land on me like a ton of brick and make me like it. I had eggs for breakfast and they haven't settled yet. Now lay off."

He walked around the room, and Hammerhorn, no weak sister himself, followed Cardigan with a glacial squint until by a circuitous route Cardigan reached the chair on the other side of the desk. Cardigan remained standing. He locked somberly at Hammerhorn for a long minute, and finally Hammerhorn, breaking a tight, hard smile, said offhand. "You're getting temperamental as a chorus girl. Unload your feet, big boy. Sit down."

Cardigan did not sit down. He placed palms on the desk, locked his arms at the elbows and leaned on his braced arms. "Did you ever have a friend that got in a tight spot?"

"Make it short and sweet, will you?"

"There's a friend of mine in a tight spot. He's in town under an assumed name. Three years ago he was a pretty big shakes in the beer trade, but he bailed out and skipped the country. He was through. He had the lousy racket up to the gills, and he was through. A lot of guys figured out beforehand that he was making to slide and told him he'd get the hot grease, if he tried to lam. He called their bluff and lammed.

"He went to Europe, had his face made over, dyed his hair. He went to Algiers and lived there. He met a doctor—a half-cracked old guy—and they became friends. One night a stranger busted into the doctor's quarters with his belly all shot to hell. The doctor did what he could for him, but the guy died. It was an incident, and for a month it was over

Then one night the doctor was stabbed and died. He left a crazy will. He left a signet ring, an old empty jewel box, his instruments, and a bulldog to this friend of mine.

"A couple of days later a guy approached this friend of mine and talked about the doctor. He wound up by pulling a rod on this friend and demanding to see what the doctor had left him. He saw. But he wasn't satisfied. He wanted five diamonds that he claimed the doctor must have taken from the guy he attended a month before. This friend got mad, and in the tussle took the gun away from the heel.

"He left a few days later for Paris. He was still in love with a jane in New York. He's a guy like that. He took a ship and came here and found the jane recovering from an operation. He asked her to marry him, and she said O. K., but they're waiting another week till she can navigate. Then they're going to Europe.

"Now who should turn up but the guy that pulled a rod on him in Algiers. He's got two pals with him and a jane. They're still after those five diamonds. This friend gets in touch with me to ask me what to do. I tell him to sit tight. They must have seen me come out of his apartment, and they make a stab at my room. One must have tried to double-cross the others. He got knifed in my room.

"Now—this friend of mine is in a tough spot. He's innocent, but if he gets tangled up in this, the cops'll find out who he really is. Word will spread, and the mob he ran with, the guys that threatened to rub him out, will get on his tail.

"That's why I'm in this. That's why I clowned around with Bone last night."

"And what, I might ask, do you intend doing?"

Cardigan straightened. "See that this pal of mine makes that boat with his frau."

"How much is in it?"

"Nothing. It's not an agency job."

Hammerhorn stood up. "Drop it. I'm not going to get mixed up with the cops. We can't afford to."

"Are you asking for my resignation?"

"I'm telling you not to be a damned fool."

"I'm not dropping it."

Hammerhorn had a glacial squint. "I still happen to run this agency, you know."

"I still happen to have an inclination to quit."

Their eyes measured each other.

Hammerhorn said flatly, "You're the best man I have. You ran the St. Louis branch swell for a number of years until you antagonized the wrong people out there."

"I antagonized a lot of cheap political grafters, and they broke my license in the State of Missouri. I'll get that license back again inside of six months. If your guts aren't equal to pressure of that kind, to hell with you and your agency."

Hammerhorn came around the desk. "Don't talk like that, Cardigan. I'm just trying to tell a thick-head Mick something for his own good. I'm telling you that you can't waltz these cops around and get away with it."

"You're telling me to leave this pal of mine in the lurch and I'm telling you, George, to go to hell for your pains. I'm strictly kosher. Nobody has anything on me. Bone doesn't worry me. None of them worries me. I didn't know the guy who was found dead in my room and I told Bone that. I had an idea, but I should go around ladling out ideas. Yes, I should!"

"Do you know now?"

"Yes."

"Then tell Bone before he gets really nasty and makes things hot for you."

Cardigan mouthed a corrosive laugh. "You're getting plain gaga now, George."

"Oh, yeah?" Hammerhorn pivoted and

went back to his chair, sat down and stuck a cigarette in one corner of his mouth.

Cardigan darkened and leaned on the desk. "If you so much as make one crack to the cops about what I've just told you, I'll cave in your jaw."

"Says you."

"What I told you I told in strictest confidence. Break that confidence, sweetheart, and you'll be an ambulance case."

Hammerhorn snapped a spurt of smoke through his nostrils and regarded Cardigan blandly. "We're both saying things we don't mean, Irish."

"I mean what I say."

"As much as I do."

"I mean what I say."

"All right, all right, I know what you mean. If you think I'd welch on you, you're just a case of arrested development. I'm just trying to tell you. I see it does no good. But I'm not Santa Claus. I've built up a good agency here, and I'm not going to take the chance. Resign now, and if you get clear in this mess, we'll tear up the resignation."

They measured each other evenly.

Cardigan said, "Sure. Thanks. Thanks for being a great big-hearted son-of-a-so-and-so. Only there's one thing wrong with your statement, honeybunch."

"Yeah?"

"Yeah. This resignation is permanent."

"You're a fool, Irish."

"You're a louse."

"O. K."

"O. K."

ONE of Cardigan's favorite hangouts was Andre's, in West Fortieth Street near Eighth Avenue. You got good steak and mushrooms there, coffee in a glass and Three-Star Hennessy straight off the French boats. There was a small quiet bar and a dining room in the rear and also three tables against the wall facing the bar. Cardigan sat at one of these tables pouring French dressing over imported endive. He had four dry Martinis under his belt, a bottle of Chablis at his elbow and a ruminative scowl on his forehead. A drunk was sitting on a high stool at the bar telling the story of his life, and an ingenue from a current Broadway success was trying to keep her eyes open while nodding mechanically at regular intervals. Emil, the barman, wore an expression of polite inattentiveness. It was a cheerful, homey bar, unlike the rowdy joints in the hinterland of Greenwich Village, miles south.

Abe Bone came in with his hands in his pockets, his Homburg sliced over one ear and his horsey face long and gloomy. He came straight to Cardigan's table, pulled out a chair, slapped it down and seated himself. He removed his hat, hung it on a prong above the table, blew his nose, and all the while kept his dark, cavernous eyes on Cardigan. Cardigan went on crunching crisp endive between long strong teeth and disfavoring Bone with intermittent glances.

"Mind if I try some of your white wine?"

"Yes."

Bone said, "Thanks," poured a glassful, raised the glass and added. "Whatever they say in French."

"Could you by any chance be at the wrong table?"

"I could, but I ain't."

A waiter swooped down. "Monsieur?"

"I'll have," said Bone tonelessly, "a pair of lamb chops, well done, some of those trick thin potatoes, some spinach and that's all."

The waiter vanished, and Cardigan said, "Don't you ever go home to your wife?"

"I haven't got a wife."

"Maybe janes aren't wise nowadays, huh?"

Bone spread a napkin, then reached for the wine. Cardigan put his hand on the bottle. "This stuff is six bucks a bottle, little boy, and times are hard."

"You don't like me, do you?"

"Oh, you're all right—in your place."

Bone said to the bar, "Bottle of that Canadian ale." He returned to Cardigan, saying, "My place happens to be smack on your tail, Cardigan."

"Yeah, I saw that keyhole artist, Fogel, tail me from the hotel. Using him for a stool pigeon nowanights?"

"I'll use anybody, Cardigan. Who was that guy?"

"Who?"

"The stiff."

Cardigan put knife and fork together crosswise on his plate and said, "It's pretty tough when I can't enjoy Andre's swell food without having you planting your ugly mug opposite me."

"Pulling a waltz-me-around-again-Willie isn't going to get you anywhere, Cardigan."

"I'm not going anywhere, Bone, so now what?"

"You're a nice enough guy, so why don't you play along with the right people? What's one job going to get your agency when you run up against us?"

"I'm not working for any agency."

Bone looked at him. The waiter arrived with the chops and went away, and Bone was still looking at Cardigan.

"You're not what?" Bone growled.

"I'm on the loose. Out of a job. Temporarily. Until I start an agency of my own . . . You don't believe me? O. K., call up George Hammerhorn. I've resigned."

"What you resign for?"

"Found the Cosmos too confining for my unusual talent."

BONE balanced three *pommes frites* on his fork, swallowed them and kept his gloomy eyes on Cardigan. "I've got a good mind to haul you over to the house and beat a little truth out of you, smart aleck."

"You'd better have your mind examined then, Bone."

Cardigan had drained his glass of coffee. He said to the waiter, "I'll take my brandy at the bar," and stood up. Bone kept looking gloomy-eyed at him. Cardigan turned his back on Bone. The drunk at the bar fell to the floor. Cardigan picked him up and helped him back onto the stool. The drunk went right on with the story of his life, and his ingenue friend seemed unaware of the fact that he had fallen. She had a rare glow.

Cardigan drank brandy and Benedictine, half-and-half, and Emil read him the latest race results. Bone finished his meal and two bottles of ale and came up to the bar for a pony of Scotch.

Cardigan called to the girl at the cigar counter, "Check, mademoiselle," and finished his drink.

He paid up and started down the corridor, and Bone was behind him. One of the waiters unlocked the front door and let them out. Cardigan reached the curb and bent his head to light a cigarette.

"Hold it," Bone said.

Cardigan held the light, and Bone got a cigar going. "Be sensible, Cardigan. You know damned well I'm going to find out who that guy was."

Cardigan tossed the match into the street and headed east past the newspaper sheds where trucks were loading up. Bone walked along beside him. They reached the whirlpool of Times Square and wedged through the eight o'clock theatre crowd. Cardigan ducked into the Times Building, went through the lunch room and took the staircase down to the subway. A northbound train was at the platform. Cardigan jumped and stopped a door from closing. Bone bumped into him.

Cardigan said, "All right, get in."

Bone hopped in. Cardigan stepped back and let the door close. Bone, in the vestibule, tried to stop it, but was too late. Cardigan tipped his hat and watched the train pull out with Bone, sour-faced, in the vestibule. Cardigan climbed the stairs and took the Broadway exit out.

At eight-twenty Cardigan tramped into the lobby of his hotel on Lexington Avenue, went past the desk and turned left toward the lounge. In the small connecting corridor there were two house phones on the right and two high-backed Italian chairs on the left. The place was very quiet.

Cardigan sat down on one of the chairs, looked at his watch, spread a newspaper and held it up before his face. Whenever he heard anyone at the phones he looked over the top of the paper and listened. At eight-thirty he heard a woman's voice say, "Mr. Cardigan, please."

He looked over the top of the paper and saw a tall, well-dressed girl in profile. She had on beige stockings of a weave called waffle, a modified Eugenie hat made of straw, and a blouselike jacket of transparent blue velvet with a skirt to match. When she hung up and turned away Cardigan raised the paper in front of his face. A moment later he was aware of another presence and, looking around a corner of the paper, saw the girl walking into the lounge with a large, bull-necked man. They disappeared around an L, and Cardigan lowered his paper and smiled to himself.

He rose, went into the lobby and caught an elevator up. He barged into his room —1115—and swung up the in-a-door bed which a maid had let down. Two doors closed and hid the bed in its compartment. The room was large, mannish and well furnished. He opened a window facing east. The night was bright, and he could see near the river the tall stacks of the New York Edison Company and the lights of Tudor City.

The telephone rang from a misplaced end table near a lowboy. "Hello," Cardigan said. "Yes, sure . . . Come right up."

He hung up, and his right hand slapped a gun's bulge on his hip. His heavy eyebrows met each other over his nose in hurried thought. His eyes glittered in deep sockets. He heaved out of his coat, put on a shaggy dressing gown. He sat down, took off his shoes and put on slippers. From the desk he took a small Colt automatic, slipped it into one of the shoes. He placed the shoes neatly beneath an armchair. He went to a south window facing an open court and looked up two stories at the rail of the solarium on the roof. He pulled the shade all the way down.

When the brass knocker on the door sounded Cardigan slushed his loose slippers across the carpet and opened the door. The tall girl stood there smiling.

"Come in," he said.

"Thank you."

He looked down at her as she sauntered past, then closed the door which locked itself automatically.

CHAPTER THREE

Russian Lallapazza

THE GIRL was an almost-platinum blonde who apparently knew the virtues of cosmetics. Her eyebrows were penciled black; her lips wore a rouge that was very dark. Worth or Patou or someone equally as chic must have sponsored the ensemble of dark blue velvet.

"I called at eight-thirty," she said. "You weren't in."

"I was taking a turn up on the roof and forgot the time. If I'd known you were such a knockout, I'd have been hours early. Smoke?"

She took a cigarette, and he struck a

match. Her fingernails were lacquered red. "I'm Lorraine Valhoff," she said.

He was lighting his own cigarette. "You came alone, I suppose."

"Why, of course."

He smiled. "That's very swell." He sat down and dropped his chin to his chest. His shaggy mop of hair flopped down over his forehead. "So now what, Miss Valhoff?"

"Well, I was desperate when I telephoned you this afternoon. I am alone in the world, and a woman alone finds it difficult to fight men. Especially when something big is at stake. You were good to grant me an interview."

"Not at all. It's my business."

She nodded. "That's what I had hoped. And I want to ask you again, Mr. Cardigan: can I be certain that whatever passes between us will remain a secret?"

"Miss Valhoff, I'll be as aboveboard with you as you are with me."

"Yes. Yes, of course— These diamonds over which the man was killed are mine."

"No!"

"Yes. Yes, they are mine. They were stolen from me in Cairo six months ago— five of them. They're of the first water. My husband, when he died, left them to me. He was a diamond merchant in South Africa. They're worth approximately ninety thousand dollars."

"Why didn't you go to the police?"

"If the diamonds are brought to light through the usual channels, I shall have to pay a heavy duty on them. I do not live in America. My home is in Paris. If I could get back these diamonds I would find a way of getting them back into France. That is why I came to you."

Cardigan said, "You probably know that a client's engaged me to protect him from a clique that thinks he has those diamonds."

She said, "I know the man who brought those diamonds to this country."

"Yeah? Who?"

"Charles Wheeler."

He leaned an elbow on one knee. "Go ahead."

"The man who took those diamonds from me was named Carl Uhl. He escaped from Cairo, went to Rome and then went to Algiers. There he was attacked by another man who was also after these diamonds. He escaped, but badly wounded, and was taken in by an expatriate England doctor. He died there. It is certain that this doctor took those diamonds, because other effects of Carl Uhl's were found in his possession. He was killed by the man who killed Carl Uhl, but this man found no diamonds, nor was there any report of diamonds having been found. But Charles Wheeler was intimate with the doctor, and directly after the doctor was killed Wheeler fled to Paris. These events I have pieced together. I am now alone against Wheeler and against a clique that is against both Wheeler and me."

Cardigan leaned back. "So then I'm supposed to get these diamonds for you."

"You would be returning them to the rightful owner."

"And how about the client I'm working for now?"

She sighed wistfully. "I am a woman— a woman alone—of gentle birth and breeding and unaccustomed to dramatics such as have been going on since Cairo. I don't know what to do. My people were exterminated during the revolution in Russia, and I fled with what jewels I could gather on short notice. These diamonds mean a lot to me. My livelihood!"

He said, "How much would I get out of it?"

"I thought—perhaps—ten per cent. Is that not usual?"

"Nothing is usual in this business, Miss Valhoff. We try to get as much as we can."

"Perhaps even—well—twelve thousand—"

He took a long time to grind out his cigarette. "My client tells me that he hasn't got the diamonds, that he never has had them and that if he did have them, he'd give them up."

She quivered. "That is a lie!"

Cardigan stood up and jammed his hands into the pockets of his dressing robe. "Who was the guy bumped off Tracy?"

She started. "I— One of the clique, I suppose. I tell you that I am all of a-twitter over these goings-on and hardly know who is who any more. Please, Mr. Cardigan—"

"Now, hold on. If you expect me to fall head over heels, you're ahead of yourself, Miss Valhoff. I'm working for a client and you want me to double-cross him."

"But I am in the right! The diamonds belong to *me!*"

"How am I to know that?"

"Because I am telling you! Because it is the truth!"

"Have you any proof?"

She rose dramatically. "In those days of turmoil when I fled from Russia, how could I take proof? I was only a little child. I fled with my uncle who later was assassinated in the streets of Constantinople." Her voice shook— "Don't you believe me, Mr. Cardigan?"

SLIGHTLY exasperated, Cardigan stood on wide-spread feet, his fists jammed against his hips. She came across to him, her eyes and lips pleading. Her long attenuated fingers gripped the lapels of his dressing gown. There was about her a faint breath of attar of roses. Back of the irises of her eyes was a translucent green shimmer.

Her voice was a throaty purr. "You are so big and strong. You would not deny a woman alone who is incapable of combating the wickedness of adventurers. Would you?"

Her hands rose and were cool against his jaw. He remained rooted to the floor, rocklike, and his eyes seemed to recede farther into their sockets until they were mere horizontal glints.

He said, "Pretty cute."

She pressed closer to him.

He said, "Before your name was Valhoff, what was it?"

She said nothing, but kept pressing her pliant body closer and staring at him with her shimmering green eyes.

"I've had many a racket pulled on me," he said, "but this is a lallapazza. I could fall for you any day, sister, if Wheeler didn't happen to be an old pal of mine. I like 'em tall like you, and good-looking —like you—but those eyes, sister, they spell trouble." He stepped back and laughed good-humoredly. "Scram while I still take it as a joke."

She recoiled and stood like a tall quivering flame. Color rushed over her face, and her hands clenched. "I did not come here to be insulted!" she exclaimed.

"You came here to try to make me one way or another, and I'm telling you to take the air. You can't sell me a damned thing. Now take it before I get nasty."

There was a sharp rap on the door.

Cardigan's hand slapped his hip-pocket. "Who's there?"

"Me—Bone."

He looked at the woman. He went close to her, muttered, "Sit down there and say nothing."

Then he went to the door and opened it, and Bone stood there with Fogel, the house dick.

Cardigan said, "Haven't you got any kind of a home? A room of your own somewhere?"

Bone's face was dull. "What the hell did you mean by giving me the slip in the subway?"

"I meant it as hint that I don't care

to have you shadow-boxing all over the city after me."

Bone pushed in, and Fogel came after him. But Cardigan pushed Fogel in the chest. "No you don't."

"I'm coming in here!" Fogel snapped.

"You're not coming in!" Cardigan laid the flat of his hand against Fogel's face and sent the house dick careening into the corridor. He slammed the door and spun on Bone. "I'm getting tired of this, Abe! It's come to a swell pass when I can't eat or enjoy the comforts of home without having you master-minding on my neck all the time!"

Bone was looking at the woman. "You know what I'm after, Cardigan, and you know blamed well that I'm a hound for punishment. I hang to a thing till I bleed."

Cardigan said. "Just now I happen to be entertaining. Miss Valhoff, this is Lieutenant Bone, one of our great modern detectives. He read Sherlock Holmes at a tender age, and it had a bad effect on his brain. He stops perfect strangers on the street and springs questions like, 'Where were you at 9:36 on the night of January such-and-such at date?' So don't pay any attention to him."

Unimpressed, gloomy-eyed Bone regarded the woman. "I'm glad to meet you, Miss Valhoff."

The woman sat stiffly in the chair, breath bated and a puzzled half-frightened look in her eyes. "How—how do you do, lieutenant."

Bone looked wearily at Cardigan. "I suppose Miss Valhoff is another client."

"Once," Cardigan said, "I tailed a Mexican hairless of hers into the fleshpots of Hoboken and brought him back. Since then we've been friends."

"Still funny, ain't you?"

Cardigan did not look so. He looked dark and mean, and his steady gaze bordered on the malignant. "When you bust into my place like this you can expect goofy answers to anything you ask."

Bone looked at the woman. "Are you here as a client, Miss Valhoff, or as—"

Cardigan stepped in front of Bone. "Listen to me, Abe. Get this. Get it straight and remember it. I don't care a hoot who you are or what you are. I wouldn't care a hoot if you were the commissioner himself, which thank God you'll never be. But get me, baby—get me. You've no right in here. You've no right to ask anybody any questions in here. You get the hell out of my place and stay out."

Bone raised his knobby chin, but his eyes remained gloomy, his face changeless. "Yeah?" he asked tonelessly.

"And don't think that strong-silent-man crap goes over big, either."

Bone said, "You had a date tonight, Cardigan—such an important one that you were in a hurry to shake me."

"I had an appointment with Miss Valhoff."

"I see that. I want to find out what it's all about."

"You've found out. Good cripes almighty, can't I even have a nice sociable date any more?"

Bone stepped to one side and looked at the woman. "Miss Valhoff, why did you come here tonight?"

She was poised again, almost languid. "To pay a friendly call on Mr. Cardigan for what you call old times' sake. If I am intruding—" she shrugged— "of course, it will be better that I leave."

Cardigan got in front of Bone again. "I mean it, Abe—by God I mean it! Get out!" His voice was low, throaty, with a subdued fierceness. "You don't get out right now, and I'll go down to the commissioner tomorrow and put up such a hot smell that you'll get kicked out into the sticks. As a private citizen I've got certain rights. You might be able to pull this noise on some punk, but I'm damned if you can pull it on me!"

Bone's voice was dull. "You're rubbing me the wrong way, Cardigan."

"As if I care whether I rub you up, down or across. You're not God Almighty! Now slide out of here, shamus —slide out!"

Bone flexed his lips once, clipped, "Have it your way, then, wiseacre," and went to the door, opened it and, going out, bumped into Fogel who had been listening at the keyhole. Cardigan booted the door shut. It banged. He barged into the little serving pantry and hove into the living room a minute later carrying a drink.

Miss Valhoff was smiling. "It is obvious, Mr. Cardigan, that you would be an uncommonly bad man to antagonize."

"Take that as a lesson then, Miss Valhoff."

"It was very good of you to conceal from the lieutenant that I came here as a potential client."

"It wasn't for your—" He stopped short, took a drink. A flush of red undermined the brown of his big face.

She said, "I am sorry you will not champion my cause. I would be very grateful. In the Midi I have a charming villa." Her eyes became seductive. "You would like the Midi." She rose, purring, "I like a man like you—dark, stormy, capable and unafraid."

He dipped his head. "Thank you. I don't blame you."

"And one who is rather—conceited. I like conceit when it is violent and healthy."

"Thanks again. But I never mix business with pleasure—especially where a woman is concerned. It took me ten years to learn that, Miss Valhoff—and sometimes I still weaken. But not tonight. You'd better watch out that Bone doesn't follow you. Change cabs at least three times on your way home."

"This, I suppose, is dismissal?"

He made a mock bow. "Much to my sorrow."

She shrugged and sauntered to the door. With her hand on the knob she turned and said curiously, "It was very strange, the way you tried to conceal from the lieutenant that I did not come here as a client."

He said nothing. She smiled, turned the knob, opened the door, sauntered out. The door clicked shut.

CARDIGAN kicked off his slippers, took the gun from one of his shoes, replaced it in the desk. In a minute he was dressed. He caught the freight elevator down and ducked out the service entrance into the street. Reaching the corner of Lexington Avenue, he saw Miss Valhoff and the bull-necked man walking north. He crossed the street and walked north also. The woman and the man crossed and headed west into Thirty-ninth Street. Cardigan stopped on the corner of Thirty-eighth and looked around. He did not see Bone.

He turned west into Thirty-eighth and walked fast to Park Avenue, reaching it in time to see the woman and the man going north past the Princeton Club. Cardigan went north on the east side of the street and did not cross till he saw Miss Valhoff and her escort turn west into Fortieth. He tailed them across Madison and Fifth, past the back of the library toward Sixth Avenue. At Sixth Avenue they entered a taxi, and Cardigan jumped one coming east on Fortieth, at the corner.

"See that yellow starting off? Tail it."

An elevated train thrashed by overhead and stopped at Forty-second Street. The yellow turned east and then south on Fifth. Turned east again on Fortieth and turned north to take the Park Avenue ramp around Grand Central Terminal. It struck out north past the new Waldorf. At Forty-seventh Street the man and the woman switched taxis.

"Pass 'em," Cardigan said, and switched cabs himself at Forty-eighth. Once in the second cab, he said, "That blue one that just passed, tail it."

Another change was made at Fiftieth and Lexington. Cardigan changed, too, and followed them west on Fifty-first street, north on Madison. At the corner of Fifty-fourth and Madison the man and the woman got out. It was a traffic stop, and Cardigan sat in his cab while paying up and saw the two head east on Fifty-fourth. He got out and reached the corner. He got behind three men walking east and saw the man and the woman climb steps to a brownstone front.

He stopped. After a minute he crossed the street and looked up at the face of the house. Lighted windows showed on the first and third floors. He waited. Presently he saw two windows on the fourth floor, at the left, light up. He caught a glimpse of the woman as she drew down the shades.

He turned and saw a familiar figure coming along in the shadows. He recognized the dumpy walk as Fogel's. As he turned, Fogel ducked into an areaway. Cardigan cursed silently for a long minute. Then his jaw tightened. He crossed the street and mounted the steps of a house two doors from the one which the Valhoff woman and the man had entered.

He pressed a button at random and after a moment the door clicked open and the lock kept clicking as he entered a large, dimly lighted corridor. He took a packet of matches from his pocket and jammed it at the bottom of the door so that it would not close completely.

Then he hid in the dark stair well. He heard a door open above, heard footsteps. After a minute the footsteps receded, and a door closed. Two minutes later Cardigan saw Fogel slip into the hallway, heard the door close gently. Fogel walked on tiptoes, reached the foot of the staircase, listened, then began climbing.

Cardigan crept from beneath the stair well, flattened against the wall on the way to the door, reached the door and slipped out. He ran diagonally across the street, went down an areaway into a speakeasy and piled into a telephone booth. He called the nearest police station.

He said, "There's a strange man prowling around the halls in a house at number —— East Fifty-fourth Street."

Five minutes later he stood in the street in front of the speakeasy and watched two cops roughhouse Fogel down the steps diagonally opposite and march him eastward toward the Fifty-first Street station. Cardigan lit a cigarette, tossed the match away with an air of complete satisfaction and headed toward Madison Avenue.

CHAPTER FOUR

Pooch Ad

WHEELER let him into the suite on West End Avenue, and Cardigan said, "Well, I hope I'm rid of Fogel for a while. He's going to have a hell of a time explaining what he was doing in a strange house in Fifty-fourth Street tonight."

Wheeler looked worn and haggard and in no mood for levity. His eyes searched Cardigan's face. "What about the woman?"

"She claims the ice is hers and tried to pull the sweetest story ever told. Only I happened to know that she didn't come alone. There was a big guy waiting for her in the lobby."

"That ought to be Bradshaw. I saw him with the woman once."

"You never saw this jane before you hit Paris?"

"No. I'm sure they connected there."

Cardigan was eyeing him keenly.

"You're sure, Charley, that you're not giving me the run-around?"

Wheeler's mouth hardened. "What do you mean?"

"That you never had anything to do with that ice."

"As far as I'm concerned there never was any ice. What the hell are you driving at?"

"O. K., O. K.," Charley. How's the little woman?"

"She'll be ready to sail—unless these lousy heels take a crack at me. What about the cops?"

"Bone's still doing a hop-skip-and-jump on my heels, but he can't touch me. You'll sail, Charley."

"What does your boss think?"

Cardigan smiled. "He's O. K.—a swell guy."

There was a knock on the door.

Cardigan stiffened, put a finger to his lips and slipped into the bedroom. After a moment Wheeler called him out.

"It was only a bell-hop. I had him take the pooch out for an airing, and the pooch broke the leash and beat it. He asked me if I wanted to put an ad in the paper."

"No, you don't," Cardigan said.

"Why not? Damn it, I've come to like the homely mongrel."

Cardigan pointed. "You keep out of the papers, kid. You always were a sentimental egg, but you're taking orders now —if you expect to bail out of this man's town. These heels may see the ad and trace you through it."

Wheeler shrugged. "Oh, all right."

Cardigan looked hard at him. "I mean it, Charley. Don't think you can put an ad in on the sly, because I'll be watching the papers. They traced you to your first address and got a line on me, too. They're trying like hell to trace you to this one."

"All right, old bohunk, all right. But the old doc was a swell guy, and the pooch—"

"Now lay off." Cardigan put on his hat and strode to the door. "So I'll be seeing you."

IT WAS eleven o'clock when Cardigan dropped from a taxi at Madison Avenue and Fifty-fourth Street. Walking east, he became aware of heels keeping time with his own. He looked around and saw a figure walking behind in the shadows. He slowed down, and the dim shape behind turned into a hall door. Cardigan went on, and a moment later turned his head about and saw the dim shape again walking. Cardigan looked up at the brownstone front and saw that the fourth floor, left, was dark. He went on until he reached Park Avenue, stopped and, looking back, saw the dim shape come to a pause. Cardigan turned south, walking fast, and when he reached Fifty-third Street saw the man idly following. Cardigan turned west and walked faster. When he reached Madison again he had dropped the dim shape. He turned north and again entered Fifty-fourth Street.

He dodged into the vestibule of the brownstone. He got the hall door open with a master key and climbed to the fourth floor. He stood in the corridor for a moment getting his bearings, then went toward a door he was certain led to the Valhoff woman's apartment. He knocked several times and listened intently. There was no answer, nor did he hear any sounds inside. He tried his master key and several others, but none worked.

He went to the rear of the hall—it was not long—and opened a solitary window there. He leaned out and saw a fire-escape platform. He climbed out, closed the window and squatted for a minute on the metal platform. He leaned way out and saw that one of the adjoining windows was open a couple of inches. He swung closer to the building, got his left hand on the ledge, stretched farther and got hold of the bottom of the open window. Holding it hard, he clung to the frame of the fire-escape with his right hand while working his left foot over to the window ledge. For a brief moment he remained spread-eagled, then kicked out with his right foot, swayed and came to his knees on the ledge, gripping the bottom of the open window with both hands. Bit by bit he raised the window, stepped into a darkened room and remained motionless, but breathing heavily.

After a few moments he began moving. From his vest pocket he drew a flashlight the size of a fountain pen. Its meager glow showed him a bedroom. He entered another bedroom and then went straight ahead into a living room. Before him were the front windows of the apartment. He cruised the living room without finding anything of consequence. Then he entered the middle bedroom, closed the connecting door and turned on the lights.

The bed had not been slept in that day. Half-packed bags were on the floor, and a man's clothes hung in a closet. Gradually Cardigan became aware of the fact that they were the clothes of two men; the suits varied in size. He plowed into a steamer trunk that appeared not to have been unpacked. Stenciled on it were the initials L. S. Apparently they stood for Sterns. In the bottom of the trunk he found an assortment of knives—five in all —of varied construction, thickness of steel and length. One he knew was a Malay *kris;* another was a stiletto; another a broad-bladed dagger with a mottled agatelike grip. All the knives were clean. He replaced them and, disappointed, closed the trunk.

The rear room was obviously the woman's. Only two dresses hung in the closet. Most of her things were packed. Cardigan went back into the middle room, searched beneath the pillows and the mattress. He flung the mattress down again, straightened, turned, and found himself looking at a man standing in the living-room doorway. The man held a gun. He was the bull-necked man, and he wasn't smiling.

"CAREFUL, Cardigan. I believe it's Cardigan." Over his shoulder he said, "Lights." Lights in the living room sprang on, and beyond the bull-necked man Cardigan saw the woman and a tall, emaciated thin man. Cardigan removed his hat and fanned himself.

"Bradshaw," he said. "I believe it's Bradshaw."

The bull-necked man said, "We are glad to meet, I'm sure."

"It's a pleasure," said Cardigan.

"For me," said Bradshaw bluntly.

The thin man, impeccably dressed, strode past Bradshaw and stood regarding Cardigan with a withering glance.

Cardigan said, "And Mr. Sterns, of course."

"And what about it?" snapped the thin man.

Cardigan said, looking past him, "And Miss Valhoff. I see, Miss Valhoff that you've stopped being a woman alone."

"Enough out of you!" Sterns ripped out. "What the hell are you doing here?"

Cardigan's smile was not genuine. He must have known he was in tough spot, but he said, "Imagine your surprise."

Sterns took two jerky steps and laid the flat of his hand across Cardigan's cheek. Cardigan did not budge. Only his head moved to one side, snapped back straight again while his eyes shone with a frigid smile.

Bradshaw said, "Cut it out, Lester," in a tone that indicated such an act was child's play.

The woman remained in the living room taking slow drags on a cigarette.

Bradshaw said, "What are you looking for, Cardigan?"

Cardigan was honest. "Some hint as to

which one of you birds bumped off Tracy in my room."

"And you found the hint?"

"Of course. Sterns did it."

The woman laughed mockingly.

Bradshaw came into the room saying, "Lester, take away his gun. Get behind him and take it."

Sterns got behind Cardigan and removed the gun from Cardigan's hip-pocket. He moved to one side and released the safety.

Bradshaw said patiently, "Lester, close that safety and give the gun to me."

"Why?"

"I am not going to have you monkeying around with a gun."

Cardigan put in, "Sure, when his game is knives."

"That's enough out of you," Bradshaw said. "You are going to talk, but not in a light vein. You are going to tell us where Wheeler is located. We are going to get those diamonds. Each and every one of them."

"You're screwy," Cardigan said.

Bradshaw said, "Tracy tried to double-cross us, you know. He hadn't the brains, though. Tracy was the one who located Wheeler, but did not tell us. But we were watching Tracy. Get in the living room."

Cardigan did not move. Sterns kicked his shins, and Cardigan grunted and stumbled forward. He went into the living room and found the woman regarding him maliciously with her green eyes.

He said, "I suppose you're waiting to see the Irish take water, huh, sister?"

She smiled. "With pleasure!"

"Go to hell," he growled.

Sterns kicked him in the spine, and Cardigan whirled, but Bradshaw was there solidly with his gun. "Nix, Cardigan," he said patiently.

Then he said to the woman, "Lorraine, turn on the radio—rather loud."

CHAPTER FIVE

Irish Blood

THE woman went to a cabinet and turned a knob. A Harlem jazz band cut loose. Bradshaw made Cardigan sit down in an armchair, then spoke to Sterns. Sterns went into one of the rooms and reappeared carrying two heavy leather luggage straps. He buckled one end to the other, then threw the strap across Cardigan's stomach, put the ends through the arms of the chair and buckled the strap behind the chair.

Bradshaw sat down on another chair with his gun, and Sterns leaned over Cardigan and said close to his ear, "Now where is Wheeler staying?"

"You want him," Cardigan said. "You go find him."

Sterns whipped his fist into Cardigan's face. Blood trickled from Cardigan's lip, but his head snapped back to an erect position, and he pressed his lips tightly together.

"Where is he?" Sterns snarled.

"The trouble with you guys," Cardigan said, "is that you're all nutty. He hasn't got the diamonds."

"If he hasn't got the diamonds, why didn't he report to the police? Why didn't you?"

"He didn't want to make trouble."

"No. He didn't report because he has those diamonds, and he knows that if he reports, that will be the end of them!"

Cardigan said, "He hasn't got the diamonds."

"Where is he staying?"

"You'll have to find that out for yourself."

"I intend to."

He kicked Cardigan's shins and kept kicking them until Cardigan lashed out with his foot, caught Sterns in the pit of the stomach and sent him smashing into a chair ten feet away. Chair and

Sterns went down to the floor, Sterns moaning and rolling back and forth on his stomach.

The woman disappeared and came back quickly, her green eyes shimmering. She carried a razor strop. She whanged it across Cardigan's face while Sterns still groaned in agony on the floor. Bradshaw took a clinical interest in the proceedings.

The woman laughed hysterically. "How do you like that, eh?"

"I'm not crazy about it," Cardigan said.

"What is that address now?"

"I told you once to go to hell; that stands."

Whang!

The buckle went clear around the back of his neck and opened his right eyebrow.

The green-eyed woman shook with rage. "You regret insulting me today now, don't you?"

Pain kept Cardigan's lips shut.

Bradshaw got up and came over and leaned close to his ear while the radio jazz band thundered. "Don't be a fool, Cardigan. We're going to get that address."

Cardigan's sneer was freighted with contempt.

Sterns got up with oaths bubbling and fizzing on his lips. He grabbed a poker from the fireplace and rushed madly toward Cardigan. Bradshaw caught the descending arm, wrenched it, and the poker fell to the floor. "Not that," he said. "We want information out of this guy, Lester." He was patient. "Now don't be an idiot."

"I'll kill him!" Sterns grated.

The woman cut loose with the strop again, and Cardigan grunted. He heaved up, lugging the armchair with him, and broke the straps with his body and arms. Fury burned red in his eyes and as the woman struck out again Cardigan gave her the flat of his hand across her mouth. She yelped and fell down, spat out a tooth.

He whirled with his fist knotted and moving uncorked it into Sterns' face, lifted Sterns off his feet and dropped him into a divan where Sterns bounced like a rubber ball and then lay chattering.

But Bradshaw stuck his gun in the small of Cardigan's back and said patiently, "This isn't going to get you anywhere."

The woman was emitting crazy chirping sounds.

The jazz band had stopped.

A voice was saying, "Late news dispatches. Here's a good one. The only one hundred thousand dollar bulldog ever found. And dead at that. An unidentified brindle bull was run over at ten tonight at Ninety-second Street and Broadway by a Broadway street car. Killed instantly. Patrolman Swenson took charge of the body and in lifting the dog noticed something fall from one of the wounds. It was a diamond. On closer inspection it was found that four other diamonds were imbedded in the dog's flesh. It appears that these diamonds had been placed in an incision, whereupon the incision had been sewn up. A doctor claimed that it looked like an expert job, probably the work of a surgeon. A cursory examination of the diamonds by an expert indicates that these diamonds are worth about a hundred thousand dollars. Some dog, folks—"

The woman had stopped mumbling. Sterns had stopped gibbering. Cardigan looked at the radio, transfixed, and Bradshaw said, "By God," dully.

The woman yelped, "Wheeler had a bulldog! The doctor's bulldog! The fool didn't know—we didn't know. Oh, what utter fools!"

Sterns said, "The diamonds are in the hands of the police!" as though making a revelation.

"Of course," Bradshaw said. He looked stunned, but he kept his gun hard against the small of Cardigan's back.

Cardigan said, "I told you. I told you Wheeler didn't know anything about those damned diamonds."

Sterns crept from the divan and stood on shaking legs. His voice was clotted. "But that doesn't let you out. You know too much. Too much."

The woman sprang up. "Too much indeed."

Cardigan said, "Tracy was a heel like the rest of you. His death doesn't mean anything to me. The case is over. Believe it or not, this will never get to the police."

"Take him out," the woman said. "Kill him somewhere. Meantime I will pack the bags."

Sterns said, "I'll wash my face first." He went into the bathroom.

Blood streaked Cardigan's face. "I'll break even on this, so help me."

"We can't take the chance," Bradshaw said. "You know too much. Start packing, Lorraine."

Sterns reappeared, carrying a slender stiletto. "This is the thing. No noise. We'll gag him in the car. Should I go and get the car?"

Bradshaw said, "Yes, get it and wait down the block. I'll bring him. Get in the bathroom, Cardigan, so Lester can wash that blood off your face." He pushed Cardigan into the bathroom, and Sterns washed Cardigan's face with mocking tenderness.

"You guys 'll regret this."

Bradshaw said, "We've got to do it."

STERNS dried Cardigan's face, and Bradshaw marched him back into the living room. Harlem was again on the air. And there was another sound. Someone was knocking. Sterns looked at Bradshaw, and Bradshaw looked at Cardigan.

Cardigan said, "There's only one guy could be out there."

"Who?" Bradshaw asked.

"The cop that met Miss Valhoff at my place this evening—Lieutenant Bone. If you think you can shoot it out with him, your crazy. He's a wizard with a gun."

Bradshaw set his jaw, and Sterns began to get panicky.

Cardigan muttered. "I said we'd break even. Turn the lights down. I'll sit in that armchair. You, Bradshaw, sit in that one. Tell Sterns and the woman to go in the back and close that connecting door. You and I are friends. Act that way. It's your only out—so take it—and quick."

"I don't believe him!" Sterns said in a whisper. "As soon as the cop comes in he'll tell. No—no!"

"So help me," Cardigan promised.

"No—no!" cried Sterns.

"What 'll you do?" Bradshaw asked.

"Tie two bed sheets together and let myself down to the fire-escape. It slants beneath the rear window."

"How about Lorraine and me?"

"I'm going," Sterns said. "You and Lorraine can make it, too. Come on."

"How about this guy?"

Sterns said, "For some reason or other this guy is just as much afraid of the cops as we are. We'll make him go, too, and get rid of him on the East Side. Come on."

"No," Bradshaw said. "Get in that room, close the door and keep Lorraine in there."

The knocking was louder.

"You hear me!" Bradshaw growled. "You bungled one job, and you're not going to bungle another. We can take care of Cardigan later. Get in there!"

Sterns winced, turned and went into the other room. He closed the door. Bradshaw turned all the lights out but a bridge lamp. He motioned Cardigan to a chair. He put his gun in his pocket.

"Remember," he said. "No tricks."

He turned the radio off and went to the door. He unlocked it, turned the knob and pulled the door open.

"Put 'em up, you!"

Bradshaw stepped back and raised his hands. Cardigan jumped up, leaped across the room and threw the bolt on the connecting door. He heard Sterns' fists pummel it. He pivoted and saw Bradshaw backing into the room.

George Hammerhorn said, "Come on, Irish."

Cardigan came up behind Bradshaw, reached into Bradshaw's pocket and took out the gun Sterns had taken from him. He crossed the room and picked up his hat, put it on. Bradshaw was speechless, dumbfounded. Cardigan walked to the door and stood beside Hammerhorn.

He said, "All right, Bradshaw. I'll give you till nine tomorrow morning to get out of town."

Bradshaw, red-faced, growled, "This man is not Lieutenant Bone!"

"I'm as surprised as you are," Cardigan said. "Remember, Bradshaw. Out of town by nine tomorrow morning.... O. K., George."

They backed out into the hall side by side, Cardigan with his left hand on the knob, his right holding his gun on Bradshaw. He closed the door.

"Go ahead, George."

Hammerhorn walked to the stairs, and Cardigan backed toward them, watching the door. The door did not open. They went down the staircase, out the front door and into the street.

"There's a speak across the street, George. Let's."

"Swell. God, but you're a goof."

"You've got a hell of a nerve tailing me around."

"Have I?"

"Yeah," Cardigan said. "And I like it."

"You're leaving on a job in Buffalo tomorrow."

"Oh, yeah?"

"What the hell do you think I got you out of that tough spot for, because I like you?"

BUOY of DOOM

by

Norman H. White, Jr.

Author of "Hot Ice," etc.

He balanced crazily and toppled over into the ice-cold water.

It floated there on the still waters of Saturday Cove—only to mark the spot where Ellwell had set his lobster trap. But when the fisherman peered down into the lambent green depths, he saw with horror that his innocent buoy had turned into an anchorage for ghastly crime.

THE fresh wind shredded the white fog hanging low above the blue-black water into ragged, cottony strips as the little auxiliary sloop, Kitty, chugged sturdily into Saturday Cove.

As the boat passed the town pier which thrust its weathered length out from the shore, Benton Ellwell flipped off the ignition switch. The final deafening barks of the single-cylinder engine bedded deep in the cockpit echoed back from the bluff above the pier. Only the swish of the following waves slapping under the stern broke the sudden silence as the boat coasted along.

Benton deftly spun the steering wheel and the sloop swung about on her heel. Defiantly she poked her stubby bow-sprit into the cold south-east breeze that breathed chill hints of icebergs which still, at that time in April, floated sluggishly not far off the broad, island-dotted mouth of the Penobscot. Not until June would the last great frozen mass be gone. The bergs left each year just as the summer visitors arrived, thought Benton grimly, and each spelled trouble in his mind.

Astern of the sloop a white dory horsed around aimlessly as the pull on the painter slackened. Benton left the wheel and went forward. A moment later the anchor splashed down into the ruffled water. Benton made the line secure to the forward bitt, set the line carefully through the starboard chock and walked aft. His gray eyes became complacent as he looked his boat over. Built by Morse at Friendship, Maine, she lived up to the proud line of tiny ships from which she sprang.

But today Benton wasted no time in admiring his boat. There ought to be a letter waiting for him up at the post office—a letter that would be of interest. He shoved the slide hatch over the companionway that led below into the snug cabin and pulled the dory alongside. Neatly, for all his hundred and seventy pounds, he slipped into the flat-sided craft and rowed toward the pier with the short jerky strokes that, to an experienced eye, would label him anywhere as a Maine man.

On the high bluff back of the weathered dock nestled the white frame houses of the town. Under the towering elm lived Benton's mother in a house that Benton's great-great-grandfather, with hands as hard as the oak he'd hewn, had built a good hundred and fifty years before.

Across the street from the Ellwell's lived a certain graceful person whose name, laboriously laid in neat gold-leaf lettering, glistened across the stern of Benton's sloop. And as he rowed toward the shore, thoughts of pretty Kitty Hopkins swept through Benton's mind and clouded his tanned face with worry.

All during the past winter while the deep snows had blanketed the pine-crowned countryside Benton and Kitty had gone to the country dances over at the Heights. When the state road had been open they'd driven up to Belfast to the movies and in the darkness of the old opera house their hands had touched and clung. Finally a month ago, with Kitty's permission, Benton had called on Mr. Doak, the jeweler, up in Belfast. Their talk had been concerning the price of diamonds.

But suddenly as the long winter shadows became shorter and the south slopes of the hills softened each noon, as the frost came up, Benton had come to a sudden worrying realization.

With the warm weather would come the summer people to the Cove. And among them Clayte Biddle and his family, as they had for years. Small chance a poor lobsterman had against the easy-mannered New Yorker with his cars and speed boats.

Benton's big hands tightened on the oars as he thought of the letter he'd written Clayte about two weeks before. There ought to be an answer by now and, knowing his fiery temper, he guessed Clayte would be plenty sore. Benton hadn't wasted words in telling him that, unless he was really serious, he wanted him to leave Kitty Hopkins alone. If Clayte was really in love—well, that was a different matter, but Benton felt sure he wasn't.

Not that Clayte Biddle wasn't a good fellow, Benton admitted grimly to himself as he rowed. He had known and liked Clayte since they'd both been kids. In the old days they'd played together, had been inseperable. Naked and brown as little savages they'd dammed the mill stream together, had shared the excitement of Clayte's first 22 rifle on his twelfth birthday. In those days Kitty Hopkins had just been a nuisance—only to be considered when their childish plans for the day's adventure called for someone to be scalped or to be held for ransom.

But as the years passed on things had changed. Benton found himself gradually resenting the college man who so gracefully appropriated the yellow-haired Kitty's favor each summer and Benton's resentment was no secret to the rest of the town. He had stood for plenty of kidding on the subject last summer. That hadn't helped but the real cause for his anger was that he felt sure that Clayte Biddle was just playing with Kitty.

So, after much thought Benton had written Clayte straight-forwardly and asked him not to come to the Cove that summer—had almost warned him against it—unless he was serious.

THE shadow of the pier cut off the afternoon sun. He shipped his oars and jumped out onto the slanting float. He was kneeling to fasten the painter to a cleat when a harsh voice interrupted his thoughts.

"You Benton Ellwell?" The question as well as the pronunciation told the lobsterman the voice belonged to a stranger. Benton stood up and turned to look down curiously from his six-foot-two at the short swarthy man who had spoken. Funny he hadn't seen him—the fellow must have been standing concealed under the rude gangway that led up from the float to the pier above.

"That's my name," drawled Benton. "What's on your mind?"

His steel-gray eyes were sharply sizing up the rough-looking owner of the voice as he spoke.

As a type, Benton placed the man at once. He was one of the many that the illicit rum-running trade had brought to such small hamlets on the Maine coast as Saturday Cove. Some of the local fishermen had also thrown in with these men from the city underworld. Byron Heald, for instance, had made a slew of money piloting in their ships among the ledges— but then a month ago he'd gotten caught and now he was in prison with eleven months to go. Benton, in desperation, had often considered the racket, but a jail sentence and Kitty Hopkins would never go together. Benton wanted money—money meant Kitty Hopkins and a home of their own—but he must get it honestly or else not at all.

"Wanta make a little spare change, Ellwell?" Black, beady eyes that reminded Benton of a rat were watching him as the man spoke—eyes that were furtive and calculating and wary. No good could come of any offer that this sort of man had to make, thought Benton.

"No, I'm not interested in having anything to do with running in booze—if that's what you mean," said Benton curtly.

For a moment the man didn't answer. He seemed to be weighing a proposition in his mind. Benton started up the slanting gangway that led up onto the pier. The other started after him hurriedly.

"Wait a minute! Want to make a few bucks if you don't have to run any rum?"

Benton stopped. "Well, what's the proposition?"

"You've got that string of lobster pots that runs down off the Cunner ledges—and ends at the Biddle place, I understand," said the man, throwing a glance behind him as though to see that no one was within earshot.

"Yes," said Benton, "I got a string that runs from a couple o' hundred yards south of here right to off the Biddle point. And those same pots need pulling. I've been fog-bound over 'cross in Dark Harbor for three days. There ought to be a nice mess of lobsters in them traps by now."

The man stepped closer, suppressed excitement in his manner. "You can make some easy money—for a favor," he said in a low tone. "Here's the set-up. A night or so ago we come in through the fog with a nice load of liquor. It was so thick that we didn't dare run right in close to the float on the Biddle place. We been using that as a landing place, you know."

Benton nodded. It had been real thick for the last several nights—thicker than mud. No weather to be fooling around rocky ledges.

The man continued. "Well, the fog was so damn bad that we didn't dare stand in as far as the pier. We happened on one of those two trap buoys of yours off the point. We dropped our load alongside it, using the buoy as a marker. It was so thick that we're not sure which buoy it was an' we haven't had a chance to pick

it up yet but we plan to get it tonight."

"Well, what do you want me to do about it?"

The swarthy man grinned confidently, dug a hand into a pocket of his soiled trousers.

"Nothing, brother. Get the idea? Nothing! Here's a ten spot for you if you simply lay off pulling either of those two traps down off the Biddle point—till tomorrow. Pull the rest of your string but lay off those two." As his beady eyes searched Benton's bronzed features anxiously the grin faded from his face.

Benton shook his head. Not that ten dollars was to be despised, but there was something in the stranger's manner that irritated the lobsterman. He had the Downeaster's instinctive dislike of outsiders. Those traps were his own, built by his own hands during the long winter months. No one was going to dictate to this Yankee whether he could pull them or not.

"Sorry, but those traps gotta be pulled this afternoon," said Benton stubbornly. "They ain't been pulled for the past three days. The marlin on some of the heads is pretty badly worn and I'm liable to lose a bunch of lobsters. They're precious this year. I've only got to lose a few to make up the ten dollars."

A QUICK flash of anger swept through the other's eyes as Benton spoke. But he restrained himself with difficulty and when the words came his voice endeavored to be placating.

"Well, I'll tell you what I'll do, brother —I'll make it twenty bucks. O. K.? You'd never get twenty dollars outa those two traps in a week o' Sundays."

But Benton Ellwell had made up his mind. "You're wasting your time," he said definitely. "Besides I figure you birds have got an all-fired nerve to use the Biddle place as a landing. I don't want any part in your dealings." He turned away but the other grabbed his arm.

"Listen to me, Ellwell. I've tried to play on the up-and-up with you. Say, you're a fine one to worry about the Biddles! You hate Clayton Biddle's guts an' you know it. An' I'm goin' to tell you somethin' else. If you try to haul those traps this afternoon, it'll be just too bad!"

Benton's thin lips had tightened at the reference to Clayte Biddle. He angrily shook off the other's clutch on his arm.

"It'll take more than you and a number of others of your breed of pole cats to stop me haulin' my traps," he said slowly. "Why, I got an almighty good mind to toss you overboard and cool you off." His big hands were twitching at his side though his face was calm.

The dark man reddened. His small eyes shot a quick glance over Benton's shoulder along the pier. The water front of the tiny harbor was deserted. His eye came back to Benton's face. Perhaps the self-control of the lobsterman misled him. Others had figured Benton wrongly to their sorrow.

With a sudden convulsive movement he whipped a hand toward his right rear pocket. But before he had the gun half out the quick surprise had left Benton's eyes and his hard fist caught the gunman on the point of the jaw. With a dazed expression the man threw up his hands and staggered backward. His knees buckled as he reached the edge of the narrow float. For a second he balanced crazily and toppled over into the ice-cold water. A moment later he came up spluttering and clawing desperately at the low edge of the float, and dragged himself onto the weathered planks, panting for breath as Benton watched him. Stooping quickly Benton pulled a vicious-looking automatic from the other's hip pocket and tossed it far out into the water.

"Now, get this, stranger," said Benton, his voice tense with suppressed anger. "I'm pulling my traps whenever I want to—and that's right now!" Benton looked up toward the bluff and then down toward the Cunner ledges that stretched their rocky length a mile and a half to the south. "An' it seems darn funny to me," he continued thoughtfully eying the panting form on the float, "that you're so darned interested in those two traps off the Biddle place. Yessiree, I think I'll pull 'em right now!"

The dripping man was on his feet. He pointed a trembling finger at Benton's lank form. "You keep away from them traps off the Biddle place or it'll be too bad," he shrilled. "You get too smart an' you're liable to end up in jail!"

"What! For pulling my own traps?"

Benton laughed harshly and took a threatening step forward. The smaller man turned and scuttled up the pier, water splashing from his clothes and shoes as he ran.

Benton jerked in the dory savagely as the man disappeared over the crest of the bluff. He got into the boat and shipped his oars between the hickory thole-pins, his face furious. He was just about to pull away from the pier when a clear sweet voice hailed him.

Kitty Hopkins came hurrying down onto the float. Her face was white and her eyes dark with excitement. As she ran toward him she kept glancing over her shoulder fearfully.

His brown face startled, Benton was resting on his oars just off the float. "What's the matter?" he called.

"Oh, Benton—Clayte's been murdered! I mean he's disappeared and dad and the sheriff both think he's been done away with! And they think you did it!"

"Me?" Benton's voice was incredulous as he worked the dory in close to the float. "Don't they know me better'n that? When did Clayte come down from New York?"

"It was that foolish letter you wrote him," sobbed Kitty. "He drove 'way down here to see you about it. He was sore, too. He showed the letter to dad the evening he got here—three nights ago. Said he was real mad 'cause you'd believe he was trifling with me. That night he went back to the Biddle place alone to sleep. It was awfully foggy and we tried to make him stay with us. But Clayte laughed and said that he knew some of the rum runners had been using his family's place to land stuff and he was going to stop them. Said he had a gun and everything. He wouldn't listen to dad.

"The next morning when dad went down to do some work at the Biddle place the front door of the house was wide open and Clayte had disappeared! Everybody in town has been looking for him since and Mr. Biddle offered a big reward to anyone who finds him." Kitty's voice broke as she finished. Benton didn't speak.

"I hurried down to warn you, Benton —about the sheriff. He's going to arrest you on sight." Kitty began to sob.

FOR a full moment Benton remained dazed. Then his brain swung slowly into action. Clayte perhaps dead—murdered—and he accused of killing him. And there was the letter.

He forced his mind to function. There wasn't much time. At any moment he expected to see the tall figure of Sheriff Frank Drinkwater coming down the pier.

The mysterious stranger's warning about the two traps off the Biddle's point came back to him. The man had admitted that his gang had been using the Biddle place for landing their stuff. And he hadn't been averse to pulling a gun! If Clayte had been foolish enough to try to prevent a load of liquor from being landed at the private dock on the Biddle estate he might well have come to some harm at the hands of the rum runners. A strange desire to pull those two traps that lay off

the Biddle place before his freedom might be taken away from him gnawed at his mind.

A few hurried words to Kitty and he bent to his oars. The white bead of foam that churned about the bow of the dory as Benton's strong arms drove it down along the mile of shore, was no more active than the thoughts that seethed through his mind.

The craft leaped ahead toward the point from which the white pier of the Biddles jutted out into the water. Benton disregarded his other pots in his speed, passing the bright red buoys, one after another as he swept along the ledges.

At first he thought it might be his imagination. But as he drove the boat along he became sure. Someone was paralleling his course in the heavy underbrush on the nearby shore as he rowed along!

Carefully concealing his interest he shot sidelong glances at the shore without lessening the quick rhythmic swing of his oars. Someone—several people—were following his progress. Vague figures keeping ominously even with him behind the thick shield of underbrush as he came nearer and nearer to the Biddle point, off which bobbed the red buoys on the two traps the swarthy stranger had warned him not to pull. These two buoys were approximately a hundred yards apart. One was on the north side of the point and one farther to the south.

As Benton rowed toward the first and northernmost buoy his eyes again swept the bushes that edged the rocky shore along which he had passed. The men were still keeping abreast of him. He forced his eyes to swing out onto the white-capped bay lest his pursuers might know that they were observed. A peculiar prickling sensation ran up and down his spine as he bent to his oars. The little swarthy man hadn't hesitated to use a gun. More and more Benton was convinced that the man had been waiting purposely for him—to talk to him before he received news of Clayte's disappearance.

His lips were tight as he approached the first buoy and shipped his oars skillfully. Trouble would come quickly now unless the stranger had been bluffing. A quick sidewise glance toward the nearby shore revealed the snubby, vicious nose of a gun protruding through the protecting foliage not a hundred and fifty feet away.

Benton hesitated, but only for an instant. He figured they wouldn't fire till the pot reached the surface. He put a hard down to the buoy. The narrow yellow streak of the manila rope descended straight as a ruled line down into the lambent green depths of the water. Not a sound from the shore but he knew if he pulled up the lobster pot a fusillade of shots would burst out. His eyes narrowed as his mind raced on to a quick decision. Then, with a sudden gesture he tossed the buoy overboard and picked up his oars again.

He rowed down to the other buoy. Still his enemies on the shore pursued him. He saw their forms—there seemed to be three of them—flitting from behind one bushy shelter to the protection of some other clump of stubby pines.

The buoy he approached was even nearer the shore than the first. There would not be as much chance now when the men began firing. And he was sure they'd fire if he pulled up the trap.

Now he was just off the long pier of the Biddle estate on the point. He steeled himself for the ordeal of the next few minutes. For a few seconds, as he rowed between the two buoys, he knew that he was safe. But if he had figured correctly that safety would be gone the instant he pulled up the second buoy.

With strange insistence the swarthy man's remark came back to him. "You're liable to end up in jail!" That remark made him feel certain that he was on the right track. He set his jaw and rowed on,

kicking off his shoes as he neared the red-painted wooden block.

AN OMINOUS red spot, the buoy lay on the sparkling water. Like a magnet Benton's white dory seemed drawn nearer and nearer to it. Now he could feel the wood thumping hollowly against the side of the dory. Laying down his oars, he reached for the bobbing red marker. In a few seconds he expected to hear the savage rattle of a machine gun coming from the nearby point.

But no sound broke the stillness save the excited chatter of a kingfisher and from far out on the bay, the distant squeal of a mackeral gull. A quietness, thick and encumbering, enfolded the lonely point like a suffocating blanket. But the silence held no peace—only menace.

Benton pulled in the slack of the crisp yellow manila and coiled it methodically on the bottom of the dory. Though outwardly cool, his arms seemed to work mechanically. Little beads of sweat glistened on his forehead as he pulled heavily on the rope and felt the sluggish weight of the trap coming slowly to the surface. Heavier than usual it seemed to him as he pulled it slowly up.

When he could see its yellow slats through the mobile surface of the water, Benton pressed the line heavily over the gunwale of the boat to hold the strain, and leaned over the side. His mind directing every move, he gazed down into the water that reflected his image back at him.

Then suddenly a gesture of horrified astonishment swept over his face—his lean figure stiffened in excitement. His eyes dilated. From his lips burst a loud ejaculation. Excitement was plainly evident in his actions and his face was grim as he stared down into the water.

With his jaw set tight he decided to bring the trap to the surface. Now trouble would begin. He took another resolute pull on the rope. The trap broke the surface of the water with its slatted side.

A deafening, raucous chatter ripped aside the silence that had hung like a thick veil over the place. Bullets screamed and spattered into the water, ripped savagely through the side of the boat.

As the first shot rang out Benton hurled himself overboard. The trap sank back ominously to the depths, the line uncoiling freely from the empty boat.

Deep Benton plunged into the cold, biting water. Down, down he forced himself. It was his one possible escape.

It seemed as if his lungs would burst. The chill of the icy water permeated into his very innermost fibre. But still he struggled to keep himself below the surface. After a dozen strokes he could feel the current that made around the point sweeping him toward the place he wished to get to. If he could only reach the other side of the point there was a chance—not much, but still, a chance. From there the men on shore couldn't see him.

Red flashes came before his eyes. His brain became numb, but still his feet and hands threshed the water down in the murky depths like an automaton. In good stead Benton's outdoor life came to his assistance. His arms, strong as live steel from the daily work at the oars and pulling his traps, urged him on. His body inured to the cold and toughened by exposure in all kinds of weather repulsed doggedly the chill of the water as he strained every muscle to cover the necessary distance.

On he went. His lungs seemed as though they were on fire. The torture of the ordeal benumbed his senses after the first few moments. It would have been easy to have released himself from that awful pain by giving himself up to the frigid waters which held him in their grasp. Then peace would have come. But Benton drove himself on.

Consciousness was losing its grasp on his mind as he finally allowed his body to come to the surface. He expected that each instant would bring a shower of leaden, death-dealing hail around his head. Then he suddenly realized that he had made his objective. He had gotten to a position around the point and was hidden from the sight of the men on the shore.

Swimming quietly, and practically exhausted, he made for the shore and lay inert for a few moments after he felt the rocky ledges of the point come up under his feet. He tried to stand and at first found that he could not lift his weight. A few minutes later, he staggered to his stockinged feet and tore clumsily across the field behind Biddle's house, making for the state road.

If luck would only break with him he might get a ride in some passing car to the Cove. The sound of a shrill horn on the Duck Trap Hill came to his ears. He turned his haggard face in that direction and stood waiting eagerly, his limbs trembling from his exertions, as the water dripped from his sodden clothes. A moment later he was seated beside an astonished stranger who drove him furiously to the Cove.

HE THREW himself from the car in front of the general store. As luck would have it the first figure that he saw was that of Sheriff Frank Drinkwater. The latter's shrewd eyes opened as they saw with astonishment the tall figure of the shoeless lobsterman swaying toward him.

"I was just goin' down the pier after you," said Drinkwater with ominous slowness. "I want to talk to you!"

"I know," cut in Benton curtly before the other could continue. "You want me 'bout Clayte Biddle's disappearance. Well, if I'm guessing right I can help you solve the deal."

Drinkwater looked at him, his leathery face cast in a mask of suspicion.

"Sorry, Benton, but I've got to lock you up. But," he added, "you can tell me what you want me to do and I'll be glad to do it. Come on, son—you come with me—we can talk it over at the jail."

Benton pulled away from him angrily. "Listen here, Frank. You know damn well I didn't murder anybody—particularly Clayte Biddle whom I've grown up with from a little shaver. I'll come back with you as your prisoner in a half an hour—give you my word of honor."

The hawklike eyes of the older man bored into Benton's. Then his lean jaw snapped shut under his tobacco-stained mustache. "If you'll give your word of honor, son, I'll play ball with you. Let's go."

Benton's big hand met the bony fingers of the sheriff. "Good," he said fervently. "Come on, Frank. We'll need guns."

A moment later with both Benton and himself armed with twelve-gauge shot guns, the sheriff's rattly flivver was hustling back along the road retracing Benton's flight. They swung down into the Biddle driveway past the big house and hurried on foot down the path toward the pier.

As Benton had suspected, the three men had put over a boat and were out at the trap. They must have thought they'd killed Benton, for on the pier lay the snubby-nosed sub-machine gun with which they had sprayed their leaden hell at him only a few minutes before. They turned in astonishment as the sheriff hailed them.

The little swarthy man took charge. "Wait," he shouted. "We'll come in for you, sheriff. Don't let him get away!"

"What's the idea?" demanded the sheriff in surprise looking at Benton, but the younger man shook his head. "Wait a bit, Frank," he said grimly. Again he remembered the swarthy man's remark earlier in the afternoon. Well, this was in line with what he expected.

"What's the trouble with you fellers?" demanded Drinkwater as the boat came alongside the float. "Ellwell here says you shot at him and damned near killed him."

The little swarthy man sitting in the stern of the rowboat spoke up fiercely. "So that's Ellwell's story? He's a fine one to talk! Well, get a load of this! We caught him pulling up a body an' when we shouted at him he tried to get away. Sure we fired at him—who wouldn't? He's a murderer!"

"A body?" demanded Drinkwater tensely, looking at Benton. "Why, that's probably Biddle!"

The little man pointed out at the red buoy. "We saw a body tied to that trap," he said flatly. "We was on the pier and when we saw him pull it up we hailed him. Then he tried to get away, so we shot at him. We claim that reward!"

"Humph," grunted the sheriff. "What do you say to that, Benton?"

"You saw a body?" demanded Benton slowly, turning on the swarthy man.

The little man nodded, his beady eyes glistening greedily. "Sure—we all did. It was sorta strapped right alongside the lobster trap when it came up."

"On that lobster trap?" asked Benton pointing to the second buoy—the one the men had just left and where he'd almost met his death.

"Sure," said the little man angrily. "Why, you saw us out there just now. What do you take us for, a bunch of fools? Sure, it was that trap."

"This looks pretty serious, Benton," said the sheriff soberly. "You didn't like Clayte Biddle any too well." He turned to the dark man. "Take us out there," he commanded.

"Come on, Benton—get busy," said Drinkwater sharply a few moments later, pointing at the buoy with a gnarled forefinger. "Haul up that trap! If there's a body there we'll soon know it."

THE swarthy man flashed an expectant look at his two companions. Benton's lean figure bent to the job of pulling up the trap which dragged heavily against the rope. It came to the surface slowly. Yellow, slatted sides showed in streaks through the greenish blue water as it came farther up. Benton stared down when it was nearly up and then dragged it to the surface without speaking.

"Why, there's nothin' in this trap, except one lobster," Drinkwater said angrily, glancing from Benton to the three men. Their faces expressed their astonishment. Their eyes were wide and they could hardly speak. "Did you see a body here?" demanded Drinkwater. "Come on, now, tell the truth. There's something funny."

"Why, sure, I saw it," said the swarthy man dully. "Didn't you see it?" He turned to his other two companions. They both nodded.

"Sure," said the younger. "There was a body there as sure as we're sittin' in this boat. Say, I'll bet he musta cut it loose when he dove over."

Benton didn't speak.

Sheriff Frank Drinkwater was confused. There was no doubt about that. Benton's feeling toward Clayte Biddle was well known to him. But he hadn't thought Benton would murder. He didn't think so yet and he welcomed this turn in affairs, even thought he didn't follow what was going on.

"Well, Benton, I don't get this deal—an' till I do, I'm going to take the hull crowd of you into custody," said the sheriff deliberately. "Might as well have this lobster," he said with real New England thrift. He reached in a hand through the hinged top of the trap and pulled out the struggling crustacean.

"Watch out!" cried Benton suddenly.

One of the men had swung a heavy blackjack directly at the sheriff's head.

The blow hit the older man a glancing one on the shoulder as he ducked in response to Benton's cry of alarm. Benton seized the gun and covered the three men who were suddenly desperately anxious to get away.

"Stick your hands up!" threatened Benton watching the men. The sheriff rose to his feet and rubbed his shoulder. "You see," Benton said to the sheriff, keeping his gun trained on the men. "There's something more in this than meets the eye. That man tried to kill you, Drinkwater. Why?"

"You're right, Benton," said the sheriff grimly. "We'll take the bunch in, and hold 'em! You keep the gun on 'em and I'll row."

Back at the county jail the three men sullenly refused to give any account of themselves. Brief inquiries among the excited crowd hanging round the jail revealed that several persons had seen the trio in the neighborhood of the deserted Biddle estate for several days before Clayte's arrival and strange disappearance. But that was no definite proof of their guilt, Benton knew only too well. If, however, his plan—already half completed—worked out, the trio would trip themselves and clear him completely.

After they were safely under lock and key and with a deputy guarding them, the sheriff turned directly to Benton. "Now, what's this about their seein' a body?" he demanded. "What did they mean? Do you know?"

"I know plenty," said Benton with emphasis.

"Humph," grunted Drinkwater. "I hope you know enough, Benton Ellwell, to get yourself clean o' this mess."

TEN minutes later the sheriff and Benton were back at the Biddle pier and rowing out toward the other buoy—the one Benton hadn't pulled.

"If I've figured right, sheriff, you'll have to help me pull this one," said Benton grimly.

Together they pulled the trap to the surface. It came up heavy and sluggish. Benton's heart seemed to stop as the trap reached the top of the water. What he had feared, yet expected, had come true.

Tied to the trap with the slack of the buoy rope was the body of Clayton Biddle, his friendly dark eyes now staring blankly over the bay he'd loved. A deep gash on his head showed how he'd met his death. Benton's face was stern. His mind had erased the past few years unpleasantness and had flashed back to the pleasant scenes of their boyhood together. And now Clayte Biddle was dead.

Without saying a word, Drinkwater and Benton deposited the body of the young man in the bottom of the boat and rowed slowly back along the coast to the town pier. Willing hands helped to carry the limp, dripping burden up the long flight of steps and into the town hall. Many glances were cast at Benton Ellwell as he strode unheedingly up the narrow lane surrounded by the curious crowd of townspeople and friends.

The glances were significant. Hadn't Benton Ellwell often remarked on his feeling toward Clayte—that he was sore at Clayte Biddle for his interest in Kitty Hopkins? Busy tongues wagged but Benton Ellwell's face was tight and grim and he gave no heed.

But Frank Drinkwater noticed.

"Come in here, son."

He took Benton into his office and closed the door on the crowd. "Now, Benton," he said slowly, "tell me all about it. You seem to know a lot more than you're sayin'. You ain't under suspicion any more so tell the whole truth."

"At first I worked on a hunch," said Benton. "If that little dark guy hadn't been so tough with me on the float—trying to shoot me and all—I wouldn't have made a bee-line for those two traps. You see he warned me to keep away from them—said he had set a load of liquor down by one of them in the fog the other night and pretended he couldn't remember which. 'Twas Clayte's body he'd sunk and when Mr. Biddle offered the reward he wanted to get it up and turn it in for the money.

"He was so damned insistent that I guess it riled up any stubborness I've got in me and I told him to go to hell."

Frank Drinkwater nodded. "I've observed a certain stubborness round these parts," he said drily. "Then what happened?"

"Well, Kitty Hopkins—" Benton colored a bit— "came down to warn me 'bout you being after me on account of Clayte's disappearance. You know I wrote Clayte a letter about Kitty and himself—" He hesitated.

The sheriff cut in. "That letter almost got you into a peck of trouble, Benton."

Benton continued hurriedly. "I wasn't really sore at Clayte," he explained. "Just wanted him to keep away from Kitty unless he was as serious as—"

"As you are, I suppose," said the sheriff with a chuckle.

"That's right," said Benton awkwardly. "Well, I started rowing down along the shore and out of the corner of my eye I saw someone following me in the bushes on top of the ledges. By this time I'd put two and two together and guessed that the traps had something to do with Clayte's disappearance. So when I got to the first trap I looked at it close.

"You know it was dead low water, Frank, extra low 'count of the moon—"

The sheriff nodded.

"And yet," continued Benton, "the line on that first trap was straight up and down! I'd left plenty of scope on those lines when I set them out and I knew right off there must be something tied alongside that trap that had used up the extra amount of slack lint. With the tide as low as that there ought to have been double the amount of scope I'd left when I set the trap out."

THE sheriff's eyes had narrowed appreciatively. "So that's how you had it figured out?" he said slowly.

"I didn't bother with that trap and I rowed right on to the next one. There was plenty of scope on this one. I pulled it up near the surface—" Benton paused. "That's where I fooled them."

"I can see how you knew the body warn't on the second trap, Benton, but I don't see in tarnation what ever made that gang of cut throats say they were certain that Clayte's body was tied to it," said the sheriff curiously. "Lucky they did 'cause it cleared you of any suspicion."

"Well, I pretended to see a body tied onto that second trap, Frank," said Benton slowly. "I stiffened right up and let out a yell looking over the side just like I'd seen poor Clayte in the water. The gang on the shore fell for it and began firing. I jumped overboard and got around the point. Then I streaked back to town and you know the rest."

A knock came at the door. A gentle knock. Sheriff Frank Drinkwater stood up and lifted the hook. Kitty Hopkins' face was framed in the doorway.

She looked with anxious eyes at Benton and then at Frank Drinkwater's weathered face. For a moment there was complete silence. Then something in the sheriff's expression reassured her. She threw herself forward into Benton's arms and burst into soft choking sobs.

"Don't take on so, Kitty," whispered Benton. "It's all right." She didn't ask for any further explanations as his arms drew her slender figure tight against him.

Hurried footsteps sounded in the short hall and Mr. Biddle, Clayte's father, threw open the door, his eyes blazing as they rested on Benton.

"I hear you've got the cur, sheriff." The wealthy man's voice came in labored gasps. His eyes glaring from behind his gold-rimmed spectacles seemed to burn into Benton's face.

"Jest a minute, Mr. Biddle," cut in Frank Drinkwater hurriedly stepping forward. "Benton didn't kill Clayte—fact is he helped me catch the murderers! They were three rum runners and they're locked up in jail right at this moment. Benton's as clear as spring water!'

Mr. Biddle stopped and his heavy jaw dropped. He reached feebly for a chair and sank down upon it. "Benton didn't do it?" he whispered. Then relief seemed to surge over his drooping figure. He straightened. "I apologize, Benton," he said slowly, looking up at the tall figure before him. "But everything—that letter —pointed at you!"

"I don't blame you, Mr. Biddle," interrupted Benton. He stretched forth his hand and the older man took it, tears unashamedly springing to the eyes of both.

Frank Drinkwater cleared his throat. "Well, Mr. Biddle," he said tactlessly, "I guess you owe Benton that reward."

Benton shot a quick glance at the sheriff. "I couldn't take it, sir."

Clayte's father nodded. "I know how you feel, son," he said. He hesitated, then glanced wisely at Kitty.

"I'm going to need somebody down at the house to take care of the place the year round. There are fine, comfortable quarters in the wing and a good salary for the right man. Would you care for the job, Benton? It would be a good one for a man and wife."

Benton nodded. "I—we'd like it, sir," he said looking down at the girl as his arm tightened about her shoulders.

GREEN GLASSES

A FEW years ago there appeared a popular song—possibly you may recall it—the refrain of which pointed a moral to the effect that if people would only wear green glasses then it wouldn't be so hard for them to see how green the grass is in their own back yards. And splendid advice that was, too, for confirmed pessimists, gloomers and others of kindred ilk.

Fortunately, the donning of such emerald-hued spectacles is one operation the editors and readers of DIME DETECTIVE MAGAZINE run no danger of having to perform. Our thrill-dotted horizons continue to remain verdant without any such chameleonlike hocus-pocus being necessary. The month-after-month fare of master mysteries goes on with ever-increasing regularity and shall continue to do so. The stories have gotten better and better each month—though that's gilding the lily a bit if we are to credit the sincerity of the readers who have written in complimenting us on the first numbers of the magazine—and if it's humanly possible we're going to see that the good work keeps up.

With your help, of course!

DIME DETECTIVE MAGAZINE wants its readers to take an active part in determining its policies and helping us to decide just what sort of yarns you like and who you like to have them by. If there are any writers whose names you would particularly like to see on the contents pages of the coming issues let us know about them and we'll see if something can't be done about it.

Constructive criticism is one of the things we're most anxious to get and if you have any to offer send it along. We'll appreciate it.

It has been our policy to offer as much variety as we could in both type and form of story while still keeping the quality standard uniformly high. In setting our yarns have ranged all the way from the swamplands of the South to the fog-bound coasts of Maine—then clear across the continent to California and out into the ocean on a yacht voyage. We've covered a lot of territory, all in all, and expect to keep moving in the future. Nothing static about that policy. Let us know what particular region of the country you'd like to have a story about. We'll try to dig it up for you and have it told by someone who knows the locale, as well as how to plot and spin the yarn.

How do you feel about stories with a setting outside this country? England—and of course that makes one think immediately of Scotland Yard—the Orient—the tropics—the Continent with the many possibilities it offers for crime and mystery fiction? Or do you prefer that we keep our malefactors and the men who dog them inside our own boundaries?

Do you relish the action story more than the deductive one? Does the terror touch and so-called horror story fit your idea of the ideal mystery yarn? Would you rather have characterization and atmosphere play a major or minor part in your detective fare? We want to know these things and you are the only ones who can tell us. How about it?

A ND now, before you begin to feel swamped by this question flood, let us introduce some of the men who made this the extra-special issue that it is. Here's John Lawrence whose *The Scarlet Comet* you have just read. We'll let him do the talking.

"Born—well, less than thirty years ago —in Windsor, Canada. Schooled in Canada and Detroit, then the Royal Military

College at Kingston, Canada, which they tell me is similar to West Point here. Law school in Detroit a while, then the newspaper business for a year. Finally the stock-brokerage racket. Ten years in that —Toronto, Montreal, Detroit, Chicago and

John Lawrence, mystery fiction writer

New York. Got my first fiction-concocting experience writing stock-market prophecies and advice. When, in due course, my customers all followed it and went broke, I grabbed the opportunity and bought a typewriter; started pounding.

"Sold my first story to the publishers of this sterling magazine (ah!) about a year ago.

"Have no other busines now but writing. It's the hardest job I ever had, but ou can't get away from it.

"My favorite author is P. G. Wodehouse. I spend as much time as I can afford at Leo's on 52nd street. I play golf, hockey and squash. Like to watch baseball, but of course, never played it myself. (We'll wager he wielded a mean cricket bat though.—_Ed._)

"Unless forcibly restrained will be back again soon with another Paul Bryant story.

"And further, deponent sayeth not."

Thank you, Mr. Lawrence. Incidentally —though perhaps we shouldn't let this out—we happen to know that the author of The Scarlet Comet is doing some intensive research in the history of poisons and their criminal uses just at this time. No, it's not so that he may wreak dire vengeance on any editor who may happen to cross him. He assures us that it's so he may have some accurate data for a yarn which we are to see in the near future. We're on tenter hooks until it comes along!

Also we happen to know—Mr. Lawrence was probably too bashful to mention it—that he did much research and used great care in getting his facts and color right for his yarn in this issue. He bearded railroad officials and publicity men in their dens, and spent days scurrying from the Grand Central to the Penn Terminal and back in his search for data on railroad methods, detail and procedure. The story is perfectly feasible in all its train action.

NORMAN H. WHITE, JR., is another of DIME DETECTIVE MAGAZINE's authors who is thoroughly familiar with the places and things about which he writes. Here's what he has to say about his story in this issue.

"The background of the story of _Buoy of Doom_ is authentic. The Cunner Ledges are known to the natives of Saturday Cove by that name and the town itself numbers many Drinkwaters and Ellwells among its citizens.

"Man and boy I sailed and swam in Penobscot Bay, though I'll admit that the sailing is better than the swimming, for the water has the chill of the far north in its depths. They're a tough, lanky race— these down Easterners who have sailed the waters of the blue Penobscot for the last two hundred years. They've got a twang all of their own in their voice, and in a rough and tumble they are bad customers. One of the reasons for a lack of important crime in Maine is the fact that big city crooks don't last very long in a competition with the enforcers of law and order.

"The editor has asked me to tell how I happened to start writing detective stories and I can simply say that I seem to fall naturally into it, having been in the secret service of the army during the war, attached to Northeastern Departmental Headquarters with the rank of Sergeant. Previous to that I put in about eight months as a Chief Petty Officer in the Naval Reserve in command of a small patrol boat out of Boston. I enjoyed both branches of the service, particularly the navy, for small boats have been my hobby for years.

"I graduated from Harvard in the class of 1920 with a war degree which cut one year off the four-year course by giving me credit for my time in service. I was damned lucky to get that credit for otherwise I'm afraid the illustrious class of 1920 would not have been able to member me among its graduates."

Mr. White—"Rusty" to his friends—is stalwart, red-headed and carries a tang of the salt sea about him. But he is equally at home on his boat or at his typewriter

Norman H. White, Jr.

as *Buoy of Doom* testifies. We hope to hear more from him later.

And now there's just room to thank all the readers who have already submitted criticism and comment on the magazine and to urge those who haven't yet done so to get busy and let us know what's what.

"If you are Ruptured, it will cost you nothing to find out if I can help you"

H. Brooks

C. E. BROOKS, Inventor

Not an idle boast on the part of Mr. Brooks is the above statement for over 3 million people have taken advantage of the unusual Brooks offer, and have found that a Brooks Appliance has aided and assisted them by acting as an agent in the control of their pain and suffering.

Mr. C. E. Brooks, inventor of the marvelous Air-Cushion Appliance which bears his name, was the first to recognize the crying need for a better, safer and more humane method of aiding rupture sufferers. He believed the old clumsy, cumbersome type of truss could be and should be replaced by a safer, more modern and lightweight type which could be not only more effective but more easily worn.

Safety *and* Comfort!

The Brooks Automatic Air-Cushion Appliance is the most widely used, made-to-measure, rupture appliance in the world. It is sanitary, clean, simple, and above all, safe and comfortable. It is fitted with a web girdle which is a masterpiece of scientific weaving and craftsmanship. There are no metal parts to rust or corrode. Why not find out if a Brooks can help you? Send coupon for facts!

"CURED" Say Thousands

We don't say a Brooks will cure you, but we do say that in many cases it has not only given safety and comfort but has also acted as an agent to assist in relieving and curing reducible rupture. Read these voluntary letters—only a few of thousands on file at Marshall, Michigan, reporting relief and cure.

Entirely Cured
"Your Appliance is all you claim for it. I have a reducible rupture and wore your Appliance for a little over one year and am entirely cured. I cheerfully recommend your firm and Appliance to any and all unfortunates who may be ruptured as I have explicit confidence in both, and the price is very moderate." Charles Roth (Mo.)

"I'm Entirely Well"
"I got one of your Appliances last January, and wore it about six weeks and then took it off and haven't worn it since. I'm entirely well. I do all kinds of work and am never bothered. My reducible rupture was about 8 years old before I got your appliance."—Dick Ruby (Minn.)

"Absolutely Healed"
"I am glad to state at this time that with God's help and your Appliance I am absolutely healed and have not been wearing my Appliance for one year. I will say it is a God-sent help for anyone suffering with reducible rupture trouble."—Thos. Erickson (N. D.)

FREE INFORMATION COUPON

Prove that a Brooks Automatic Air-Cushion Appliance with firm but gentle "finger-tip" support, will help you by testing it personally for ten days without risk. More than 3 million men, women and children have already taken advantage of our liberal 10-Day No-Risk Trial Offer. A trial at our risk will convince you that never again need you be without proper support day and night—at work, at sleep, at play. Send coupon for details of 10-Day No-Risk Offer and Free Rupture Book.

Send it Now!

BROOKS APPLIANCE CO.,
167 State Street, Marshall, Michigan

Please rush to me in plain wrapper your Free Book on Rupture, details of your 10-Day No-Risk Trial Offer and complete description of the Brooks Automatic Air-Cushion Appliance with "finger-tip" support. This costs me nothing and does not obligate me in any way.

Name _____

Street _____

City _____ State _____

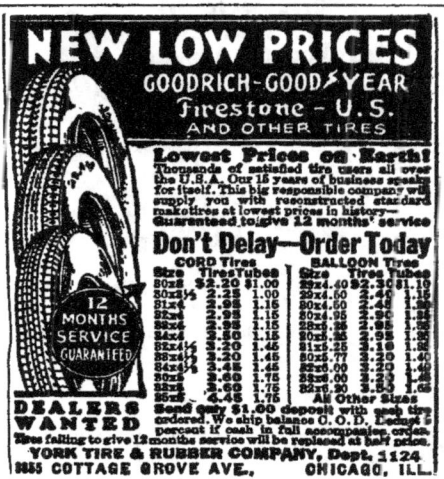

www.ingramcontent.com/pod-product-compliance
Lightning Source LLC
Chambersburg PA
CBHW080912020726
47502CB00008B/2429